“What are yo

Ike crossed his ar
chest. The bandages that covered his arm from
fingers to shoulder hampered his movement.
“I’m suffering enough without you adding to my
misery.”

Ignoring the little sting his words gave her, Tracy smiled sweetly at him. “Ever the charmer, Ike. I thought I’d give the nurses a break from your delightful personality.” She flicked her finger at his hospital gown. “By the way, the pastel-blue flowers suit you.”

The gown should have looked silly on such an obviously masculine body. Instead, it actually emphasized his honed chest and arms, making him look more manly, rather than less.

Still, he didn’t need to know that. Nor that he’d made her pulse skip.

Dear Reader,

It's time to drop the puck on another story about the dedicated and delicious hockey players of the New Jersey Ice Cats! Welcome back to readers who've enjoyed the series so far, and thank you for your many lovely comments. If this is your first Ice Cats book, hello, and thanks for stopping by.

They say if two people are meant to be together, they'll end up together. But what if for some reason the timing isn't right? Although there are tragic stories of missed chances, you also hear many heartwarming stories about people finally getting together after many years. I like to believe that love will always find a way, although sometimes fate has to give a helping hand.

The moment Ike and Tracy appeared in *A Perfect Distraction*, I knew that for them the timing the first time around was definitely not right. It was also clear fate would have to use both hands to get this stubborn couple back together!

I love to hear from readers. Please write to me at anna@annasugden.com or Box 174, Regis House, 23 King Street, Cambridge CB1 1AH, England. You can also find me on Facebook and Twitter.

Anna Sugden

ANNA SUGDEN

A Perfect Catch

ISBN-13: 978-0-373-60898-0

A Perfect Catch

This edition published by arrangement with Harlequin Books S.A.

For questions and comments about the quality of this book, please contact us at CustomerService@Harlequin.com.

Printed in U.S.A.

Former marketing executive **Anna Sugden** loves reading romance novels and watching films with happy endings. She also loves watching hockey and football, where she prefers a happy ending for her teams. When she's not researching hockey players (for her books, of course), she makes craft projects and collects penguins, autographs and memorabilia, and great shoes. Anna lives in Cambridge, England, with her husband and two bossy black cats. Learn more about Anna, her books and her shoes at annasugden.com.

Books by Anna Sugden

HARLEQUIN SUPERROMANCE

A Perfect Distraction
A Perfect Trade

Visit the Author Profile page
at Harlequin.com for more titles

For Keith, all my love always

For Favourite Nephew, Matthew,
and Favourite Niece, Hannah—love you xx

Acknowledgments

My wonderful agent, Jill Marsal,
for all her support, advice and help.

Donna MacMeans and Cassondra Murray—
plotting has never been so much fun!

Beth Andrews, Terri Garey, Kathleen Long,
Janice Lynn and Tawny Weber—who are always
there for me.

The Romance Bandits—who make this
roller-coaster ride a blast!

CHAPTER ONE

"WHY DOES IT take so long to have a baby?"

At her niece's question, Tracy Hayden looked up from the stack of invoices she was logging into her business's accounting system.

She smiled at Emily, who was playing a game on the other home-office computer. "They don't have bar codes on their bums, so you can't just pick them up at a grocery store."

Tracy's sister, Maggie, had gone to the hospital early that morning, when her water had broken. The latest update from Maggie's anxious husband, Jake, at 5:00 p.m., had been that all was progressing well, if a bit slowly.

Now, at seven-thirty, ten-year-old Emily's excitement was stretched thin by the lack of action.

"Very funny, Auntie Tracy." The soon-to-be older sister rolled her eyes. "Do you think Mummy's having a girl or a boy?"

"Hmm." Tracy pretended to consider the question seriously. "I have a feeling the sproglet is a boy."

Her niece leaned forward eagerly. "Why?"

Tracy lowered her voice conspiratorially. "Your

mum put sugar in her cup of tea yesterday. They say you need extra sweetness if you're having a boy."

Emily's eyes widened. "She also ate a whole bar of Cadbury's chocolate from her stash."

"Aha." Tracy snapped her fingers. "That settles it."

"A baby brother would be okay," Emily mused. "He wouldn't want any of my things. Plus he'll like sports. I could teach him to skate and play hockey."

Tracy clipped the invoices together, then slipped them into a folder marked November Bills. She'd allocate them to the appropriate accounts tomorrow. "That would be nice."

"Maybe he'll even get to play on the Ice Cats like Daddy Jake."

Jake "Bad Boy" Badoletti was a star defenseman for the local professional hockey team, the New Jersey Ice Cats. He and Maggie had gotten together after his transfer from Chicago a few years ago, when Maggie had helped him find a place to live. Though she'd been wary of falling for another pro athlete after escaping an abusive marriage to Emily's father—an English Premier League soccer player—Jake had eventually won the hearts of both mother and daughter. As well as being an avid fan of her stepfather's team, Emily had also become a good mites' hockey player.

The child pouted. "It's not fair that girls can't play for the Ice Cats."

"You never know. Maybe you'll be the second woman to play in the NHL."

"But Manon Rhéaume was a goaltender." Em wrinkled her nose. "I want to be a forward and score lots of goals."

Naturally. Her niece was all about action.

The phone rang, startling them both.

Tracy's heart leaped into her throat as she saw Jake's number. She snatched up the receiver. "Is everything okay?"

"Yeah." He sounded a little befuddled. "We have a boy. Eight pounds, six ounces. Mom and son both doing well. Dad's not sure he ever wants to go through that again."

"Isn't that supposed to be Maggie's line?" Tracy said drily.

"She had an epidural. I did the whole thing without anesthetic."

She laughed. "A tough guy like you can't handle childbirth. I'm shocked."

"I can't believe, having survived it once with Emily, she'd be willing to do it again." He paused and Tracy could almost feel his shudder down the phone. "Maggie's one tough cookie."

"She certainly is."

Despite what she'd been through, Maggie had not only managed to make a fresh start in the US, but she'd also embraced marriage again.

Something Tracy couldn't do after her own disastrous experience.

That mess wasn't something she wanted to think about. Not when there was a new life to celebrate. "So, are you up for visitors?"

"Sure. Whenever you can get here. I'll call my parents next and get them to pass the news to everyone else."

After she'd hung up, Tracy turned to Emily. "A boy," she said smugly.

"You rock, Auntie Tracy." Emily reached across the back-to-back desks to fist-bump her. "When can we go to see him?"

"Right now." Tracy saved her files, then switched off her computer and stood. "Get your coat and we'll head over."

Em dashed out of the office. A moment later, she stuck her head back around the door. "Don't forget the teddy bear."

"I won't. He's already in the gift bag by the front door."

The drive to the hospital passed quickly, with Emily chattering like a magpie about her new sibling. As they walked across the parking lot toward the hospital entrance, Emily squealed and darted toward a tall dark-haired man getting out of a black Mercedes SUV.

"Uncle Ike!"

Tracy's pulse hitched at the familiar figure of Ice Cats goaltender Eisenhower "Ike" Jelinek. She wasn't surprised to see him. The four Jelinek boys had grown up with Jake, and the men were like brothers. Still, she'd hoped she'd get lucky and miss him.

Back when Tracy had been starting Making Your Move, her relocation business, she'd helped Ike find the perfect town house and they'd had a hot and heavy fling shortly after. Even though they'd been great together in bed—and a whole bunch of other places—the fire had burned out quickly when they'd realized they'd wanted different things from a relationship.

The flip side of all that passion meant they rubbed each other the wrong way ever since. Unfortunately they couldn't avoid each other. Even ignoring the family connection, Making Your Move managed all the Ice Cats' relocation, travel and accommodation projects, so Tracy spent a lot of time with the team.

What surprised her was that every time she saw Ike, her body reacted to his broad shoulders, his powerful legs and his crooked grin as if they were still lovers.

No way. She knew better than to go down that road again.

"Hey, princess." Ike caught Emily as she threw herself at him, lifting and twirling her around, much to the girl's delight.

Laughing, they headed toward Tracy.

Ike's smile faded when he spoke to her. "Congratulations."

"Thanks," she replied politely.

Emily skipped between the two adults as they

walked toward the hospital entrance. "Auntie Tracy, did you see that Uncle Ike bought exactly the same bear as you?"

Sure enough, the stuffed toy Ike clutched awkwardly by the arm was identical to the one in her gift bag, right down to the yellow ribbon tied jauntily around its neck.

"You can't have too many teddy bears." She kept her voice light, even though she wanted to snap childishly at him to take his back.

Ike arched an eyebrow. "I wouldn't have thought you'd get something as *old-fashioned* as a bear."

The emphasis was intended to goad her. One of the reasons she and Ike hadn't made it was she'd thought his attitude toward women and life were stuffy and old-fashioned. "Teddy bears are *traditional*. There's a difference."

The look in Ike's green eyes said he begged to differ. "Uh-huh."

"Auntie Tracy got me the same bear when I was born. Except mine has a pink ribbon."

"A family tradition." Tracy smiled sweetly.

"My *tradition* for new Ice Cat babies is to get them one of those all-in-one things with feet, with the team logo on it."

"Shouldn't they be called Ice Kittens, Uncle Ike?"

"I guess they should. But you wouldn't want to confuse them with the girls who clean the ice for us."

"Why? They're only cheerleaders on skates." Emily's lip curled.

"Just because we don't like their job doesn't mean we should disrespect the ice girls, Em," Tracy chided gently.

Ike shot a look of surprise at her. "I thought you'd disapprove of them. Women being used as—" he paused, glancing at Emily, who was following the discussion intently "—entertainment for the predominantly male audience."

"I wouldn't want to be one and, if I owned the team, I wouldn't have them at all, but the job exists. As long as they're not being exploited, good luck to them. Besides, I've seen how hard the Ice Kittens work. They have a lot of promotional and charity duties, on top of what they do at games."

"Be careful—they'll be taking away your feminist badge."

Tracy shrugged. Ike had always thought she was a bra-burning radical, rather than a woman who didn't like to be pigeon-holed, dictated to or discriminated against because of her sex. "I believe in equality and that if you can do the job, you can do the job."

"That means if I can play well enough, I can be an Ice Cat, not an Ice Kitten." Emily nodded, with a satisfied grin.

Tracy bit back a smile as Ike clamped his jaw shut. Clearly, he didn't agree with women playing in the NHL. Luckily, they arrived at the hospital entrance, so Emily's attention turned to which floor her mother would be on.

A blast of warm air hit them as the automatic

doors swished open, and the three of them hurried inside out of the chilly November evening. The lift was crowded with the start of evening visiting hours, but by the time they got to Maternity there were only a few people with new-baby gifts.

Jake met them in the waiting room, looking tired but exhilarated. They exchanged hugs and congratulations before he led them down to Maggie's room. Emily rushed ahead, chattering a mile a minute.

Ike caught the door and held it open for Tracy. She nodded her thanks as she walked past him into the room.

While Tracy appreciated his gentlemanly gestures, manners didn't make up for the control issues that went with them. In the first flush of their romance, she'd believed Ike was different. But after only a few weeks, he'd shown her how naive she'd really been. No matter how much she might have wished otherwise, Ike had turned out to be as bad as her father and her ex-husband.

Besides, the only male she was interested in loving and having in her life permanently was the one in the pastel blue cap that her sister cradled in her arms.

"He's a bit funny-looking." Emily wrinkled her nose, disappointment in her voice.

"Poor lamb's had a rough few hours." Maggie stroked the shock of dark hair on her son's head. "You didn't look much better when you were born. In fact, he looks very much like you did."

"Mu-um," Emily huffed, rolling her eyes.

"She's right, Em." Tracy grinned. "You turned out fine, so he'll be okay, too."

"Kid clearly takes after his mom, not his dad," Ike said.

Jake laughed. "Fine by me."

"Do you want to hold him, sis?" Maggie asked her.

"Of course." Tracy sat on the edge of the bed while her sister passed the precious bundle over. "Come to your auntie."

Her throat tightened with love as his warmth filled her arms. "He's gorgeous. Have you named him yet?"

Maggie smiled mistily at Jake. "Joe. Not Joseph—just Joe."

"A good, solid name." Ike leaned over and gently ran his finger over Joe's soft cheek.

Tracy stiffened. It felt weird to be holding a baby with Ike so close beside her. His unique, spicy scent mingled pleasantly with the smell of the infant, making her feel even more unsettled.

Ike brushed Joe's little fist with his finger. Almost immediately, her nephew curled his tiny fingers around Ike's. Somehow, it felt as if the three of them were now connected. A strange prickling feeling danced across Tracy's shoulders. She wanted to order Ike to move away, but knew that would sound crazy. Instead, she gritted her teeth and focused on her nephew.

Joe must have sensed her discomfort because his eyes popped open. Her heart squeezed at his solemn expression as he studied her. He then shifted his unfocused newborn gaze to Ike, giving him the same unblinking stare.

She hated to give the baby up, but she had to break the connection. Get away from the cozy tableau that had formed.

"Would you like a turn, Ike?" she asked politely.

"Sure." He sat beside her on the bed and reached for the baby.

Ignoring the heat of Ike's thigh pressed against hers, Tracy kissed her nephew's forehead and passed him over.

She was surprised by how confidently Ike handled the small bundle.

"Goaltenders have the safest pair of hands," he said smugly, as if he'd read her mind.

"Of course." Her smile felt forced as she jumped up and went to sit in the chair on the opposite side of the bed.

"Ike used to help my mom look after Linc while Aunt Karina was at work," Jake added. "He was a whiz at changing diapers, making bottles of formula and burping the kid."

Tracy knew one of the reasons Ike was so serious was that he'd had to learn responsibility at an early age, after his father had walked out. Even though Jake's parents had helped Karina Jelinek a lot—Jake and the four Jelinek boys had been raised together—

it had been a struggle as Ike's mum had worked several jobs to keep her sons fed and clothed. Ike and the next oldest, Tru, had done their part to help look after their younger brothers, Kenny and Linc.

It was touching to see the brawny goaltender holding her tiny nephew so tenderly, his green eyes looking fondly at the gurgling baby. Someday, he'd probably hold his own children with the same confidence. Look at them with the same affection.

She ignored the tug in her chest.

Tracy didn't want to be the woman who gave him those children. She was happy with her life and her business; she answered to no one but herself. She enjoyed the freedom of doing what she wanted, when she wanted. Sure, she dated. Some guys had even lasted a few months. But every time things had started to turn serious, she'd felt hemmed in and backed away.

As for children… Well, she was a fantastic aunt and that was enough for her.

Really, it *was*.

Tracy turned to Maggie and asked brightly, "How are you feeling?"

"Pretty good, considering." Her sister lowered her voice. "I don't want to upset the men by telling you about my stitches, so I'll give you the gory details later."

Tracy bit back a laugh as the two hockey players winced. "At least we're in the right place if they pass out."

"I'll go and check if anyone else is in the waiting room," Jake said quickly.

"I'll come with you." Emily hurried after him, already bored with her new brother. "I wonder if Nonna and Poppa brought me a big-sister present."

Maggie shook her head indulgently. "Jake's poor parents have been bombarded with helpful suggestions for gifts."

"Em's thrown a few ideas my way," Tracy said.

"Mine, too." Ike nodded.

"The little monkey. We had a talk about that and I told her not to try it on."

Tracy patted her sister's arm. "Emily's excited about Joe's arrival, which is nice, given she's been an only child for so long."

"I know. She's a good kid, just a little cheeky."

"I don't blame her. It's not like our parents ever spoiled her." When their father was alive, Em had been lucky to get a birthday card, let alone a present. Dominic Hayden had believed gifts were frivolous. Since his death, their mother had continued to abide by his rules. God forbid she should have a thought of her own.

"True." Maggie grimaced. "I suppose I should let Mum know about Joe."

"Don't worry. I'll call her later." Tracy deliberately changed the subject. "Have the doctors said when you can go home?"

"Tomorrow, assuming everything's okay." Her sister sighed. "I'm sorry. This has messed up our plans at work for the next few weeks. I can't believe I went into labor so early. Everyone kept telling me I was bound to be late because it had been so long since I'd had Em."

"Babies come when they want to," Tracy reassured her. "I'd factored in the possibility. Which is why the intern we recruited is starting ahead of schedule—on Monday. Carla's grateful for the extra money and I'm happy to pass over the admin duties, so it's all good."

"Even more reason for you not to pay me while I'm off work."

"Don't start that again. You know how well the business is doing and there's more than enough in the budget to cover your maternity pay, so relax. Besides, didn't I read somewhere that worrying turns a mother's milk sour?"

"That's an old wives' tale."

Tracy shrugged. "I wouldn't want to risk it."

"Okay." Maggie laughed. "Can I at least ask if you heard back from those two new business pitches we made this week?"

"Not yet, but I'm sure they'll let me know before the weekend," Tracy lied smoothly, not wanting her sister to start fretting again about her workload.

Both contracts were in the bag, which would be a nice boost to their bottom line and another step closer to Tracy's goal of getting their business to number one. Even with Carla's help, she'd be working flat out until Maggie returned. But the extra hours would be worth the financial cushion it would give them for next year.

"How will you cope if we win them both?" her sister asked.

"I thought we just agreed that everything was under control," Tracy scolded.

"Yes, but..."

Thankfully, Maggie's protest was interrupted when Jake's parents bustled into the room, followed by Ike's mum and stepfather.

As the older folks exclaimed excitedly over Joe, Tracy was touched by the joy and love in the room. So different from when Emily was born, when Tracy had been the only family member to visit. Their father had hated London and refused to travel south. Even though it had broken their mother's heart not to see her first grandchild, as usual she hadn't fought her husband's decision. Horrified, Tracy had sworn then that she'd never let a man control her life. Sadly, only a short while later, she'd fallen into the same trap.

Tracy's phone vibrated against her hip, breaking into her dark thoughts. Grateful for the interruption, she stepped away from the bed to check the caller ID.

Bloody hell. She'd missed a call from Glen at the Brooklyn Bridgers, one of the local Major League Soccer teams. She and Glen had played phone tag all day. The Bridgers were interested in the Helping Hand services her business had recently begun to offer. They had a new French star, Marcel Chabal, whom she'd been helping to relocate from France. Marcel's wife didn't speak much English and needed support for the transition to living in a new country.

As she listened to Glen's voice mail, she saw Ike frown at her. His obvious disapproval made her bristle. How dare he judge her? Her business was successful because she was available to meet her clients' needs 24/7. Unscheduled calls like this one were rare, but right now, time wasn't on her side. She needed project and budget approval so she could have everything in place for when the couple arrived this weekend.

"I'll be available until eleven tonight." Glen signed off. "Call me."

If she phoned right now, she might catch him. Since no one other than Ike—and he didn't count—was paying her any attention, Tracy slipped out of the room.

Luckily, the waiting room was empty, so Tracy could call Glen in privacy. This time, they connected and he approved both the proposal and the budget. "Send over the revised paperwork and I'll sign it."

Tracy kept her voice calm and professional, though she wanted to fist-pump the air. "Great. I'll get that to you first thing tomorrow."

Once she'd hung up, Tracy decided to celebrate with a coffee. As she waited for the machine to do its thing, she gave a happy wiggle. Major score! And a very nice boost to her turnover. Hopefully, once the Bridgers saw how Helping Hands enabled Mme. Chabal to settle more easily and eased Marcel's stress, they'd extend the contract to cover all their foreign players. Their positive reference would be invaluable for pitching the service to her other clients.

Collecting her coffee, Tracy glanced at the clock. Visiting hours would be over shortly and she wanted another cuddle with her new nephew. It had been a good evening all around.

"Excuse me."

Ike's deep voice, close to her ear, startled her.

She jerked her head around as he leaned forward to program the machine. Their gazes clashed.

He was too close. Tracy could feel the heat radiating from his body. Prickles of awareness danced across her skin. Her pulse skipped as emerald fire flared briefly in his eyes.

Then he blinked and the flames disappeared. "Finished your business?" Ike reached past her for his coffee.

Tracy jerked away from him. Hot coffee splashed over her hand.

She swore and sucked on the sore patch before answering. "Yes, thank you. A client needed me," she added, before she could stop herself. Damn it. She didn't owe him any explanations.

"What kind of relocation *emergency* can there be?"

Her earlier irritation returned at his sarcastic tone,

but she fought to stay polite. "You, of all people, should know that problems don't just happen between nine and five. As I recall, you liked me to be available whenever you needed me."

A muscle twitched in his jaw. "I had to work viewings around the Ice Cats schedule."

"Then you should understand when other professional athletes need flexibility, too."

"Sure, but there are times when business should take a backseat. Like when your sister's just had a baby."

He was acting as though she'd abandoned Maggie and Joe. She'd stepped out briefly, leaving a room full of people to fuss over them. "Really? So you've never had to leave a family event to get to a game or missed a family occasion because you've been on a road trip?"

"That's different. I don't get a choice about where I have to be or when. I thought the whole point of running your own business was that you were in control. I remember how vital being your own boss—in every part of your life—is to you."

His bitter tone brought up memories she'd rather had remained buried. Arguments better forgotten. "You're the one who wouldn't compromise."

"You didn't want compromise—you wanted things all your own way."

"I didn't want them all *your* way. Big difference."

"What was so wrong with expecting you to take me, our relationship, as seriously as your career?"

Once again, he was twisting the facts to make everything her fault. Irritation turned to anger. "That wasn't what you expected at all. You wanted my career to take a backseat to yours."

"I never said that." He drained his coffee and threw the cup in the bin.

"Maybe not exactly, but you made it clear that you thought my business was only something to keep me occupied until I had a husband to look after me. Meanwhile, you chasing around after a puck was—" she used air quotes "—'so much more important,' even though you only had, at best, another ten years."

He clenched his fists by his sides. "I'd make enough money in those ten years to keep you living comfortably for the rest of your life."

"I didn't need you to take care of me and I didn't need your money." Tracy worked so hard because she never wanted to be dependent on another man or his money again. "I can bloody well look after myself."

"Yeah, you've made it pretty freaking clear there's no room in your life for a man."

"Not quite true—there's no room in my life for *you*."

"Trust me, babe, I'm glad," he drawled. "I had a lucky escape. I get banged up enough on the ice—I don't need a ballbuster in my bed."

Tracy gasped at his cruel words. Then she tossed her coffee over him. She'd show him a ballbuster.

IKE SWORE AS he wiped down his sweater and jeans with his handkerchief. From the heat around his zipper, the coffee had got too close to the family jewels for comfort.

Tracy Hayden had been a major pain in his ass from the moment she'd strutted into his life on those killer legs. With a toss of her dark hair and a glint in her brown eyes, she'd challenged him in every way. Still did. Damn woman was as irritating as grit in an oyster, except he never got a pearl. That said, a coffee shower was a first.

"I should apologize." Tracy's crisp tone, which emphasized her still-strong English accent, was grudging.

"Why bother, if you don't mean it?" He stripped off his sweater. Beneath it, his T-shirt was damp but wearable. "I thought the one thing we had left was honesty."

Her gaze lingered on his chest before flicking up to meet his. Color tinged her cheeks. "You're right. Your remark was uncalled for, but I reacted badly."

His conscience pricked him, taking the edge off his anger. It was partly—okay, largely—his fault. One minute Tracy had been cooing over her nephew and the next she was desperately checking her phone. Since she'd just told Maggie that everything was under control, what could be so freaking important?

Ike hadn't deliberately followed Tracy into the waiting room. The cozy family image Jake, Maggie and Joe had presented had scraped on his already raw nerves, reminding him of the life he'd once hoped he could have with Tracy and making the hospital room feel claustrophobic. He'd escaped to get some air. He'd been surprised to find Tracy by the coffee machine and had nearly turned back. But then he'd seen that damn wiggle. That sexy hip-shimmy she always did when she was happy. The one that always fired up his pulse—and his groin.

He'd barely got himself under control when she'd spilled coffee on her hand. He'd wanted to kiss the burn better. The thought of putting his lips on her had sent desire rocketing through his body once more. Frustration had fuelled his annoyance. After all this time, he hated that he was still so pathetically affected by her, while all she felt for him was aggravation. And he'd snapped.

"No harm done," he said stiffly. "I should apologize, too."

"Okay." Tracy dropped her empty cup in the trash and turned back to the coffee machine.

As she tapped in her selection, Ike stifled the urge to offer to buy her a drink. He turned to go when her voice stopped him.

"I know you won't believe this, but I wouldn't ordinarily let business intrude on such a special occasion."

"So why the exception?" He was pleased his question held no hint of his skepticism.

"It was a time-sensitive issue."

"Aren't they all?"

"I suppose so." Tracy smiled ruefully as she collected her drink. "But in this case, it would have been a costly mistake. The Bridgers are a major client."

He frowned, unsure how one phone call could be that important. Unless she'd been about to lose the soccer team as a client. "Is Making Your Move in trouble?"

"Not at all. In fact I'm trying to broaden the range of services we offer with the new Helping Hands package." Tracy explained the extra support her company wanted to give players and their families.

Ike obviously had a different definition of *emergency*. If her company had been struggling, he'd have understood. But how could adding business when her company was already successful be more important than celebrating a new member of the family?

Don't go there.

What was the point? It would only lead to another fight and he probably wouldn't survive another dousing unscathed. Besides, all of this only reinforced what he already knew—the two of them would never work. He couldn't be with someone who put work ahead of everything and everyone else. He sure as hell wouldn't compete with a woman's career.

Ike acknowledged that his own childhood colored

his thinking. Not just the weight of responsibility that he'd carried from too young an age, but also the way his mother had worked herself to exhaustion to provide for the family after his father had walked out. Ike was determined that his future wife and children would not struggle or suffer. Which was why he firmly believed the traditional male-female roles were necessary. Men provided and supported so that women could take care of the family.

Tracy would never be that type of woman.

Now if only his body would get the message.

"So you can see why I couldn't risk messing up and not getting the Bridgers on board." Tracy wound up her explanation and looked at him expectantly.

He was damned if he understood. Luckily, Ike was saved from having to come up with a suitable reply when his younger brother, Kenny, ambled toward them. "So, this is where the sane people hang out. The kid's cute and all, but do we really have to sigh over every gurgle and dribble?"

"I'm afraid so." She patted his shoulder sympathetically. "Give it a few weeks and you'll be doing the same. I've seen harder men than you going gaga over a cute baby."

"No way." Kenny gave an exaggerated shudder.

Tracy laughed. "Well, I'm not afraid to say I want another cuddle."

"Good luck prying him away from the grandmas." Kenny rolled his eyes. "I'll grab a drink and wait until the bloodshed is over."

"Coward." She waggled her fingers in farewell.

Ike and his brother watched Tracy walk back down the corridor.

Kenny punched him in the arm. "I don't know why the two of you don't just sleep together and get it out of your system."

Ike choked. "Where the hell did that come from?"

Kenny smiled smugly. "So you don't deny you're hot for her."

"Because it's too dumb to bother denying."

"Ike's got the hots for Tracy," Kenny added in a singsong voice.

"Mom must have dropped you on your head when you were a baby. You're seeing things that aren't there."

"And you're protesting a little too much, especially since you still haven't taken your eyes off her admittedly great legs."

"Leave her legs out of it," Ike growled.

Kenny held up his hands in mock surrender. "She's all yours. Or would be if you'd get your act together."

"Trust me, the last thing Tracy or I want is a relationship."

"Who's talking about a relationship?" His brother plugged change into the soda machine. "I'm talking about doing the horizontal mambo until neither of you can move or snipe at each other."

Damn it. Even Kenny's teasing words were enough to spike Ike's temperature. He did not need to remember what that had been like with Tracy. "I know for a fact we're not compatible."

"How do you know unless you give it a sho—" Kenny stopped and stared at him. "Holy cannoli. You already did it, didn't you?"

Although Ike had never told anyone what had happened, Kenny and his other brothers had picked up on something between him and Tracy—perhaps the electricity in the air whenever they were together—and delighted in giving him crap about her. Maybe if he admitted it, they'd lay off. "A long time ago. It didn't work out. Game over."

Kenny studied him, his usually happy-go-lucky expression serious. "That sucks."

"Yeah." His brother didn't know how much.

By unspoken agreement, they walked back toward Maggie's hospital room.

"Are you starting in goal again tomorrow night, bro?"

"For sure." Ike appreciated the change of subject. "What about you? Are you playing? Did the extra practice sessions help?"

Kenny's confidence had been knocked when Coach Macarty had made him a healthy scratch for the past couple of games. Ike had reassured him that it wasn't unusual for a player in his first season with an NHL team to struggle—the game was much faster and harder than in the minors—but his brother wouldn't be happy until he was back in the lineup.

"Coach said he'd let me know in the morning."

Kenny sighed. "It wasn't so bad. Watching from the press box gave me a different perspective on how the game is played here, so my positioning on the wing should be better. I just need a chance to put what I've learned into practice."

Ike clapped his brother on the back. "Keep at it, kid, and after the All-Star break in January, it'll click."

"I hope so. I want to do my part, but I feel like I'm a step slower than everyone else."

"Right now, we all need to pick up our play, and that includes our big-money guys."

The Cats' start to the new season had been okay, but not great. They were fourth in their division and a couple of places out of a playoff spot in the Eastern Conference. But their points tally masked the real win-loss picture; the extra points they'd gotten for going to overtime or a shoot-out blurred the fact that they'd lost every freaking one.

Man, he hated shoot-outs and not just because he was 0-for-4 so far. Damn skills contest. They might as well toss a freaking coin. The Cats had lost a couple of their shoot-out stars when his brother Tru had moved to Denver and Vlad had returned to Russia, and to date no one else had stepped up. Sure, Ike could do better, too, but he needed a little help from his teammates. Like at least one of them could score. Then again, they weren't scoring much during regulation, either. Worse, they couldn't hold on to a one-goal lead. The number of times the Cats had given up the tying goal in the last two minutes of a game was plain crazy.

They were all adjusting to the new coach's "run and gun" style. The veterans, like Ike, Jake and the captain, Scotty Matthews, preferred a more defensively responsible system, where even their best forwards would back-check to help out. The kids liked the focus on offence, but tended to be a bit wild. Shots on net hadn't gone up. Goals sure as hell hadn't, either. Ike had had to play out of his mind to scrape the wins they'd got.

Still, Kenny needed reassurance from his oldest brother, not a lecture. "The season's only a month old. Things'll get better. Besides, everyone has to sit out at some point in their career. Even JB Larocque."

"Sure, but no one's going to send a superstar like JB down to the minors if he doesn't deliver. I don't want to go back to riding the bus now that I've made it to the show."

Jake came out of Maggie's room in time to hear Kenny's words. "Hang in there, bro. It'll work out."

Kenny grinned. He didn't stay down about anything too long. "If you old guys say so, I guess I'll be okay."

Ike cuffed his brother around the head. "You need to learn to respect your elders and betters, brat."

"Yeah, but I'm only seeing elders here."

"We old guys have clout with the boss. You don't want to be benched because you gave us too much lip." Despite Ike's ribbing, he was proud to have Kenny playing alongside him.

"This is why I need Tru here." Kenny shook his head. "*He* has a sense of humor."

"Speaking of which, I called him to give him the news," Jake said. "He's going to try to stay an extra day when the Avalanche comes east in December."

"It'll be good to see him." Ike grinned. "It feels weird not to have him skating with us."

They'd all been shocked when the Cats had shown Tru the door during the off-season instead of re-upping his contract. Hardshaw and Macarty had favored the Canucks' stud defenseman, Troy Davidson, over the second-oldest Jelinek brother. Unfortunately, Davidson hadn't yet shown the form he'd had in Vancouver, which had made Tru's absence more difficult.

"Yeah." Jake sighed. "At least he's enjoying Denver. He's slotted into the team well and the Avs are doing better than anyone expected."

"That's because we taught him everything he knows," Ike said loftily.

They all laughed as they headed back into the hospital room.

Despite his best intentions, Ike's heart squeezed when he saw Tracy cradling baby Joe. Her expression was soft and adoring as she murmured nonsense to her drowsy nephew. The maternal look suited her. He couldn't understand why she preferred contracts and clients over a child of her own.

Perhaps Ike was projecting his own feelings. His career wouldn't last forever. He hadn't considered what he'd do once it was over; he didn't like to think about it. That was tempting fate. The hockey gods had a funny way of knocking you on your ass when you thought everything was set. But as retirement loomed closer, he'd begun to feel frustrated that his personal life had stalled. It wasn't as if he were a monk—he'd dated lots of nice women. Seeing Jake and Tru so happy in their marriages had made Ike question why he hadn't been able to find anyone special.

The answer was simple. He hadn't thought seriously about a woman since Tracy. Because of Tracy. Even now, four years later, the shock of her turning him down flat ricocheted through him. He hadn't even proposed, just asked if she wanted to move in with him.

"Your turn. I have to go."

Ike blinked as Tracy handed him the baby. The little dude snuggled into Ike's neck; the scent of baby powder laced with a hint of Tracy's perfume assailed him.

"Leaving so soon?" He hadn't meant the question to sound accusing.

"I need to phone my mum and let her know she has a grandchild." Tracy's icy tone was the stinging rebuke her words weren't.

"Right. Sure." He stumbled over his words, but

she'd already turned away and was saying goodbye to the others.

Crap. Why was it that when he was around her he couldn't open his mouth without sticking his big foot in it?

Tracy didn't acknowledge him again before leaving. Not even when she gently caressed baby Joe's head. Ike didn't need his kid brother's censuring look to know he'd screwed up again.

Maybe it was time to admit he couldn't handle being around her. He should treat her like any other problem. Do them both a favor and steer clear of her. Out of sight, out of mind. That might even open the door for him to find someone who was better suited to him.

Pleased with his solution, he gently rubbed Joe's back. The loud burp that erupted from the little guy startled them both. The timing was coincidental, not a commentary on his plan, Ike reassured himself, even as he hoped the kid wasn't right.

CHAPTER TWO

"WHAT'S WRONG WITH ME?" Tracy muttered as she spooned food into two cat bowls.

Moppet, the more sociable of her black cats, replied with a meow.

Poppet licked a white-tipped paw and washed one of her pricked ears.

"It's crazy," Tracy continued. "I can handle any other man, except Ike bloody Jelinek. Whenever I'm near him, he winds me up and I do something stupid."

With impeccable timing, Moppet hacked up a hairball.

Tracy laughed as she cleaned up the mess. "Maybe tossing coffee on him was a tiny overreaction." She held up her thumb and forefinger to show a small gap. "But it annoys me that there's one rule for his career and one for mine."

Despite Tracy's determination to marry someone completely different from her father, she'd ended up with his twin—only with a more polished veneer. She'd left home at eighteen and headed to Manchester, where she'd waitressed by day and studied business by night. Hank Turner, a visiting academic from New Jersey, had been one of her lecturers. She'd fallen hard for the charming American, marrying him within weeks. It had taken much longer to realize her mistake.

At first, Tracy had overlooked the warning signs, attributing them to the difficulties of adjusting to life in New Jersey. It had taken Hank's affair to rip the blinkers from her eyes. To Tracy's chagrin, she realized she'd become exactly the kind of acquiescent wife she despised.

Poppet head-butted Tracy's ankle, reminding her to hurry up with her food.

Tracy put the bowls down and the two felines dived right in. "Why do I still let Ike get to me? Why can't I ignore him?"

Because he was a hard man to ignore. His presence, even when he wasn't speaking to her, sent that delicious hum through her. The problem was he always did something to turn that hum into a jarring buzz.

When they'd first met, his charm had swept her off her feet. His gentlemanly manners and serious nature were rare in a business full of inflated egos. And their physical connection had sizzled. A touch, a look, a smile and they'd been all over each other like sex-starved teenagers. Ike had treated her as if she were special, both in bed and out. It was only later that his courtliness had begun to feel controlling. Caring suggestions had become polite demands. Compliments about her work had sounded more like criticism.

When Ike had asked her to give up her house and move in with him, she'd panicked. First her house, then her business, then her self-respect. Terrified that history would repeat itself, she'd refused. That final argument had been brutal; the bitter words they'd each said were still a thorn in her heart.

Trying to escape the memories, Tracy went upstairs to her office on the middle floor of her Victorian and sought refuge in work. But as she waited for her computer to power up, her mind went back to Ike.

That he still couldn't understand that her company was more than just an income for her had confirmed that she'd made the right decision. Making Your Move might not keep her warm at night, but it enabled her to sleep soundly—secure in the knowledge that the only person who controlled her life was her. Good or bad, success or failure, she made the decisions. When Making Your Move was number one, she'd have proved to everyone who'd doubted her that she was strong and capable on her own.

Speaking of which, the sooner she got the paperwork to Glen, the quicker he'd sign. Tracy pulled up the Bridgers' proposal document and began to make the changes she and Glen had discussed.

She'd just emailed him the revised copy when she looked at the clock and saw that it was already after eleven. Surprised it was so late, Tracy suddenly remembered her mother.

Damn it. Tracy had been so wrapped up in work, she'd forgotten to call her. She grabbed the phone.

Doris Hayden answered after a dozen rings. "Do you know what time it is?"

Tracy puffed out a frustrated breath. "I'm sorry, Mum. But…"

"You know I don't like calls after ten."

Actually, that had been one of Tracy's father's edicts. Despite his death eighteen months ago, her mother still clung resolutely to every blasted one. Ordinarily, Tracy would have challenged this, but she wasn't in the mood for a row that would only rehash ground they'd covered many times before.

Especially as she'd already had one of those tonight.

"Congratulations," she said with determined brightness. "You're a grandma again."

"Maggie had her baby, then?"

"A gorgeous boy." She filled her mother in on the details. "Jake took loads of pictures and he said he'll email them to everyone in the morning." Before her mother could complain that she didn't know how to use the computer—Dominic Hayden hadn't seen the point in his wife learning—Tracy added, "I'll print them off for you and pop them in the post."

"I won't get them for a week." Her mother sniffed. "I don't know why you girls have to live so far away."

No. She never had.

Tracy tried to head off the waterworks she knew were coming next. "Both Jake and I offered to pay for you to come over here. I can still book you a flight."

"I don't like to fly by myself. Can't you come over and get me?"

Tracy gritted her teeth at the pathetic tone. "I'm sorry, but I can't get away right now. We can organize a car to pick you up at home and someone to help you through the airport. Then we'll meet you when you land."

"I couldn't. It's too much on my own. And Maggie and Jake won't be able to fly to England until the summer. I'll miss out on seeing Emily and Joe for so long."

That's when the tears started, her mother's usual ploy for getting her own way.

Tracy held firm, even when Doris Hayden hit all the guilt-trip hot buttons. Tracy was emotionally wrung out by the time her mother gave up and hung up on her.

Unfortunately, she was also too wired to sleep. Tracy had a glass of wine, hoping that would help her relax, then went to bed. She tossed and turned for several hours. Finally, she admitted defeat and rose. After making a large cup of tea, she went back to her office and focused on the one thing she knew would settle her mind—work.

IKE WASN'T AS superstitious as most goaltenders, but he knew it was a bad sign to fall flat on his ass in the pre-game warm-up before he'd even made it to his crease.

He jumped up and made a show of poking at a nick in the ice, then called for a water bottle from the bench.

Kenny brought one for him, laughing. "I was expecting a freaking crater the way you wiped out, bro."

Ike let his brother's comment slide. He knew Kenny was excited to be back in the lineup after having been a healthy scratch again for the past week's games. Kenny had only played once—the night after baby Joe's birth—before Coach had benched him again. The rationale had been that they'd needed one of the tougher fourth-line guys in Kenny's place for the harder, more physical games, against those opponents. Facing a younger, faster team tonight, Kenny had earned his place back.

"Do you need salt to throw over your shoulder?" Jean-Baptiste Larocque added as he joined them. "We don't want to start the game with bad mojo."

Ike flicked the bird at the star forward, then poured water into the divot. "Nah. No bad luck involved. I must have caught it funny."

Jake skated over and tossed Ike a puck to smooth off the newly frozen patch of ice. His blue eyes were rimmed with red and he looked like he hadn't slept in a week.

"Has your son been keeping you from your beauty sleep again, Bad Boy?" he said, to deflect the attention from himself.

Jake's glare didn't have its normal cutting edge. "Yeah. I'm thinking of getting a hotel room so I can get my pre-game nap in peace."

"You can always crash at my place, bro."

"Thanks." Jake leaned on his stick. "I may take you up on that. Especially when we play Detroit and Toronto."

Both teams were riding winning streaks and had strong road records. The way the Cats had been playing lately, they'd need to bring their A-game to have a chance of getting any points off either team.

"Anytime. There's a bed with your name on it."

"As long as you don't take a nap while you're on the ice, Bad Boy." JB punched Jake in the arm and skated off.

The captain, Scotty Matthews, frowned at them as he glided past. "Stop flapping your gums and get some action going. The Oilers are going to come out hard tonight."

The Islanders had handed Edmonton their butts last night in a game the Oilers should have won. Edmonton's players would be looking to redeem themselves, which wasn't good news for the Cats, who desperately needed the win.

Ike tossed Kenny the water bottle, then kicked the puck at his net. "Just fixing the ice to make sure no one else falls on their ass."

"Aye aye, captain." Kenny saluted Matthews, before dumping the bottle at the bench and joining the rest of the guys skating drills.

Scotty skated back around, then stopped. "So, do you need to sacrifice a chicken or something to ward off the bad luck after your tumble?"

Ike rolled his eyes. "Not this time."

Scotty slapped him on the back. "You sure? We could razz that new kid on the equipment team."

They both laughed. For a moment, Scotty looked like the young rookie he'd once been, rather than the grizzled veteran he was now. As Scotty skated off, Ike knew he'd miss him when the captain retired at the end of the season.

Retirement. Even though it loomed on the horizon at some point for Ike—sooner rather than later—it wasn't something he looked forward to.

Pushing that thought from his mind, Ike warmed up, easing the stiffness from his muscles as he prepared to face shots. He practiced sliding between the pipes, right side, then left side, then right again. He'd need to be on his guard for fast break-outs tonight, especially with the speedy Oilers' wingers.

He put his fall out of his mind and focused on seeing the puck as it began to fly at him from all angles, courtesy of his teammates. Strangely, after a dozen shots, he still didn't feel on his game. Biscuits sailed past him when he should have stopped them.

He frowned, holding up his glove to stop the drill, and took a long drink from his water bottle. After squirting water over his face, he got back into position and nodded to start the routine again.

After another round of shots, he adjusted his stance and his grip. But things still didn't feel right. He forced himself to focus harder, to visualize success. Gradually, he dragged himself into the right mental zone and settled into a comfortable rhythm. He was satisfied he'd be ready for the game, but something still felt off.

Ike left the ice early and headed back to the locker room. Maybe he needed to start over. He stripped down to bare skin and started to dress again, from the jock up. Right sock, then left. Right pads, then left. Pants. Skates. His trusty old chest-and-arm protector, the one he'd worn ever since he'd come up from the minors. He probably should replace it next season—it had been patched so many times—but he hated breaking in new gear.

Finally, he slipped on a clean jersey and got his mask and gloves ready. He downed his pre-game Sprite as he listened to last-minute instructions from Coach Macarty.

Confident he'd done everything so he could go back out onto the ice with a clear head, Ike began to slip into game mode. As the locker-room clock counted down, his mind became sharper, more focused.

At the three-minute mark, Scotty rose and headed to the front of the locker room. As he had every game since becoming captain, he said, "Let's go out there and show them the Ice Cats play the best damn hockey in the world."

Ike joined him, ready to lead the team out. When the doors swung open, he tapped the doorframe for luck and strode forward. The roar of the crowd, along with the announcer's introduction, welcomed him to the ice. This time, he made it to his crease without mishap. Satisfied, he roughed up the blue paint and repeated his post-to-post sliding ritual.

"Good game, bro." Bad Boy tapped his stick against Ike's pads.

He nodded. "You, too."

The horn sounded and Ike removed his mask for the national anthems.

As the singer began "O Canada," Ike's gaze slid over to the family seats. His heart warmed to see his mom and Rory, her husband, and Jake's parents, with Emily between them. It felt weird to see the gaps for the women who weren't there. Maggie, who couldn't leave Joe yet, and Tracy, who always joined her sister and was a staunch Cats' fan. It was unusual for Tracy to miss a game, even for work. Was she okay?

Not your business.

The singer switched to "The Star-Spangled Banner" and Ike forced all thoughts other than those of the players he was about to face from his head.

The first period started quickly, with Ike facing a shot within seconds of the puck dropping. He snatched the biscuit out of the air, stealing a scoring opportunity from the Oilers' rookie wonder kid. Throwing it back out to the corner, he allowed himself a satisfied grin. Whatever had been bothering him earlier was out of his mind now.

All around him, his d-men and the Edmonton top line chirped at each other as they fought for the puck. The air was filled with grunts as bodies thudded into each other. Ike poke-checked and blocked, shoved and kicked—anything to keep that hunk of rubber out of his net.

Finally, Jake broke free and hit Kenny with an outlet pass, clearing the zone and starting a rush to the other end.

Ike kept his eye on the action while steadying his breathing and rolling his tight shoulders. A whistle stopped play. He grabbed a drink from his bottle and skated around his crease before resetting his position.

The Cats lost the face-off, but regained the puck. The battle at the other end of the ice was fierce. A linesman's arm shot up, alerting Ike to a delayed penalty against the Oilers. Ike started to head to the bench for an extra attacker, but they touched up almost immediately and play was blown dead.

The Cats' power-play unit cycled the puck well, but didn't get any clear-cut chances.

"Get shots on net," Ike muttered. "Their guy has a rebound problem."

In the blink of eye, everything changed. One of the Oilers intercepted a sloppy pass and a breakaway was on. Two on one. Kenny and JB raced back to provide cover.

Ike watched the rush unfold, making sure he kept the puck in sight.

The shot stung as it bounced off his chest. He corralled the puck and sent it out to Kenny, but once again it was intercepted by the opposition.

There was a wild goal-mouth scramble.

Bodies went flying. Sticks clashed.

The Oilers' agitator, "Steeler," planted himself on the edge of the crease, his huge body screening Ike's view.

"Get your ass out of my face," Ike growled.

The crude reply involved an anatomically impossible suggestion, followed by a creative one involving a sheep. Ike jabbed the guy with his stick and tried to find the puck.

All of a sudden, play seemed to unfold in slow motion.

A Cats' player was tripped and fell into one of the Oilers. They both caromed toward Steeler, who got hit from the other side by Kenny.

Ike, his gaze glued to the puck on the wonder kid's stick, got sandwiched between the tumbling players. He saw the shot and stretched out with his catching glove to snag the biscuit as the mass of bodies hit the ice in a pile.

The whistle blew.

Steeler fell on top of Ike.

A skate blade flashed.

A sharp pain shot through Ike's arm.

Shocked, he stared at the cut that had gone through both his jersey and his protector. A thin red line marred the skin beneath.

Around him, players peeled off and got to their feet.

"Crap, man. I'm sorry," Steeler said as he helped Ike up.

"Are you okay?" a linesman asked.

Ike nodded, but the pain in his arm worsened. "I think I'd better get this looked at."

He'd barely finished speaking when the cut suddenly widened and blood spurted out.

Ike clamped his other hand on his arm and started to skate to the bench.

He was almost there when his legs went weak. His vision blurred. His legs crumpled.

The arena went silent. Then, there was a collective gasp.

Someone in an Oilers jersey wrapped an arm around his waist. An Ice Cat grabbed him from the other side. Between them, they pulled him to the bench and shoved him through the gate into the care of the trainers.

Stars danced in front of Ike's eyes as the trainers helped him stumble toward the locker room. Fire burned in his arm. He was vaguely aware of blood, wet and warm, pulsing though his fingers. Bile rose up his throat.

Once in the locker room, he gave up his loose grip

on consciousness. As everything faded to black, he wondered just how much bad luck that damn fall had brought him.

CHAPTER THREE

"I REALLY APPRECIATE you staying late to get those invoices finished, Carla." Tracy smiled wearily at her intern, then pushed her chair back from her desk and stretched. "You're a star."

Carla snapped a rubber band around the stack of envelopes and tossed it into the box, ready for posting the next morning. "No problem. Happy to do it. Now that I know what I'm doing, it'll be a lot easier next month. I'll be able to take that job off your hands completely."

"You're already proving yourself to be indispensable. I can't believe you've only been here a week." Tracy turned off her computer and took a sip of her long-cold coffee.

"Is it too early to ask for a permanent job?" Carla asked teasingly.

Tracy laughed. "We'll see how you do for the rest of the month. There might be room in the budget, if those two new pitches for Helping Hands come off."

Impressed with the younger woman's skills and initiative, Tracy was already looking into ways for Carla to stay on once her internship was over. If she continued to be as good as she seemed, she'd be a great addition to the company.

In return, Carla would get invaluable experience at a time when other college graduates were struggling to find even part-time jobs. There were also ways in which Making Your Move could support her if she wanted further education and training. Tracy liked the idea of helping someone else achieve their dream.

"Cool." Carla pulled on her coat and slung her purse over her shoulder. "Are you sure I can't do anything else for you before I go?"

"Thanks, but no. I've kept you late enough as it is."

"In that case, I'll head off. If I'm lucky, I'll catch the third period of the Cats' game on TV when I get home."

"I'm sorry we both had to miss the game. I promise we'll make the next one."

Tracy had offered to take Carla, an avid Cats' fan, to the arena using Maggie's ticket. Unfortunately, an issue with the Chabals' air shipment from Paris had meant a frustrating day with long conversations with Tracy's French counterpart and a lot of chasing around. Although the problem had finally been resolved, it had been midafternoon before she and Carla had been able to tackle the invoices.

"Can't wait." The younger woman grinned. "See you tomorrow."

Carla was barely out the door when Tracy's phone

rang. Her stomach dropped when she heard Maggie's voice; it sounded like her sister was crying. "What's wrong, Maggie?"

"You haven't been watching the game?"

"No. Carla and I have only just finished. Why?"

"There's been an accident. On the ice. It's bad."

"Was it Jake? What happened?" Tracy leaped up and rushed out of her office.

"It wasn't Jake, sis. It was Ike."

Tracy's throat seized. Her knees went weak. She gripped the banister at the top of the stairs.

"Tracy?" Her sister's voice sounded far away.

"Ike?" she managed to force out. "What? Who?"

"There was a goal-mouth pile-up. He was cut by a skate."

Tracy clapped a hand to her mouth, feeling slightly nauseous. "Where?"

"His left arm."

Tracy released a breath. Ike wore special gear that covered his chest and arms. "How's he doing?"

"They don't know. He's in surgery. The team doctor managed to stop the bleeding, so the paramedics could get him to the hospital."

Tracy frowned. "He was cut that badly, even through his protector?"

"The blade sliced through a weak part in the padding—where it had been patched before—cutting Ike's forearm almost to the bone."

"What?" The word came out as a squeak.

"Apparently, his protector was over ten years old.

You know how athletes get about their lucky equipment."

"How can someone so obsessive about everything else be so blasé about his protective gear?" Fear sharpened her tone.

"They all think they're invincible."

"Until something happens to them." Tracy's mind raced. Ike injured... Cut... Surgery.

Anyone who followed hockey knew that skate injuries to players' arms and legs—even on one horrific occasion, a player's neck—were not unusual. There would be stitches by the dozen, months-long recovery periods and scars that would make Frankenstein's monster look like a wimp.

Her stomach rolled at the thought of Ike suffering. His arm. Probably season-ending. Could even be career-threatening.

She didn't question the urgency that finally drove her to move. She had to know. To see for herself that he was all right.

"I'm heading to the hospital now." Tracy ran down the stairs, grabbed her purse and keys and hurried toward her car. "Is anyone with him?"

"Yes. Karina and Rory followed the ambulance, along with Jake's parents. They should be in the waiting room. The guys will be along when the game is over."

"They're still playing?" Tracy shouldn't be shocked. She knew that's what generally happened. Still, it didn't seem right. "How can either team be in any state to think about the game when a player is so seriously injured?"

"I don't know, but they'll tough it out. The Cats will try to get a win for Ike." Maggie sniffed. "Will you call me when you know what's happening? I can't be there myself because of Joe."

"Of course."

Tracy made it to the hospital in record time, thanks to lights in her favor, little traffic on the roads and breaking the speed limit at every possible opportunity. Luck was even on her side with a parking space right near the entrance.

Members of the hockey media were milling about the reception area when she pushed through the doors. From their concerned expressions, she got a sense of just how bad Ike's accident must have been. These guys had seen it all and they looked shaken.

Even though no one but family or team personnel were allowed in the surgical waiting room, Tracy persuaded the receptionist to call through and get permission for her to go back there.

Ike's mother wrapped her in a hug as soon as Tracy walked into the large gray room. The tiny older woman looked as if she'd aged overnight. Her body felt frail, yet her hug was tight. Tracy had always admired her strength, knowing what Karina had been through in her life, but never more so than now.

"I'm glad you're here." Karina's voice wobbled. "Ike will be, too."

Tracy sent Rory a worried look over his wife's head. "Has there been news?"

Rory's weathered face looked ashen as he gently turned Karina into his arms. She laid her head against his barrel chest with a hiccupping sigh.

"Not yet," he replied. "Ike's still in surgery. The nurse said it would be another couple of hours."

"He's in good hands," Jake's dad, Gio, added. "Dr. Gibson is one of the best."

Tina Badoletti nodded. "The Ice Cats made sure Ike got the top guy."

They all stood silently for several moments, lost in their own thoughts.

Desperate not to dwell on what was happening to Ike and knowing they were all in for a long wait, Tracy ushered the two couples over to the dark gray couches and encouraged them to sit. "Can I get anyone a coffee or tea or anything?"

She took their orders and went in search of vending machines. As she waited for the drinks to dispense, Tracy sent a silent prayer heavenward that Ike would be all right.

"IT'S BEEN TWO HOURS."

Karina's quavering words broke the tense silence of the waiting room and jolted Tracy out of her mental debate.

Should she stay or go? She felt out of place sitting here. Technically, she wasn't family and she was hardly Ike's friend. Not that anyone had made her feel unwelcome. Still, the longer they waited, the more awkward she felt.

Tracy wanted to know for sure that Ike had got through the surgery and his arm was fixed. That he'd be all right. She didn't want to wait to hear about it on the news or through social media. Plus, she'd promised Maggie. It wouldn't do any harm to wait a bit longer.

The room was more crowded now. They'd been joined by a couple of trainers from the Ice Cats. Callum Hardshaw was there, too, though just outside the room where they allowed cell phones, getting updates from the team. The game had ended with a 2–1 win for the Ice Cats and Tracy expected Jake, Kenny and the rest of the team to join them shortly. They'd be pleased to have won for Ike, but she doubted anyone was celebrating. Ike's youngest brother, Linc, was on his way from college. Tracy had arranged his transport.

"It'll take as long as it takes, love," Rory reassured his wife. His calm conviction seemed to bring the level of anxiety in the room down a notch.

"The nurse said they were almost done." Jake's mum patted her friend's arm.

"But it can't be good that it's taking this long," Karina fretted.

"Better the surgeon takes his time and does a fine job," Gio Badoletti said.

Rory squeezed his wife's hand. "He's probably making sure his stitches are extraneat."

Karina managed a watery smile.

Gio added, "Ike needs his catching arm fixed right the first time. We all know he'll want to be back between the pipes as quickly as possible."

Tracy could see from Karina's expression that the last thing she wanted was for her son to strap on his skates again. But Karina was a hockey mum; she knew it was futile to expect anything else.

A commotion from outside the room had everyone starting nervously. Kenny pushed through the door, followed by JB Larocque, Scotty Matthews and several other Ice Cats players. A larger group of players hung back, waiting in the hall. Coach Macarty stood in the doorway talking in a low voice with Callum Hardshaw.

"Any news?" Kenny wrapped his mother in a big hug.

"Not yet," Rory replied as Karina shook her head. "But we should hear soon."

Jake brought a burly guy into the waiting room. From his damp hair and the scar next to his mouth, Tracy assumed the man was a player, but she didn't recognize him. The guy hung back, watching anxiously, as Jake went across to the family group.

"I hope it's okay, Aunt Karina, but I brought Darren Steele with me. He and Ike played together in juniors. Steeler feels terrible about what happened and asked if he could come with us."

"Of course it's okay. I remember Darren." Karina waved the man over, hugging him when he joined them. "It's not your fault. Accidents happen. On another day, it could have been you injured. Though I pray that never happens." She crossed herself, then kissed her fingers and sent the kiss heavenward.

Steeler shifted uncomfortably, looking down at his feet. "I appreciate that, ma'am. I'd never hurt Ike intentionally. We always grab a beer whenever we play each other. In fact, we'd planned to go out tonight."

"You can have that drink if..." Karina caught herself. "No, *when* he goes to Edmonton in the new year."

"For sure."

A tall gray-haired man in surgical scrubs came into the waiting room and captured everyone's attention.

Tracy's chest tightened as she scanned the man's face. He looked tired, but she couldn't tell whether his news would be good or bad.

Dr. Gibson cleared his throat. "I'm sure you all have a load of questions for me, but let me give you the good news first. Ike came through surgery well. Although there was extensive damage to his forearm, we were able to repair it all."

Relief flooded through Tracy.

Even so, she felt ill as the surgeon went on to describe the injury—three severed tendons, one partially severed tendon, a sliced artery and some nerve damage. "Thankfully, the prompt attention of the Ice Cats medical staff meant that Ike's arm was in the best condition it could have been for us to work on. That made my job a lot easier."

"Will he make a full recovery?" Rory's quiet question reverberated round the room.

The surgeon gave a weary smile. "It's too early to tell, but the signs are good and there's no reason he shouldn't eventually be as good as new. I'll know more in a couple of days, once the swelling has gone down and his arm has begun to heal."

"What kind of recovery time are we looking at, doc?" Kenny asked.

"Hard to say for sure. Everyone's different. I'd expect Ike to be back on the ice in three to four months."

The room took in a collective breath. *Months*. That meant Ike would be out pretty much for the rest of the season. A huge blow for the Ice Cats.

On the bright side, at least he *would* be back.

"When can I see my boy?" Karina asked.

"He's in recovery right now. Once he's back in his room, he'll be allowed visitors. But only family tonight. The rest of you can see him tomorrow when he's had a chance to rest."

His words broke the tension that had hung like a pall over the room. Everyone started to talk at once as relief washed over them.

Ike was going to be okay. Tears burned in Tracy's eyes. The tightness in her shoulders eased. She felt weak, as if she had nothing left in the tank. Thankfully, no one was paying any attention to her, giving her the chance to pull herself together.

As she got to her feet, getting ready to leave since she wouldn't be able to see Ike tonight anyway, an arm dropped across her shoulders and pulled her close.

"How're you holding up, beautiful?" JB Larocque's dark eyes searched hers.

The Ice Cats star had been an honorary member of the Badoletti and Jelinek clan since Jake had helped him out of trouble in his rookie year. Both Maggie and Tracy had a soft spot for the young charmer, too, thinking of him almost like a younger brother.

"I'm okay, thanks." She managed a half smile, though her lips felt stiff.

"Uh-huh." JB wiped a tear from her cheek with his forefinger. "I can tell."

"I'm relieved. It sounded like a terrible injury. Maggie was worried, so I said I'd find out how Ike was doing for her. Though these days, she'll hear about it more quickly through social media than waiting for me to call." Damn it. Why did she have to babble mindlessly?

"Yeah. Hardshaw just left to update the press. They'll be keen to air his statement, given they've been running the footage of the accident almost constantly."

Tracy's stomach churned. "That's a highlight I don't want to see."

"It was bad enough being there. Scared the crap out of me."

"I don't know how you managed to play on."

"We had to get the *W* for Ike." JB scrubbed a hand across his jaw. "Hardest thing I've ever done."

She tilted her head against his, so their temples touched. "He'll appreciate what you did."

He sighed heavily. "It still sucks."

They stood that way for a few moments, each lost in their own thoughts. Then JB straightened and dropped his arm. "I'd better hit the road. I'm wiped."

"I'll walk out with you."

"Don't you want to see Ike?" He frowned, surprised.

Tracy shook her head. "I'm not family."

"You're as much family as I am."

Though she felt herself wavering, Tracy shook her head again. "I can wait. It's more important for Karina to see him. She's worried sick."

"And you're not?" There was that probing, all-seeing look again.

"Of course I'm concerned. As I would be if any of you got hurt." She hated that her voice shook on the last word.

JB held her gaze silently, as if waiting for her to change her mind. When she didn't, he shrugged. "Whatever you say."

"If you're ready to go, I'll walk out with you."

"Okay." He pressed a kiss to her forehead. "I bet Ike would appreciate you stopping by tomorrow."

About as much as he'd appreciate being sidelined for the next few months. Maybe that's why she was so hesitant about seeing him. She wasn't sure he'd want her there. That thought tugged at her heart. "I…uh…should say goodbye to Karina, but I think I'll just slip away."

"Then let's bug out."

Tracy managed to hold herself together as she walked through the media throng and out of the hospital doors. JB walked her to her car before heading off to his own. Once he'd gone, she lowered her head to the steering wheel, taking several deep, shaky breaths to calm her jittery pulse.

When she got home, Tracy called Maggie to update her on Ike's condition, fed Moppet and Poppet, then poured herself a glass of wine and sank onto the couch. She switched on the TV, hoping to watch something light.

Unfortunately, she caught the sports news, which led off with the story about Ike. Tracy should have changed the channel, but she couldn't look away. Her throat burned as she saw the blood spurt from Ike's injured arm. His pale face and confused expression made her heart ache. A chill went through her as he collapsed and those around him rushed to help. The network kept replaying the moment of the injury. It looked almost harmless. It wasn't like Steeler had stamped on Ike. A quick swipe and the damage was done.

The coverage switched to the press conference

at the hospital. Hardshaw kept details to a minimum, briefly summarizing what the surgeon had told them. Coach Macarty braved the barrage of questions, though he clearly looked as shaken as his players. He shut the interview down when a thoughtless journalist asked about the Ice Cats' goaltending situation while Ike was out.

"This isn't the time for that question. Right now, our thoughts and prayers are with Ike and his family," he snapped before stalking away.

Finally Tracy flicked off the television. Her mind kept replaying what she'd seen in all its glory. Despite the surgeon's reassurances, she couldn't quite believe that Ike was all right.

Her hand trembled as she lifted her wineglass to her lips. Perhaps she'd been a bit hasty, rushing out of the hospital. Maybe if she'd seen Ike, she'd be able to move past the gruesome images etched into her brain.

It would only take a few minutes to stop by and see him tomorrow. Hopefully, he'd still be too groggy from the operation to pay much attention to why she was there. If not, she could claim that Maggie wanted reassurance. Regardless, it was something she had to do. She'd worry about any fallout later.

CHAPTER FOUR

Everyone was laughing at him.

Ike tried to skate across to his crease, but he kept losing an edge and falling over. Meanwhile, the Rangers players jeered at him as they fired pucks into the open net. The score kept flashing up—rising and rising—more like a basketball tally than hockey.

The laughter grew. Ike looked up to see himself on the Jumbotron. Why was he wearing a hospital gown? The other players catcalled as they pointed at his bare ass on the screens.

Determination burned in his gut as he crawled across the ice. He would make it to his goal if it killed him. Inch by painful inch, he drew closer, until he could grab one of the posts to pull himself up. But before he could, the red pipe turned into skate blades, gleaming in the lights of the arena.

Pucks flew at him from all sides. He tried to block or catch them, but kept missing. Finally, one came at him at the perfect angle. He reached out to snatch it from the air, but as he did, his arm went back into the goal and those skate blades closed around it.

He screamed in agony as they sliced his arm with the finesse of a sushi chef and the crowd mockingly chanted his name.

"Ike. Wake up."

Ike felt himself jolt, but couldn't move. His limbs were heavy, as if weighted down. His arm hurt like a son of a bitch. Sweat beaded on his forehead. His heart pounded furiously against his ribs. He tried to swallow, but his mouth was too dry. His eyes opened, but the bright light hurt, so he shut them again.

"It's okay." A gentle hand wiped a cool, moist cloth across his forehead.

The comforting touch helped push the nightmare from his brain until all that remained was the sharp, throbbing pain in his arm. He frowned as he recognized the soothing voice. A familiar scent teased his nostrils, light and fresh above the antiseptic smell.

There was no way Tracy would be mopping his brow.

"You were dreaming." Definitely Tracy's voice. "The nurse said the anesthetic can have that effect on some people."

He must be dying; no way she'd talk that softly to him otherwise. A sorrowful pang tugged at his chest as he mourned lost chances. Why hadn't he done more to try to win her back?

Then, as she wiped his forehead again, reality crashed into his brain. Because no amount of trying would have made a damn bit of difference.

Still, if he was dying, he might as well enjoy his last moments with her. He forced his eyes open, despite the glare of the sun through the window.

"Let me close the blinds a little." Tracy walked to the window.

Ike breathed a sigh of relief as the light faded.

A nurse came in and checked his vital signs and his IV, then adjusted his pillows and showed him how to raise the bed. "If you need more pain relief, you can press this button." She touched the control lying beside his left hand. "Don't be a martyr. It doesn't do you or me any favors."

He nodded his understanding, grateful that the drug took effect almost immediately—seeping into his veins and making him feel light-headed. He didn't like the wooziness, but he ached all over and his arm felt as though those blades were still slicing him.

Once the nurse had left, Tracy returned to his bedside. She hovered uncertainly. If he didn't know better, he'd say she was nervous.

"I…uh…should probably go. I just wanted to check you were okay. For Maggie and…" Her voice trailed off. She cleared her throat. "Anyway, I hope you get better soon."

He didn't want her to leave. "Si—" he tried to speak, but struggled to get a sound out.

"Here." Tracy put a glass of water in his good hand, twisting the straw so it was against his lips. "Dry mouth is another side effect."

The cold water was blissful against his raw throat. After several sips, he said hoarsely, "Sit. Stay. Please."

She hesitated for a few seconds, then perched on the edge of the chair, looking like she might jump up again at any moment. "How are you feeling?"

"Like I got ran over by a Zamboni. Twice."

"That second time is always the killer." Her lips curved briefly. "You gave everyone quite a scare. Poor Steeler was beside himself."

As she spoke, memories began to flood back. But Ike's mind was still muddled and he found it hard to distinguish between what had really happened and what had been a dream. Clearly the whole "bare-assed in a gown" thing wasn't true. The damage to his arm, though, was all too real.

"I remember the pileup and making it off the ice. After that, it's a blank until I woke up in this room." He frowned again. "I don't even know if the Cats won."

"They did, and Kenny got you the game puck. Though I don't know why you'd want a souvenir of *that* game."

Ike shrugged. "It's one to add to the collection, I guess. It's not like I get hurt too often."

"I think you've made up for your lack of injuries with this one."

"For sure. The doc said it'll be a long time before I can even practice, let alone play."

"I know that's tough, but once your arm heals, you'll be as good as new. You're lucky."

"Real lucky—I'm out until at least March." Everything was clear now, even the things he wished he could forget.

"You could have been out permanently." Tracy's voice softened. "You'll be back on the ice before you know it."

"In the meantime, I'm not freaking allowed out of bed until I get the okay from the doc. I can't even twiddle my thumbs." His laugh was edged with bitterness. "Then when he does let me up, all I can do is physio on my arm. I can't work out until I'm cleared from that—which could be weeks."

How the hell was he supposed to keep himself game-fit if he couldn't exercise? Not even a stationary bike. Ike had promised he'd be careful not to do anything that'd damage his arm—damn it, he wouldn't risk setting his recovery back further—but Dr. Gibson had been resolute. Ike's arm was the first, the only, priority.

The one glimmer of hope had been the surgeon's confidence that Ike's overall level of fitness would mean his recovery should be faster than for a non-athlete. But even that had come with a caveat—as long as Ike followed instructions to the letter.

"I'm sure it'll pass more quickly than you think," Tracy said with a reassuring smile.

Ike shot her an incredulous look. "The hell it will. It'll be worse than waiting for the play-offs to end when you haven't made the cut. You just want them to freaking award the Cup already, so you can start thinking about the next season. This..." He clenched his jaw against the urge to yell. "This will be pure torture."

And he'd suffer alone. He couldn't hang with the team. Though, truthfully, he wasn't sure he wanted to. It'd be the worst kind of torment—being around the guys but not able to practice or do anything to help the team. Having to wear a suit and sit in the press-box for every home game—man, he hadn't done that since his rookie year. Nah—better to stay away altogether until he had the green light to skate.

"All you can do is take it one day at a time."

"I don't have a choice, do I?"

"No. Sorry."

Ike slumped back against the pillows. "At least if I was a horse, they'd shoot me to put me out of my misery."

"For heaven's sake." Tracy rolled her eyes. "It's not the end of the world."

"Isn't it?"

"You act like you've been told you can't ever play again. Think of those poor blokes who suddenly develop medical conditions—like heart irregularities and strokes—that are career-ending. Your injury isn't even *season*-ending."

Her lecturing tone brought out her English accent. It made him feel like a petulant child.

It also made him hot.

Not that he could do anything about that right now. Instantly, his brain filled with images of how they could take advantage of the bed without jarring his arm. It would require a little athleticism on Tracy's part. If she climbed up and positioned herself…

Stop! What was wrong with him?

He shifted, hoping she wouldn't notice his distraction. "I'll be fine once I can get out of this bed. Even better once they let me go home. At least I don't have to wait on Physio to sign my discharge papers."

"Can I do anything to help?"

His mind zipped back to the fantasy he'd had only moments ago. Crap. That wasn't what he needed to be thinking about. Embarrassed by his one-track mind, he replied more harshly than he intended. "What do you mean, 'help'?"

"I don't know. Anything you need doing for you at home? Whatever will make life easier while you're not able to do much for yourself."

"You're kidding," he snapped. Her offer scraped his already sore ego. He hated feeling helpless. Useless. That's all he needed—Miss Freaking Superwoman feeling sorry for him and treating him like an invalid. "I've been in hospital less than twenty-four hours and you're already touting for business."

Tracy reared back as if he'd hit her. "That wasn't what I meant at all."

"Yeah, right. I know you—Making Your Move is all you think about. Well, I'm not going to be a guinea pig for your new services. You'll have to find some other way to get the Ice Cats interested."

"Where the hell did that come from? I never mentioned my company or my services." Tracy pushed the chair back and stood. Hurt darkened her eyes. "I was trying to be friendly. I should have known better."

Ike knew he'd made a big mistake, but couldn't bring himself to back down. "Come on, you're not telling me you wouldn't have offered me a special discount?"

"Actually, I'd have helped you for free." Her tone was icy. "I'd have done whatever you needed out of the goodness of my heart."

Way to go, numb-nuts. What's your next trick?

He opened his mouth to apologize, but she held up her hand to stop him.

Tracy stalked to the door. She reached for the knob, but instead of turning it, she marched back to the bed. She then took a glossy brochure out of her purse and slapped it down on the bedside table. "I might as well get hung for a sheep as a lamb. Should you require any assistance during your recovery, this is a list of the services Helping Hands provides. Feel free to call and make an appointment and I'll see if I can fit you in." Her lips twisted. "Assuming I'd even accept you as a client. One of the perks of being the boss is that I get to choose who I work for."

It was a good thing hospital doors didn't slam, though Tracy closed it with enough force to show that she was pissed—as if Ike hadn't already got that message. Even injured, he couldn't do anything right with Tracy. Made him wonder why he kept trying.

WORK DIDN'T PROVIDE its usual distraction. Tracy finally had admitted it to herself after reading the same document three times and not taking in a word. She tossed down her pen and headed downstairs to the kitchen.

She'd been a fool to visit Ike this morning. Why hadn't she listened to her inner voice when it had yelled that she was making a huge mistake the moment she'd walked into his hospital room? Or when it had kept yelling, as her heart had softened at the sight of him asleep, his body so still, his arm heavily bandaged and immobilized from shoulder to fingertip. The beeping monitors and IV drip had made him seem vulnerable. What harm could sitting with him for a few minutes do?

She grimaced as she stuck her mug of stone-cold tea in the microwave to reheat. Those few minutes had stretched to half an hour. She'd kept telling herself she'd leave as soon as he awoke. But when he'd finally begun to surface, he'd been so restless that Tracy had been worried he might hurt himself. Though she was relieved that she'd been able to soothe him, she'd felt awkward and a little foolish once he was fully conscious. Especially as he'd been more or less his normal self—if a little grouchy.

His horrible accusation had shocked Tracy because she'd always thought that despite their differences, he'd at least respected her. How could he believe that turning his injury into a business opportunity would ever cross her mind? Knowing that he thought her capable of such heartless behavior had really hurt.

When had things between them deteriorated so badly?

Could it be fixed? She may not want to marry Ike, but would like them to be able to have a conversation where they weren't ripping each other apart.

As Tracy was contemplating whether a truce was possible, Carla walked into the kitchen.

"Is there a reason you're not answering your phone?"

Tracy frowned, confused. "No. Why?"

"Callum Hardshaw's assistant called me when she couldn't get ahold of you."

Reaching into her pocket for her mobile, Tracy remembered that she'd turned the phone off when she'd visited Ike. She turned on the phone to see several missed calls from clients, including the Ice Cats.

"Bloody hell. Is there a problem?"

"No. She just wanted to know if you'd stop by and see Mr. Hardshaw when you go to the Cats' offices later."

"I wonder why now. Maggie and I have been trying to get an appointment with him since his appointment over the summer, but he always fobs us off with one of his underlings."

Carla shrugged. "His assistant didn't say there was an issue. Maybe he wants to congratulate you on doing a great job."

"Hmm. Somehow I don't think so. He isn't one to waste time with praise for doing what you're supposed to."

A little unnerved by the GM's request, Tracy headed back up to her office and did a quick review of the current Ice Cats projects, even though she knew there weren't any issues. Everything was running on or ahead of schedule. Making Your Move had even come in below budget on several recent projects.

Oh, well. She'd find out what this was about soon enough.

It felt weird to walk into the Ice Cats' headquarters that afternoon. Tracy's eyes were drawn to the team photographs that covered the walls of the reception area. It was as though Ike's face was highlighted in each one, from the posed annual pictures to the familiar celebratory photo from a few years back of the team sprawled on the ice around the Stanley Cup.

It was stranger still to be part of a meeting as Cats' management discussed the measures they'd be putting in place for Ike's absence. Her role was to ensure that the goaltender they wanted to bring up from their AHL affiliate was where he had to be on time and had a place to stay. She also had to make sure the contingency plans could be put into action smoothly and quickly, as required. Tracy couldn't help feeling guilty. As if somehow she were being disloyal to Ike.

"Don't be ridiculous," she muttered to herself as she walked down the long corridor toward the offices. "It's all part of the job."

About that, at least, Ike would be pragmatic.

Tracy was shown into the GM's office straight away. She didn't pick up a bad vibe about the meeting, but she was still on her guard.

Callum Hardshaw rose to greet her, smiling. He was a smartly dressed, big man, with graying hair and a broad face. The scar that bisected his jaw was the only visible sign that he'd been a player himself, though only in the minor leagues.

"Good to finally meet you." He shook her hand. "My staff has told me positive things about your company."

"Thank you. That's always nice to hear." Tracy took the seat he indicated.

"I appreciate your making time to see me today. I'm taking the opportunity, now the season's fully underway, to meet all our suppliers. While I'm not a hands-on manager, I like to have a clear understanding of how things operate in my organization."

"Of course," Tracy said politely. Hardshaw's tone and body language were genial, but she still didn't relax. "What would you like to know?"

"Tell me about your company and how you came to be working for the Cats."

As Tracy explained what Making Your Move did, she sensed she was being evaluated more closely than the casual conversation might suggest. Hardshaw seemed particularly interested in her other clients and the kinds of projects she did for them. Naturally, she didn't reveal specifics, but gave him a general picture. He made a point of his approval that she didn't work for rival teams in any sport, in order to avoid any conflict of interest.

"I understand your sister is married to Jake Badoletti."

"That's correct." She deliberately didn't say anything further, waiting to see if the GM would make an issue of it.

He didn't, moving on to the projects she was currently working on. Yet Tracy filed away the fact that he'd raised it for future reference.

"I understand you'd like us to consider your new service, Helping Hands." Hardshaw pointed to the brochure on his desk. "How do you think it could benefit our organization?"

Pleased by the opportunity to pitch directly to the GM, Tracy sat forward and told him about the kinds of things they could offer: from employing and managing household services, to grocery shopping. She used the Chabals as an example and offered Glen as a reference.

"I see." Hardshaw steepled his fingers and tapped them against his chin. "Given how much business we do with you, isn't this a service that should be included for free?"

Now the negotiation started. Tracy smiled. "Naturally, we value your business highly, which is why the Ice Cats already get a number of extras thrown in. In the case of Helping Hands, we feel the returns far outweigh the investment." She went on to explain not only the benefits to the players, but also how Helping Hands could be used to offset player bonuses.

The interest he showed in that particular argument made her wonder if there were financial issues she wasn't aware of. Professional hockey was an expensive business.

The meeting ended shortly after. As she walked back to her car, Tracy couldn't shake the feeling that there was another, less pleasant reason behind Hardshaw's questions. She wasn't naive; relocation was a competitive market and there were a number of good companies who could provide the same services she did. That was why she and Maggie worked hard to ensure Making Your Move provided added value with every project. And why it was vital that Helping Hands was successful.

Losing the Cats' business would be a major setback. Not just financially, but for her longer-term goals. Without the turnover from the Cats, she'd drop way down the market rankings. She wouldn't let that happen. Not when she was so close to cracking the top three, at last.

Even though she'd had no specific indication that the contract was under threat, it never hurt to be prepared. That, after all, was how she'd made her company a success. Time for a contingency plan of her own.

CHAPTER FIVE

GAME DAY. THE RANGERS. In our barn. Bring it on.

For a few seconds, when Ike awoke, his heart pumped fast as adrenaline shot through his body. Then reality sank in. He wouldn't be strapping on his pads or lacing up his skates. He was stuck in this freaking bed, just as he had been for the past couple of days, unable to do anything—not even take a piss—without supervision and assistance. Hell, the only thing similar to a normal game day was that he'd taken a nap this afternoon.

This sucked. It didn't help that the wall clock was opposite his bed, so he couldn't avoid seeing the time. Four o'clock. His teammates would be arriving at the arena for their pre-game preparations. He could visualize the locker room: equipment laid out in each player's stall; crisp, clean sweaters hanging on pegs. He could practically hear the grinding of skate blades being sharpened and smell the acrid aroma of heated sticks.

Ike's chest squeezed as he imagined Kenny and JB cracking terrible jokes, Mad Dog and Blake arguing over what music to play to pump up the team, and Jake and Scotty swapping stories about their kids. Coach Macarty would be scrawling key points for the game on the large whiteboard at the front of the room, while Patrick "Beefy" DuBoeuf, the goal-tending coach, would be going through last-minute notes with the Cats' number-two net-minder—Chaz "Monty" Montgomery.

Ike had to restrain himself from reaching for his phone to call and add his own advice. Not that Beefy would forget anything, but this was an important game and Ike had more experience than anyone at facing their cross-river rivals. He hadn't missed a game against the Rangers in more than a decade and his record against them was strong.

Monty could handle it—he was a solid goaltender—but he didn't know the opposition as well as Ike. Although they trained together, reviewed video and discussed players and tactics, being theoretically well versed wasn't the same as having hands-on experience.

Truth was, the only person Ike wanted between the pipes for the Cats was himself.

Get over yourself! The guys would cope without him.

Doesn't matter if they can't. They have no choice.

Just as Ike had no choice.

Like it or not—and he sure as hell didn't—he wouldn't be minding the net for months.

He tried to cross his arms across his chest, but

only succeeded in bashing himself with his cast. Pain shot through his arm, setting his teeth on edge.

Why hadn't he listened to the trainer's advice about his protector? Ellis had warned that Ike was taking a big risk every time he went out onto the ice. The padding was wearing thin, so Ike had felt every puck that bounced off the snow leopard's head on his sweater. With the speed that some of those guys fired shots these days, it had stung. More often than not he'd had the bruises to prove it.

But Ike had kept putting off replacing his protector. Finding new gear, then wearing it in was a pain in the ass. Plus he felt uncomfortable changing something that worked for him. Not because of superstition, really, but to be practical. He'd figured one more season wouldn't hurt. *How's that working out for you, dumbass?*

"A positive mental attitude is half the battle when it comes to healing." Dr. Gibson strode into the room. "I'm not seeing much of that in here."

Ike's smile felt like a grimace. "Yeah, yeah. Happy, happy. When can I get out of here?"

"The answer won't change just because you keep asking me." The doc examined Ike's arm, pressing gently in various places. "When I'm sure you've healed enough for you to be able to move around without doing any damage. A couple more days. Enjoy the rest and the great food."

Dr. Gibson's cheery tone bugged the hell out of Ike. "Can I at least get out of bed?"

The surgeon made some notes on Ike's chart. "Assuming you don't develop any problems, you can get up tomorrow. But I want you to take it very easy."

As if he were going to start a street hockey game in the hallway. "About time. I'm sick of staring at these damn four walls."

"From what the nurses tell me, you've had plenty of visitors."

Ike knew he was lucky so many people had stopped by—his family, his teammates, the backroom staff. The problem was that after asking him how he was, nobody knew what to say. The guys hovered uncertainly, looking guilty every time they mentioned hockey. "I hate lying here doing nothing."

"I know it's frustrating but it'll be worth it. The more care we take at this stage of the process, the quicker you'll be able to get back to normal activity."

"So you keep telling me."

"Then maybe today you'll listen." Dr. Gibson clicked his pen and shoved it into his shirt pocket. "Have you figured out what you're going to do when you go home? You know you won't be allowed to drive or do anything with that arm for at least a month. No lifting, no carrying, no holding, no exercise—nothing that might risk reinjuring your arm."

Ike shrugged. "I'll work something out."

"You can't take this lightly. I'll want to be sure you can cope before I discharge you, so I'll expect to see what arrangements you have in place. I don't want to have to get the Ice Cats management involved, but I will if I think you're not taking me seriously."

"I won't do anything to jeopardize my recovery, Doc. Trust me. The occupational therapist has already been to see me and I have a list a mile long of what I need to do before I go home."

"That's what I like to hear. Nothing warms my heart like a model patient."

Once the surgeon had gone, Ike puffed out a frustrated breath. Now what did he do? There was nothing worth watching on TV and he was tired of reading and playing games on his iPad. A few more days of this and he'd be certifiable. The evening stretched out ahead of him like a desert. There wouldn't be any visitors tonight since everyone would be at the arena. He hadn't made up his mind whether or not to watch the game. He wanted to support the guys, but it might be too painful.

"You're looking better today." Ike's mom bustled into the room, followed by Rory.

She rushed forward, then halted abruptly by his bed, as if unsure how to hug him without doing any damage. Ike sighed inwardly. She'd done the same thing each time she'd visited.

"I won't break, Ma," he said gently.

Karina looked anxiously at her husband, waiting for his encouraging nod before wrapping Ike in her arms. Her familiar scent—a combination of sugar and spice from baking and apple from her perfume—warmed his heart.

"Your mother made your favorite." Rory set a bag on top of the bedside cabinet. "Enough baklava to feed the entire floor."

"That's great. Thanks." Ike hugged his mom with his good arm.

She kissed his forehead, as if he were still a small boy. "Food is the best medicine. Make sure you don't eat it all. Let your nurses have some, too."

"But there won't be any left if I let them near it."

"They deserve a reward for putting up with you, boyo." Rory patted Ike's right shoulder.

"I'm sure he's been as nice as gold," his mom said earnestly, though there was a twinkle in her green eyes.

"As *good* as gold, Ma," Ike corrected gently.

"Or as nice as *pie*," Rory added with an indulgent smile.

Karina threw up her hands. "Pie, gold, nice, good. It's all the same, no?"

Ike and Rory exchanged amused looks. "Sure."

"You boys." His mom shook her head at them, her gray curls bouncing. "Anyway, what did the doctor say about you going home?"

Ike made his tone upbeat. "I should be out of here in a few days. I can't wait."

"Rory and I think you should come stay with us. You need somewhere to rest and I can look after you until you're better."

He loved his mom, but he really didn't want her

fussing over him. "I appreciate the offer, Ma, but I'll be fine."

She frowned. "But who's going to cook for you and make sure you have groceries? I don't want you living on takeout. And who'll look after your place and do your laundry?"

"I have a cleaning service. The rest I'll figure out." He was saying that a lot today. "Besides, you guys are newlyweds. You don't want me around, cramping your style."

"Your mum would feel better if she had you under her roof." Rory crossed his arms over his chest, making it clear that whatever his wife wanted he'd make damn sure she got.

"I appreciate that, but I'll be out of action for several weeks. You can't look after me for that long. What about your trip at Thanksgiving?"

Ike and his brothers had all pitched in to send their mom and Rory on a visit to see his family, followed by a belated honeymoon in southern Ireland.

"We'll delay it." Karina waved her hand dismissively. "I'm not going anywhere until I know you're okay."

"That's crazy. It's all planned and you've both been looking forward to it."

His mom planted her hands on her hips. "I can't leave you by yourself."

"I'm a grown man, Ma. I'll find someone to help me out."

"Who can look after you better than your mother?"

He rolled his eyes at her. "Jeez. There's no good answer to that question."

Her lips twitched, but she shook her head. "Unless I take care of you myself, I can't be sure you won't overdo things."

"There's no chance of that. Anyway, the doc has said he won't let me out of here until I have the proper support in place."

"At least someone is being sensible," she huffed.

"It'll all be covered. Trust me. There's no need for you to postpone your trip."

He'd make damn sure; he wouldn't ruin his mom's first vacation in years. "So, have you got some new outfits to take to Ireland?"

His mom gave him a look that said she'd allow him to distract her. The rest of the visit was spent talking about the upcoming trip.

All too soon, it was time for his mom and Rory to go to the arena to watch the game. Kenny was in the lineup again and they wanted to support him.

Ike shoved down his envy. "Have a good time."

"It won't be the same without you in net," Rory said, understanding in his eyes.

"Tell everyone to give the Blueshirts hell and tell Kenny to have a good game."

His mom hugged him. "I expect to hear what you've 'figured out' tomorrow."

"Yes, ma'am." He picked up the list the occupational therapist had left him. “See, working on it now.”

Ike waited until his mom and Rory had gone before reading the papers. There was a crap-load of stuff to arrange and not much time to do it. His frustration grew—he couldn’t use his freaking arm, but the list made him sound like an invalid.

Still, if he wanted out of here, he had to get it sorted. Starting now. It wasn’t as if he had anything better to do.

Ike went down the checklist to see what he could cross off easily. The cleaning service. They might do extra chores for him, like laundry. He reached for his cell and dialed their number. Unfortunately, no one answered, so he left a message and continued down the list. But he only got halfway through the page before tossing it aside in frustration. He couldn’t check anything off without a crazy amount of internet research to find out which companies were reputable. Then he’d have to check references and get quotes. How the hell was he supposed to manage all of that from here?

The simple answer was he couldn’t. But he knew someone who could.

Ike reached for the Helping Hands brochure Tracy had left him. It was the perfect solution. She’d do the legwork and present him with options and prices. All he’d have to do was say which ones he wanted and write a check.

Unfortunately, the chances of Tracy working for

him were probably close to zero after the way he'd treated her. Bad enough that he'd been an ass when she'd visited, but he'd attacked the very thing he needed—her business. She wouldn't spit on him if he was on fire.

Ike hadn't had the chance to apologize because she hadn't been back to see him. He'd planned to fix things once he was out of the hospital. Clearly, he couldn't wait that long.

The problem now was that she'd think the only reason he wanted to apologize was that he needed her help.

Ike swore. Just like every other damn thing to do with his injury, he had no choice. He *did* need her help. And fast.

Perhaps she'd soften toward him if he showed he respected her business. He might not like that work always came first, but he admired what she'd achieved with Making Your Move. He could offer to spread the word about Helping Hands. Not just within the Ice Cats' organization, but other NHL teams, too.

He should also grovel. Yeah. Probably do the groveling first.

Before he could change his mind, Ike grabbed his cell and dialed.

HELL HAD FROZEN over and Satan was skating on his personal hockey rink.

Why else would Ike's name be on her caller ID?

What did he want? She rolled her eyes. The easiest way to find out was to answer. She was tempted to let his call go to voice mail and see what message he left. But returning his call would put her on the back foot. Making him drive the conversation put her in control.

She took a calming breath and answered. "Making Your Move, Tracy Hayden speaking."

"Yeah. Hi." He sounded startled, as though he hadn't expected her to answer. "It's Ike."

She kept her tone civil but cool. "Hello."

Silence. Tracy could hear him breathing. He was probably waiting for her to say something, but she was determined not to speak first.

"So," he said finally. "I…uh…owe you an apology."

"You do."

More silence.

He sighed heavily. "I was a jackass."

Tracy blinked, surprised. "You were."

"I'm sorry."

She bit her lip, not prepared to let him off that easily. "I see."

"I could blame the drugs—damn pills make me dopey as hell. Truth is I've been feeling sorry for myself and I took it out on you. Your offer touched a nerve and I reacted badly."

His honesty took her aback. "Next time I'll remember not to be helpful."

"I hope this is the last time I'll be in this situation. Anyway, I said some things I didn't mean and I'm really sorry."

From his stilted delivery and his clear discomfort, Tracy believed his regret was sincere. Still, she got the feeling there was more to his call than an apology. "Okay."

"Am I forgiven?"

"Your apology is accepted," she said politely.

"Good. Great. Thanks. So, are you going to the game tonight?" he asked.

"I'd hoped to, but I have too much work." She hadn't meant her answer to be a test, but she was interested to hear his response.

"That's a shame. Should be a good tilt." He didn't sound chastising or snide. Full marks for effort.

She continued cautiously. "I wouldn't normally miss a game against the Rangers, but I have a lot to do before Mme. Chabal arrives this weekend. She wants everything I proposed and the Bridgers have agreed to fund it all."

"Congratulations. That'll be a nice boost for Helping Hands."

Ike was batting a thousand. Not only had he remembered the name of her new service, he actually sounded pleased for her. Yet she couldn't help waiting for the other shoe to drop.

"Thanks. The team are considering extending this service to other players, so I'm pleased. Hopefully, from there, we can expand to our other clients. Even so, I'll be sorry to miss the game. I take it you'll be watching on TV?"

"Probably not. It's hard enough when you're sitting on the bench as backup. At least then there's the chance of being called on to help out if things go south. It's hell knowing that if the Cats are losing I can't do anything about it. I hate feeling useless."

"I can understand that."

"The flipside is it'll be a long evening, stuck here in this bed. Watching the game will help the time pass more quickly."

Tracy felt sorry for him. He sounded miserable. "You're still not allowed up?"

"Nope. Maybe tomorrow. I just have to get through tonight." He paused, then said, "If you get your work done early, it would be good to have some company."

That was the last thing she'd expected from him. His deliberately casual request, with just a hint of hopefulness, made her heart clench. She wanted to say she'd be there, but something made her cautious. "I don't know. I'll see how it goes."

"For sure. No problem either way."

His tone was so like her mum's—the pathetic one that said it *did* matter—yet Tracy didn't feel the irritation she should have. Ike wasn't into manipulative guilt trips. He had no problem calling a spade a bloody shovel. He was trying to be polite.

Which made her feel even sorrier for him. For someone who needed to be in control, his situation must be terrible. What harm could there be in a short visit?

"Actually, I have to pick up some documents from a client near the hospital later. I could stop by to see you after that." It wasn't strictly true—she didn't have to pick them up *tonight*—but he didn't need to know that. She didn't want him to think she was rushing in to see him just because he'd asked. Even if that was exactly what she was doing.

"Great. I'll look forward to it."

Tracy sat staring at the phone for a few moments once she'd hung up.

She couldn't shake the feeling that Ike had a hidden agenda, but she couldn't figure out what it would be. Perhaps when they were face-to-face it would be easier to see. Until then, she'd give him the benefit of the doubt. She didn't acknowledge the hope sparking within her that Ike's apology and desire to see her were just what they seemed.

For the next hour, Tracy worked solidly to finish the comprehensive information package she'd been compiling for Lise Chabal. Tracy was proud of how well it had turned out.

Tracy would've loved to have had something similar when she'd first arrived in the States. Even though she spoke the language, unlike Lise, everything had been so different and Tracy had floundered. With the benefit of hindsight, she knew that was when her reliance on Hank had started. His guidance had smoothed the way for her and it had been easy to slip into the habit of doing whatever he said.

There was a certain smug satisfaction in knowing that Hank's lump-sum divorce settlement had helped her start Making Your Move. And in knowing that she'd proved him—and her father—wrong when they'd said she couldn't make it work. She'd not only survived, but if Helping Hands was the success she thought it could be, she'd be sitting pretty at the top of that market.

On that cheery note, she should get to the hospital. Tracy switched off her computer and grabbed her coat and purse.

When she got to Ike's floor, Tracy nipped into the visitors' bathroom to put on some lipstick. Just to tidy up. She pulled a face at the mirror. Who was she kidding?

As she signed in on the ward, the nurse in charge greeted her cheerfully. "Watch out. Ike's in a grumpy mood. Something about his team already losing."

"Not just losing, but down 2–0 after only five minutes." Tracy smiled. "Sorry, you probably don't care about the details."

"Not really." The nurse grinned. "But when it affects your patient, you have to be 'interested' in all kinds of things. Hockey's better than fly-fishing or ultimate cage fighting."

"That's true." Tracy laughed. "Hopefully a visitor will cheer him up. Though even that won't work if the Cats get blown out."

"I'll keep my fingers crossed for a turnaround, then."

Tracy had just reached Ike's room when she heard him roar.

"I don't need a freaking straw in my drink and I don't want you to cut up my food."

A young blonde volunteer in a striped uniform rushed past Tracy, her face flushed. "Perhaps you'll have better luck with him."

Tracy smiled sympathetically, then strode into the room. "Someone's in a foul mood."

"You'd be miserable, too, if you weren't even allowed to use a freaking knife and fork," he growled, crossing his arms awkwardly over his broad chest. The bandages that covered his arm from fingers to shoulder hampered his movement.

The flowery pastel-blue gown should have looked silly on such an obviously masculine body. Instead, it emphasized his honed chest and arms, making him look more manly, rather than less. But Ike didn't need to know that.

Nor that he'd made her pulse skip. "Good job I'm here to give the staff a break from your charming personality."

He narrowed his gaze. "Do *not* push me."

"Seriously?" Tracy rolled her eyes. "That might work on a sweet young thing like that candy striper, but I'm immune."

Ike's green eyes turned fiery, challenging her to take him on.

She tamped down her body's instant heated response. Besides, she shouldn't tease a wounded man. Especially one whose pride probably hurt as much as his arm.

"How are you feeling?" she asked brightly as she sat in the chair beside his bed. "Are you at least being sensible about taking painkillers?"

"I've been better," he admitted grudgingly. "And yes, I'm taking the pain meds. My arm aches and throbs like a son of a bitch if I don't. But it's improving, so I won't be on them much longer."

"Has the specialist said when you can go home?" She grinned. "I bet the nursing staff are pushing for tomorrow."

"If only. I'll be out of here by the weekend."

"So soon? I thought you'd be in here for a few more weeks. Maybe even a month."

"Not a chance. No way am I sticking around here for the next four weeks."

"Four *to six* weeks." The nurse she'd spoken to earlier bustled into the room and cleared away his dinner tray. "And you're lucky you're young and healthy or it would be a darn sight longer than that."

Ike shrugged. "My season's pretty much done either way."

"That's no way to look at it." The nurse tutted. "And this behavior is unacceptable. If you can't treat my staff with respect, I'll come in here and stick a feeding tube down your throat. Got it?"

Tracy's lips twitched. She could tell Ike wanted to dare the nurse to try it, but wisely bit his tongue.

"Yeah," he huffed. "Tell the girl I'm sorry. It burned my butt to have a kid treating me like I was some old dude in a wheelchair."

"It's your own fault. How exactly had you planned to eat steak by yourself?"

"I didn't think of that. I was sick of soup—I'll float away if I eat any more—so I ordered something I could get my teeth into. Next time, I'll order a sandwich or something I can eat one-handed." He made it sound like cyanide with a side order of arsenic.

"How will you cope once you get home?" the nurse asked. "You won't be able to cook anything."

"My mom will fill my freezer with meals I can nuke. And there's always delivery. It only takes one finger to dial." He smiled cockily.

"Fast food will do wonders for your figure when you can't exercise," Tracy said helpfully. "You need to be careful you don't turn into the Michelin Man."

The nurse laughed as she walked to the door. "I know I'm leaving you in good hands."

He glared at her. "You're all heart. I thought you were supposed to be concerned for my health and well-being."

"I am. To show I don't hold grudges, I'll order a couple of sandwiches for you."

"Thanks." Once she'd gone, Ike muttered, "Man,

I'll be glad to be out of here so I can get back to normal, without people watching my every move."

That whole exchange had reinforced how much Ike wouldn't be able to do for himself with his injured arm. Tracy also knew that he wouldn't be above ignoring instructions if he got frustrated. "At the risk of being accused of touting for business, how *are* you going to manage when you go home?"

His gaze flicked away briefly, then returned. "Actually, that's something I wanted to talk to you about."

The earlier feeling about Ike's hidden agenda returned. "Oh?"

He hesitated, then blew out a breath. "I need your help. Please."

"To do…what exactly?" Tracy frowned.

Ike's expression became earnest. "I'm not dumb. I accept that I'll need support when I go home. Finding the right services will be tough when I'm stuck in here. But I need everything in place for when I get out. Helping Hands is the answer."

Tracy should have been pleased, but she couldn't help feeling disappointed. It really stung that his apology had been driven by his need for her professional services, rather than a genuine desire to repair their relationship. "I see."

He smiled charmingly. "I'll pay your going rate and give you a great reference. I'll even promote Helping Hands with the rest of the guys."

So now her business was okay…when he needed

her help. How bloody convenient. Still, she was damned if she'd be anything but professional about this.

"Has the occupational therapist given you a list of what you'll need?"

His smile faded at her cool tone. "In the drawer." He pointed at the bedside table.

She made no move to get the list. "I'm guessing your orthopedic surgeon is playing hardball and threatening not to sign your release until you have that support system in place."

"Yeah." Ike's green gaze dipped and he looked uncomfortable. "The Cats are behind him one hundred percent."

That explained Ike's sudden change of heart. She'd been a fool to believe that he was genuinely sorry. And to hope they could finally stop being at war with each other. "Naturally. You're a valuable asset. They won't want anything to jeopardize your recovery, least of all you."

"I want my arm to heal as quickly as possible, too. I sure as hell wouldn't do anything that might delay my return to the ice."

Yes—he'd made it pretty clear how much that return mattered.

"So, what do you think?" he asked expectantly.

CHAPTER SIX

"I JUST WANT to be clear about one thing."

Something in Tracy's tone made Ike wary. "What's that?"

"Your apology was a ploy, wasn't it? To make me feel sorry for you and forget how you've sniped about my work, so I'd help you get out of here quickly."

Damn it! "It wasn't like that."

"Really." Angry amber sparks flashed in her eyes. "How was it, then?" She crossed her arms over her chest.

Frustration bubbled inside him, like lava in a wakening volcano. Why did she always think the worst of him? Why did every conversation have to become an argument? Was it so hard to believe that he wanted them to stop rubbing each other the wrong way and actually get along?

It didn't help that his body had reacted the moment she'd walked into the room. His pulse had kicked up when she'd sat beside his bed. Her scent had floated around him like morning mist rising from an outdoor rink, clouding his mind.

Ike shifted, trying to conceal his arousal. This conversation was too important to be derailed by his body's personal agenda. He imagined an ice bath—like the ones he'd taken over the years after grueling games—and tried to figure out his next move.

Honesty was usually the best policy. Why not now?

"I should have apologized sooner and if I hadn't been stuck here, I would have. But I kept hoping you'd stop by to see me, so I could do it face-to-face."

Tracy arched an eyebrow haughtily. "Why would I come by, when you were rude last time?"

"I finally figured that out." He gave a self-deprecating smile. "Then, the longer it went on, the harder it got to call. We've always argued, but we got over it quickly. This time was different. I knew a simple 'I'm sorry' wouldn't cut it."

"So buttering me up by being nice about my business was the answer?"

"Yes. No." He sighed. "I guess I thought it couldn't hurt."

Tracy studied his face, but Ike wasn't sure what she was looking for. Finally, she asked, "Why go to the trouble of asking me to visit tonight? Why not ask me straight out for help?"

"Because I didn't want you to think that's all I was after. Look, whether you like how I approached it or not—whether you like *me* or not—I'm sorry for being a jackass. We don't have to be friends, if you don't want." He wanted to add that that was what he wanted, but her expression gave nothing away and he couldn't risk making things worse.

He plowed on. "I really need your help. If you'll work with me, I'll make sure it's a good deal for you, and I don't just mean financially."

Tracy said nothing for a few moments. She hadn't walked out, so she had to be considering what he'd said. He couldn't resist trying to sweeten the pot. "I'll accept whatever terms you want to give me."

"Any terms? Seriously? You really are desperate."

"You try being stuck here with every move monitored and observed. I'm not even allowed to have a shower. Do you know how humiliating a sponge bath is?"

Her mouth twitched. "I'd have thought there would be women lining up outside your room for the chance to give you a sponge bath."

"Yeah, well, the ones who 'lucked out' are either old enough to be my grandmother or young enough to be my kid. It's a nightmare and one I'd happily not go through again. Once I'm allowed up, I can shower, though I'll have to be accompanied. Just in case."

He caught her gaze and held it. The hint of sympathy in those brown depths spurred him to continue. "It's bad enough being sidelined for the next four months. I really don't want to spend a second longer in here than I have to."

"I can understand that. But you probably have

a disgustingly fast healing rate and will beat your surgeon's predictions."

"It'll still feel like forever. You can see why people would be willing to cheat and take a little something extra to help speed the process along."

Tracy looked shocked. "I can't see you doing that, Mr. Everything-by-the-book. Heck, you probably wrote the book."

"Hell, no. I wouldn't touch the stuff. I guess I didn't get the appeal before, because I've only ever missed a few games in my career. Man, am I making up for that now."

Tracy leaned forward, her expression earnest. "Don't try to look at your recovery as one big chunk. Think of it more as a series of stages and try to get through those stages one at a time. Kind of like on the ice, one shift at a time."

"I'm trying. It's easier said than done." Ike hated the whine he heard in his voice. This damn injury was making him soft and pathetic.

"Isn't it always?"

"I guess." He shrugged. "Anyway, I want to go home and I'll do whatever it takes."

"Including being nice to me." This time, there was no bite to her words.

"Including throwing myself on your mercy and appealing to your generous soul and kind heart." He put on a woebegone expression. "I'm also prepared to beg."

"Now, that I'd like to see." Tracy laughed. "I'm almost tempted to hold out just to see how far you'd go."

"All the way."

The words hung in the air between them, taking on a meaning he hadn't intended. A deeper, hotter meaning. One that made the room feel smaller, more intimate, and that challenged the control he had over his body.

Tracy lifted her gaze to meet his. She swallowed hard and licked her lips. So he wasn't the only one who felt the electricity between them.

She cleared her throat. "I'm not stupid enough to cut off my nose to spite my face."

His heart jolted. "You'll help me?"

"I will." She sounded like she'd agreed to fight a gladiator in the middle of the Colosseum.

Relief swept through him. No matter how she felt about him personally, Tracy would deliver whatever he needed. "Great. Thank you. I promise you won't regret it."

"Don't make promises you can't keep."

He wanted to argue, but knew he should quit while he was ahead. "All right. How about I'll do everything I can to make sure you don't regret it?"

"Fair enough." She rummaged in her purse and pulled out a notepad and pen. "I warn you, I'll want a full and detailed reference from you for my services. I'll also want to be able to quote you in all my promotional materials."

"No problem."

"And not being friends is not a deal-breaker?"

Her casual question was like a stick spear to the gut. "We got along okay—better than okay—once. But if that doesn't work for you, then I'll cooperate." He wouldn't be happy about it, though.

She tilted her head and gave a half smile. "We don't have to be friends for me to work with you, but it would certainly make things more pleasant if we weren't enemies."

It was a foot in the door. He'd take it. "I'm willing to give our—" what should he call it? "—relationship a reboot, if you are."

"Instead of a reboot, which sounds as though we could repeat the mistakes we made before, how about a fresh start?"

"Sounds perfect." He stuck out his good hand to seal the deal. "I'm all for not repeating past mistakes."

Tracy grasped his hand. Her touch was the best medicine he'd had in days. He could feel warmth flooding through his veins, easing the tension that seemed to have taken hold of his body since the accident.

Neither of them moved to break the connection. They sat quietly, lost in their own thoughts for several moments.

His thumb stroked the back of her hand. Hers did

the same to his. That simple touch seemed to do more to heal the rift between them than anything they'd said. He could see the pulse beating at the base of her throat. He longed to lean forward and press his lips to the spot.

Tracy slipped her hand away and retrieved the papers from the bedside cabinet. "Since you're keen to get out of here, we should get started," she said crisply.

Ike missed her touch instantly. His mind started thinking about ways he could get to hold her hand again. Or more. His erection sprang to life again. Damn. *Not now. Focus.* "Yeah. Sure."

Tracy scanned the list, making notes here and there. Ike was fascinated by the change in her as she slipped into business mode. Her body became stiffer, more upright, and her movements were as brisk as her tone.

"It seems to me that your life would be much easier over the next few months if you had a housekeeper—someone to manage and coordinate all your household requirements."

He frowned. "I don't want an old lady living in my house, telling me what to do."

"First of all, most of them aren't old. How else could they do the work? Second, she or *he* wouldn't have to live in."

"He? There are male housekeepers?" His lip curled. What kind of man put on an apron and played with a feather duster?

"Of course there are." She laughed. "It's not that different from a butler. Anyway, I can provide a list of suitable candidates and you can select the one you want."

"I'm still not sure why I need a housekeeper. Can't my cleaning service do what I need?"

"They might do laundry and ironing, but they won't cook or buy your groceries. A housekeeper could do all of that and more. It's efficient and cost-effective."

"All right. Sounds good."

"I'll also check out both a car service and a driver, since you can't drive yourself."

Crap. "Nice catch. I'd forgotten about that."

Tracy stood and stuffed her pad and pen back in her purse. "The sooner I get onto this, the sooner I'll have a costed proposal and the sooner you'll be able to get out of here. If there's anything else you need, just let me know."

"Thanks again for doing this. I can't tell you how much I appreciate it."

"Don't worry, I'll make sure it's worth my while." She smiled. "Start working on that recommendation and don't stint on words like *outstanding* and *excellent*."

He grinned. "Yes, ma'am. Whatever you say, ma'am."

"And try not to piss off any more nurses."

Ike blinked with mock innocence. *Who, me?*

Tracy laughed and, shaking her head, waved goodbye as she left.

After she'd gone, Ike felt surprisingly buoyant. He could rely on Tracy to get the job done. She would never let a client down. He was as good as out of here. Once he got home into familiar surroundings and away from the hovering nursing staff, his recovery would progress quickly.

He'd work with the Ice Cats staff to pull together some form of training routine. He wanted to be back on the ice in three months, not four. That would give him a month of the regular season to get game-ready for the playoffs. This was doable.

Eager to watch the game, Ike flicked on the TV. He groaned. Four–nothing. With his luck lately, the Ice Cats would already have been eliminated by then.

"THREE NEW CLIENTS? I should be upset that you're doing so well without me."

Maggie's exaggerated pout made Tracy smile. "Your mummy is being silly," she said in a singsong voice to baby Joe, who lay contentedly her arms. "Isn't she?"

He blinked and smacked his lips, as if agreeing with her.

They were enjoying a casual lunch in Maggie's living room, sitting with their feet up on the sofa, while Jake was at practice. After the previous night's loss, Coach Macarty had called all the players in early and told them to expect to stay late.

"Your mummy knows I couldn't have done it without her." Tracy kissed Joe's button nose. Joe gurgled and kicked his legs. "Helping Hands was her idea, wasn't it? Yes, it was."

"But you're the one who made it a reality." Maggie pointed a slice of buttered baguette at her. "Today the Bridgers, tomorrow all the major sports franchises in the tri-state area."

"I like your optimism. It's a start. We should get a great reference from Mme. Chabal. She's already singing our praises and she hasn't even arrived yet."

"Trust me, global domination will be ours." Maggie gave a witchlike cackle.

Tracy laughed, startling her nephew, who scrunched up his face and looked ready to bawl.

"It's okay," she soothed, lifting the baby up and resting him against her shoulder. She rubbed his back gently, loving the way he snuggled into her neck. "We probably can't even manage domination of northern New Jersey, so Mummy won't turn into an evil villain."

"I don't know. Lack of sleep may yet do me in. Young sir is feeding every couple of hours at the moment and barely sleeping in between. Good job he's cute, or I'd be trading him in for a kitten."

"I wouldn't let you do that to my gorgeous nephew." Even if he was drooling onto her shoulder, creating a damp patch on her sweater.

"Change his nappies and you'll see how not-gorgeous he can be. It's easy being the adoring aunty. You get all the nice bits, then hand him back to me."

"Them's the breaks, kid," Tracy teased, but her heart squeezed.

Every time she cuddled Joe, she lost another piece of her heart to her nephew. He'd awakened maternal feelings in her that she hadn't felt since her marriage ended. Not for the first time since his birth, Tracy found herself wondering what it would be like to hold her own baby.

A loud burp from Joe cut those thoughts short. The chances of her having a baby were nonexistent. Heck, she wasn't even dating. And she firmly believed in doing things the right way round—husband, then baby. Besides, there wasn't room in her life at the moment for either a husband or a baby, let alone both.

Maggie's heavy sigh cut into Tracy's thoughts. "Mum called yesterday evening."

"I got a message from her, too. Do I want to know what she had to say?"

"Same old, same old. We live too far away. We don't visit enough. It isn't fair that she can't see her grandchildren, when Jake's parents can."

"We've offered countless times to pay for her to visit and she makes the same excuses."

"We made our beds when we went over there and brought her here for a visit after Dad died." Maggie grimaced. "I admit I didn't try too hard to convince her this time. As sorry as I feel for her, I don't really want her here. The last thing I need right now is her telling me I'm doing everything wrong or rearranging the house to be the way she thinks it should be. Rather, how Dad thought it should be. Does that make me a bad person?"

"Well, if you are, I'm just as bad. I don't want her here, either. I'm actually more afraid of Mum deciding she wants to stay permanently." Their mother's dependence was hard enough to take in small doses. Especially as she wasn't as helpless as she liked to pretend.

"We won't let that happen. No matter how much she whines or cries."

The sisters exchanged determined looks and nodded. They were united about that; none of their mother's guilt trips would sway them. Besides representing a painful past for both sisters—in seeking to avoid turning into their mother, they'd each made terrible mistakes—Doris Hayden had never given them even an ounce of motherly support.

"Speaking of difficult people, you haven't mentioned your visit to Ike last night."

"How did you know?" Tracy's eyes widened with surprise.

"I have my sources." Maggie gave her a superior look, then grinned. "Actually, Jake told me. He's been worried that Ike might be a macho idiot and try to do everything himself once he's released. When

Jake raised it with him a few days ago, Ike put up a big front about how he was okay and shot down any suggestion of needing help. I don't know why they have to pretend to be so tough. Admitting they're not invincible doesn't make them any less men."

Tracy laughed. "Dr. Gibson was smart to make Ike's discharge contingent on him having support."

"Ike told Jake this morning that everything was under control. That you're going to look after him," Maggie said questioningly.

Tracy nodded. "He'll pay the going rate and it's a foot in the door with the Cats for Helping Hands."

"Uh-huh. I seem to recall you telling me repeatedly that you'd never work for Ike again. Something about hell freezing over."

"Oh, look—a snowflake."

"Funny." Maggie's lips twisted. "Come on, give."

Tracy wasn't ready to discuss the reasons for her changed attitude, even to her sister. Partly because she wasn't quite sure how things between her and Ike had ended up in such an optimistic place.

Convinced that nothing Ike said could appease her, she'd been prepared to tell him to stick his excuses where the sun didn't shine. Yet, once again, his openness and his sincerity had disarmed her. She'd sensed his desperation about going home; he hadn't tried to hide it. Perhaps it had been the catalyst that had driven his apology, too. But she'd also believed his desire to put things right between them was genuine. For the first time, it had felt like there could actually be something between them other than antagonism.

Still, it was all too new. Her emotions were all over the place. She wasn't sure how she felt about any of it.

Maggie's expectant look said she wasn't going to let the subject drop.

"Okay, so Ike wouldn't have been my first choice of client," Tracy admitted. "But it seemed crazy to turn down a great opportunity because we don't get along. Under the circumstances, I think it's a win-win situation. It won't be a huge amount of work." Tracy explained what she and Ike had discussed. "And Ike's reference for Helping Hands will be invaluable. Such a high-profile professional athlete raving about our services will carry a lot of weight with other players and other organizations."

In an attempt to distract her sister, Tracy stroked Joe's head and said, "I think he's gone to sleep."

Maggie took the bait and stood. "Let me try to put him down."

Tracy missed the weight and warmth of her nephew once she'd handed him back. "Speaking of other organizations, there's some possible good news on the horizon. I've had an inquiry from a bloke at NBC. They're reorganizing some of their departments, which will involve senior staff relocating in and out of New Jersey, and are keen to hear what we can offer them."

"Ooh, that sounds interesting." Maggie's face lit

up. "I wonder if we'll have to work with any of their big stars."

"It'd be tough, but I'm sure we'd make the sacrifice for the good of our company."

"Absolutely."

They both grinned.

"There's one thing I don't understand," Maggie said as she laid Joe in his Moses basket. He didn't stir.

"What's that?" Tracy smiled at her sleeping nephew.

"What exactly Ike said or did to make you change your mind about working with him."

Tracy groaned inwardly. She'd hoped her sister had forgotten that particular subject. "I told you—it was a smart business move."

"And that's really all there is to it?" Maggie's tone was skeptical.

"Of course." But even as she spoke, Tracy's mind flipped back to that moment in the hospital room when she and Ike had shaken hands to seal the deal.

She could almost feel the electricity that had tingled the palm of her hand. When his thumb had caressed the back of her hand, that tingle had spread all the way up her arm. Her heart jolted now, as it had when their gazes had met and she'd seen the fire in his green eyes.

Tracy fought the urge to moisten her lips. That would be too much of a giveaway. Instead she took a deep breath and tried to look unaffected.

"Why do I think there's more to this than you're telling me?" Maggie tapped a finger against her lips, as if musing.

Feigning innocence, Tracy shrugged. "Ike and I have always rubbed each other the wrong way."

"I think the problem is that you rub each other the right way."

"The physical side of things was never the issue," Tracy admitted reluctantly. "Our relationship didn't work because we were too different. Once the lust faded, we didn't have much else going for us." Still, it had been glorious while it had lasted.

"As you once asked me, why do you need to have a relationship? Can't you guys have another hot fling, then go back to annoying each other?"

Tracy smacked down her body's reaction. "I won't mix business with pleasure."

"Ah, but you said yourself the business won't take long. This could be an opportunity for you to give things another go."

"I don't know that I want to try again. The end was awful last time. Let's face it, Ike hasn't changed and neither have I."

"That's not quite true. You've both mellowed since I came to the States."

"All right. Maybe we haven't changed enough or in the right way." Was that why she felt so unsettled? Because she couldn't be sure.

"But maybe you have. Isn't it worth finding out?"

Tracy didn't want to admit that she was scared—

if it didn't work out, she sensed the pain would be far worse than the last time—so she hedged, "Let's see how things pan out. If Ike and I haven't killed each other by the time our business is done, maybe I'll consider it."

"Good grief. For someone who encouraged me—I'd go as far as to say practically bullied me—to take a chance on Jake, you're being ridiculously coy."

"And for someone who was gun-shy about dating again, especially a hockey player, you're being ridiculously gung ho about me and Ike. Not that there is a 'me and Ike.'"

"*Yet*. But I wouldn't rule it out. If you gave it a shot, you might be pleasantly surprised. At least you'd have a hot few days." Maggie waggled her eyebrows suggestively.

Tracy shook her head at her sister's antics. "I wonder how much time I'd get for justifiable homicide."

"I don't know. But remember—as Joe's godmother, you'd inherit nappy duty."

"Joe, you just saved your mother's life."

Maggie leaned forward and placed her hand on Tracy's. "You deserve to be happy. I want you to have what Jake and I have."

"I'd love that, too. I just don't think it will be with Ike." No matter how much she might want it to be.

Tracy's pulse jumped. Where had that thought come from?

Before she could analyze that any further, Maggie squeezed her hand. "Promise me that if the opportunity arises, you won't reject it straight away."

Tracy hesitated. Was she really considering another go round with Ike? Her head told her that would be foolish, but her heart whispered that she'd be a fool not to try.

The stunning truth was that Tracy wanted to listen to her heart. "I promise."

CHAPTER SEVEN

IKE STOOD AT the window of the hospital ward's sunroom the following afternoon and watched a plane climbing into the wintry sky.

He didn't know if it was the jet carrying his teammates out to the west coast for a four-game road trip, but it might as well be. He wouldn't see anyone from the Ice Cats for at least a week. Even once they were back in town, they had a pair of back-to-back games, so no one would have time to stop by.

Ike used his good arm to rub the ache in his chest. He hated feeling left out. And he hated feeling alone.

He'd heard other players talk about how hard it was to be out with a long-term injury—the loneliness, the isolation—but he'd never experienced it himself. Even on the few occasions he'd been unable to play, Ike had always been with the team. He'd gone to the practice arena, seen the trainers and medics, hung around with the healthy players.

This was different.

He was on his own. Away from the action. Away from the guys. The inactivity was bad enough, but the silence was hell.

It hadn't even been a week since his accident and he was going crazy. He had months of this to look forward to. At least it was only months. There had been a couple of dark moments over the past few days, especially late at night, when Ike had felt so weak and been in so much pain that he'd wondered if his arm would ever be right again. The thought that his career might be over terrified him.

Even now, in bright daylight, with all Doc Gibson's assurances, Ike couldn't help wondering how he'd cope if this wasn't just temporary. If he never played again. If this isolation was permanent. Hockey was all he'd known for so long, he couldn't get his head around life without it. Worse, who he'd be if he didn't have hockey.

He wouldn't think about that or he'd drive himself nuts.

At least he'd finally been allowed out of bed, even if he couldn't wander farther than the end of the hall. He'd been shocked by how shaky his legs had been walking to this dayroom. He'd almost stumbled several times, as though he'd been bedridden for months, not a few days. Perhaps he hadn't made up for all the blood he'd lost. It was easier to think that than to admit how seriously he'd been hurt.

It felt good to be back in his own clothes, too, though having the young nurse help him was another indignity he could have done without. She'd had to massacre the Ice Cats sweatshirt Kenny had brought him; she'd split it down the left seam, chopped off the sleeve, then safety-pinned it all together to allow access for his immobilized arm. There had been no way to pull his jeans on one-handed other than to ask for help. Right after that, he'd called his mom and asked her to bring him sweatpants next time she visited.

Ike was beginning to realize he was in for a rougher ride than he'd thought. Every action reinforced how tough it was to do even simple things with only one arm. He was no longer as confident as he'd been about how he'd cope at home by himself.

At least by Friday, he'd be figuring it out in the privacy of his own home. Assuming Tracy came up with a plan that would convince the tight-assed surgeon to sign the damn release papers.

Ike's heart kicked at the thought of seeing her again. He looked up at the clock on the gray wall. Less than an hour to go.

They were like oil and water every time they were together. Or was it fire and dynamite? Either way, he shouldn't be grinning like a freaking Cheshire cat.

He forced his curved lips into a straight line. Tracy was coming to see him on business, not to party between the sheets. She'd be quoting figures and terms, not whispering sweet nothings. Not that she'd ever whispered *sweet* anything. Hot and spicy, for sure, but not sweet. Like the night he'd moved into his house, when she'd asked him to choose which room he wanted to christen first. He'd practically lost it right there in the front hall as she'd described—in tantalizingly explicit detail—what his options were.

Ike swore and leaned his forehead against the cool windowpane, willing his body not to react to the memories. He had to remember that all she cared about was growing her business and keeping her independence. One day, he'd find someone who heated his blood *and* wanted marriage and kids. He didn't need to settle for anything less than the whole package, no matter how great Tracy was at the first part.

His cell rang. Grateful for the interruption, Ike reached for it. The stiff fabric of his new sling rasped against the back of his neck, reminding him that he wasn't supposed to move his arm. Swearing under his breath, Ike used his good hand to pull the damn phone out of his pocket before grinding out a hello.

"Is it a good sign that you're growling like a grizzly?" Tru teased.

Ordinarily, Ike would have given his brother the verbal equivalent of the bird, but he was so pleased to talk to someone who wasn't on the medical staff, he let the comment slide. "You'd be pissed, too, if you were stuck in this place."

"Aww, aren't those lovely nurses cooing over you enough?" Tru laughed.

Ike bit back the urge to whine about them being mean to him. His brother had enough to rag him about.

"I have to fight them off with a stick," he drawled. "But you can have too much of a good thing."

"Uh-huh. Well, they do say women love to take care of a helpless, injured man. Guess that's true even for a miserable SOB like you."

"If you weren't in Denver, I'd show you how helpless I am. Even one-armed I can still kick your butt, little brother."

"Brave words when you can't act on them."

"Back at ya."

"I can handle whatever you throw at me, net boy." Tru's tone became serious. "I wish we weren't so far away, so we could help you."

"I appreciate the thought, but you and Jenny should be focusing on my soon-to-be nephews or nieces, not worrying about me."

Tru's wife was expecting twins in the spring. "We are. Everything's going smoothly."

"Glad to hear it. Take good care of her."

"Trust me, I plan to spend a lifetime doing just that."

The warmth in his brother's voice tugged at Ike's heart. He was pleased that Tru and Jenny had finally overcome their traumatic past of terrible secrets and bitter betrayal, and found happiness together. They seemed to complement and complete each other. Whatever happened, whatever lay ahead, they'd face it together.

Even as their love made him envious as hell, it gave Ike hope that someday he might find the right woman, too. If he ever got out of this damn hospital. "Yet another downside of this injury is that I'll miss seeing you guys when the Cats are in Denver on Monday."

"Yeah, that sucks. Maybe you can fly out during the All-Star break, since you won't be playing this year." Tru stopped, as if realizing what he'd said. "Crap, man. I'm sorry."

Ike hid his disappointment with his own jab. "At least I'll know I wasn't selected because I'm injured. What's your excuse?"

"My stats are looking damn fine this season. Either way, since the All-Star game is in Denver, I'll be around."

"Nice catch."

"Almost as good as one of yours."

Ike sighed. "As good as I was. Who knows how my arm will work once I'm healed up."

"The doc said you shouldn't have any problems, right?"

"Sure. But plenty of players have found their reflexes weren't as sharp after a serious injury. You never know until you get out there and start playing again."

"*I* know, because I know *you*. Whatever it takes, you'll make damn sure you're good enough again."

Ike hoped so. The alternative wasn't worth thinking about.

Tru continued. "Don't think negatively or you'll drive yourself crazy. Turn your mind to something positive. Find a new hobby. Oh, wait, don't you need two hands to knit?"

"Good thing you can skate, bro, because you'd never make a living at stand-up." Ike paced back and forth across the room, suddenly feeling restless. "You sound like Ma. She said this is the perfect time for me to start thinking about my future outside the game."

"Seriously? I know she mixes up her words, but I can't believe she'd want you to consider retirement."

"Not retirement—dating." Ike waited while his brother laughed his ass off. "She thinks that since I can't catch pucks, I should focus on catching myself the perfect woman."

"That's not a bad idea. Your injury will win the sympathy vote."

"Right. Except I can't do anything about it because I can't move my arm."

"Let her do the work, bro. As they say, 'lie back and think of England.'"

Ike's mind made the connection between England and Tracy and in a flash was back where he'd started before the phone rang. He didn't need his imagination to picture Tracy "doing the work." He had the memories. Blood-pounding, groin-tightening memories. "Maybe. Once I'm out of this place."

"When will you be discharged?"

Ike stopped in front of the window again. Another jet was taking off. "I want to be out of here on Friday."

"So soon?"

"I'll be ready. Hell, I'm ready now."

"Mom said Tracy's helping you."

"Yeah, so? That's her business. Why shouldn't I hire her?" He winced at the defensive note in his voice.

"You two don't exactly get along. Just saying."

"We can put our differences aside for mutual benefit."

"That's very mature and adult of you." Tru's tone was mocking.

"What can I say? It goes with me being the eldest. Besides, it's the only way I'll get out of here on Friday."

Behind him, someone cleared her throat.

Ike whipped around to see Tracy standing in the doorway.

His mouth went dry at her intriguing blend of professional and sexy. The fitted red jacket, nipped in at the waist, and black pencil skirt were elegant, yet emphasized her delicious figure. Sheer black hose and black high-heeled pumps completed the picture. No-nonsense, yet at the same time, distinctly feminine.

Man, how was he supposed to concentrate on business when his brain had just shorted out?

"Gotta go, Tru," he said quickly. "I'll catch you later."

"Keep me posted and follow the doc's orders. We all want you back to full health ASAP."

They exchanged goodbyes, then Ike slipped his phone into the front pocket of his jeans. "Tru says hi."

Tracy smiled warmly as she came toward him, making him wish she would smile like that for him.

"How are he and Jenny doing? Last time I spoke with Jenny, she was struggling with the altitude and morning sickness."

He grimaced. "Uh, yeah. I think that's all done with now. Sounds like they're pretty settled."

"Great. Moving out to Denver was a big enough upheaval for them both, without having to worry that Jenny might lose the babies."

"I know the way your company managed everything for them and made it go so smoothly was a huge help."

"Thanks. We do our best." She sounded pleased. "Now, let's sort you out so you can go home."

"The sooner, the better. Can I say again how grateful I am that you're doing this for me?" Ike touched her shoulder, then realized she might think that was a little personal and dropped his hand.

"Oh." Surprise widened her eyes and a hint of color brushed her cheeks. He wasn't sure if it was because of his words or his touch. "You're welcome. Shall we get started?"

"For sure." He indicated the couch with a coffee table in front of it. "Over here looks good—we can spread out the papers."

Tracy took the seat across the table from him and opened her briefcase.

Ike pretended not to notice the way her skirt hiked up, showing even more of her legs, before she smoothed it down again. "Uh, would you like a drink?"

"I'm good, thanks." She pulled out a thick red folder, extracted a couple of documents and slid one across the table. "Why don't I talk you through the main points and you can give me your thoughts on them?"

"Sounds good." He sat and picked up the sheets. "Shoot."

Once again, Ike was fascinated to see the transformation as Tracy slipped into work mode. She looked very much the successful businesswoman. He hadn't seen this side of her the last time they'd worked together; she hadn't yet developed this professional persona. He wasn't sure he liked the change, though he couldn't say why.

Even the way she spoke changed, becoming brisker and more formal. "Per our discussion, I've provided information and given detailed pricing options for three services—a driver, a housekeeper and yard maintenance. I've also screened potential candidates for you. My recommendations are highlighted. Feel free to ask questions as I go along."

As Tracy went through her proposal, Ike was impressed by how thorough it was, after little more than a day. She'd always been good at her job. Now she was slick, organized and efficient. Clearly, she'd kicked everything up a gear. No wonder her business was thriving.

Still, he couldn't help missing the old Tracy.

Ike forced his attention back to the proposal. He needed to be released. If the new Tracy could make that happen, fast, that was all that mattered.

Turning to the last page, Tracy tapped the costing summary with her finger. "The housekeeper service has to be for a minimum of three months. You'll also get a much better deal if you have the same driver for a specified period. Yard maintenance is flexible, but again, a fixed-period contract will work out better financially."

He frowned at the papers. "The housekeeper looks kind of expensive."

"He or she will do everything you need at home, including managing your cleaning and yard services. Given that you'll need all the help you can get for the first month at least, the rate is reasonable, especially for someone who doesn't live in."

"But once I'm past that first month, will I really need that extra 'support'?"

"Do you want to focus on mundane household details or your recovery?"

Tracy certainly knew how to sell her business. "Okay. What about the yard work? It's November and I've already raked the leaves."

"They provide a useful winter service. They'll keep your paths and driveway clear when it snows, and make sure they're salted. The last thing you need is to fall." She leaned forward, warming to her task. Her light perfume teased his nose. "You could call them when you need them, but priority goes to their contracted clients."

Distracted by the fact that her fragrance was one thing that hadn't changed, he gave up on trying to concentrate on the details. If she said it was the best option, it would be.

He closed the document and laid it on the coffee table. "This looks great. I'll go with all your recommendations. How long will it take to set this up?"

"Most of it can be up and running tomorrow."

"Perfect." He grinned. "I can't wait to get out of here."

She held up a hand. "I said most. I've pulled out all the stops to make things happen as fast as possible, but the housekeeper won't be in place until the middle of next week."

No. Freaking. Way. He could *not* stay in the hospital for another week. Struggling to keep his voice even, he said, "You can't get anyone sooner than that?"

Tracy sat back in her seat. The whisper of her stockings as she crossed one leg over the other made his pulse jump, even as it made him grit his teeth. "It's better to take the time now and get the right person for your needs than to make a mistake and be sorry later."

Intentional or not, the double meaning in her words fueled the fire burning in his belly. "I'm not staying here until next Wednesday. Fix it faster."

She thought for a moment. "I really think you

should interview the candidates. However, you could bypass that stage, if you wanted. Then, if we complete the paperwork tomorrow, the housekeeper could be in place on Monday. That's the best I can do."

"It's not good enough." Ike leaped to his feet. "I'm going home on Friday. If you can't get it all signed, sealed and delivered by then, our deal is off."

"You're being unreasonable."

"Do you say that to all your clients when the job is harder than you thought?" He regretted his words immediately, especially when she paled, but he wasn't going to apologize. Not this time. Not if it meant being stuck here for the weekend.

"My other clients don't behave like spoiled brats when things don't go their way," she snapped back.

Their gazes clashed, neither of them prepared to give an inch.

"I don't care how you do it—you can play housekeeper yourself, if that's what it takes—but my deadline stands."

"Oh, you'd love that, wouldn't you?" Her laugh had a bitter edge.

"If it gets that damn specialist to sign my discharge papers, I'd welcome the Wicked Witch of the West and her flying monkeys."

"Charming as ever. No wonder the nurses are desperate for you to go." Tracy jumped up and shoved her folder into her briefcase.

The snap of the case's locks echoed in the room,

jolting Ike out of the haze of anger, frustration and fear. In that moment of clarity, he realized that if Tracy walked away, he'd be stuck in here for far longer than a few extra days.

His temper subsided like a deflated balloon.

Ike slumped onto the couch. He went to put his head in his hands, but the damn sling got in the way. "This stupid thing is driving me bat-crap crazy." He waved his arm in the air, only to have the sling rasp and tug against his neck. "Aargh!" he growled.

Tracy's expression softened fractionally. "It would drive me nuts, too."

"I'm sorry I'm being a jackass. Jeez, I've apologized more in the past few days than I have in the past year."

"That's surprising how?" Her words were only mildly sarcastic, her animosity gone.

Looked like he was back to groveling. "There must be a compromise, so I can get out of here. All Dr. Gibson needs to know is that I have the support in place. Can't we fudge it somehow?" He sent her a desperate look. "Please. Whatever you can do, whatever it takes, to see me through to Monday—just get me out of here on Friday."

Tracy was silent for a few minutes. Finally, she sighed. "I suppose I could arrange what you need myself until the housekeeper can be there."

"I'll be eternally grateful."

"Keep up your end of the deal and we'll be all

square." She buttoned her jacket and smoothed her skirt; the professional persona was back. "I'll send over revised paperwork and contracts for you to sign in the morning. I'll check the house, then bring in basic groceries. When you know what time you'll be discharged on Friday, I can arrange for your driver to pick you up. Once you're settled at home, I'll stop by and we can figure out what else you need me to do. Are you sure you're happy to go with the housekeeper I recommended, without even speaking to her?"

Since she'd compromised, he decided to do the same. "You're right. I should meet her. As long as it doesn't affect the timing of my release."

"All right. I'll arrange the interview for Monday morning."

"Sounds like a plan." Ike stuck out his hand. "Thanks, Tracy. I know it doesn't seem like it, but I really do appreciate everything you're doing for me."

She hesitated, but shook his hand quickly. "That reference had better be gold-plated."

Once she'd gone, Ike returned to his spot by the window and stared out at the darkening sky. This time he wasn't thinking about his teammates jetting away from him, but the woman who—despite his best intentions—had somehow landed squarely back in the middle of his life. Strangely, he didn't feel quite so lonely anymore.

THE GRANDFATHER CLOCK in the hall struck four. Its deep chimes sounding through the empty house reminded Tracy of the stadium anthem the Ice Cats skated out to at the beginning of a game. Fitting, she thought, as Ike would be arriving home from the hospital shortly. His driver had texted ten minutes ago to say he was en route.

Tracy took one final look around Ike's kitchen and quickly ran through the printed to-do list in her client file. She'd worked her socks off for the past twenty-four hours since Ike had signed on the dotted line, and managed to complete everything she'd promised to do.

Groceries—bought and put away. Check.

Dinner—cottage pie—made and ready to be reheated. Check.

Assortment of takeout and delivery menus on the kitchen table. Check.

Client folder with housekeeper application, also on the kitchen table. Check.

Cleaning service—been and done a thorough job throughout the house. Check.

Laundry—done (apart from his hockey gear—there were limits!) and put away. Check.

Fresh sheets on the bed and towels in the bathrooms. Check.

"The mind I lost when I agreed to do this job myself..." Tracy grimaced as she strode out into the hall for one last walk-through. "No-bloody-where to be found."

Everything looked fine downstairs, so she headed up to the second floor. Ike's home office, the spare bedroom he'd converted to a workout room and the two guest rooms and baths were all in good shape. Which only left Ike's bedroom.

Tracy took a steadying deep breath. It wasn't the first time she'd been in there. Yet, each time, she'd hesitated on the threshold.

When she'd agreed to work with Ike, Tracy hadn't been sure how being in his town house again would affect her. After all, Tracy had helped him buy the place. Helped him choose the decor for all the rooms.

Helped him christen those rooms.

She quickly pushed aside those particular memories. That history was never going to repeat itself.

Tracy gave a short laugh. That was what she'd said about coming back here. That was why it had felt weird yesterday to use Ike's key and walk into his home, as if she belonged there. Knowing she could have belonged here, if she'd accepted his offer. She'd stood in the front hall for several minutes, feeling like an intruder, until curiosity had taken over.

Tracy hadn't seen the finished result; she hadn't been back to Ike's town house since they'd split. As the afternoon shadows had lengthened yesterday, she'd walked from room to room, ostensibly to check out the house from a professional standpoint. Really, she'd wanted to see how it had come together. Would it be as she'd imagined?

She'd been surprised not only that it was, but that Ike had followed through on every one of her recommendations, giving the house a cozy feel. Sure, there was the usual guy stuff—the humongous plasma screens, the futuristic entertainment center, the sports memorabilia on the wall of the wet bar in the basement—but it hadn't felt like a bachelor pad. More like a home, waiting for its family to walk through the doors.

Now, as it had the day before, her chest squeezed as an image of Ike with a wife and children, laughing and happy, flashed into her mind. The wife's face wasn't clear, but it clearly wasn't her.

Why did that bother her so much? That wasn't the future she wanted.

Or rather, it was a future she couldn't have—because it wasn't real. That happiness was a fairy tale that didn't exist. Couldn't exist. At least, not for her. She'd have to give up too much, especially of herself.

She'd done the right thing when she'd said no to Ike.

Angry words echoed in her head as she relived that final argument and the fear that had driven her. She'd realized that she'd already started to slip into dangerous territory with Ike. She'd recognized the signs. They'd become too close, too quickly. Their lives had already started to intertwine. There had already been expectations...assumptions.

She'd had to end their relationship before she lost herself completely.

She'd done the right thing. No matter how much it had hurt.

Don't think about the past. Think about the future you're building for yourself.

Tracy blew out an unsteady breath. Part of that future was making bloody sure everything was spot-on for Ike's return. She walked into Ike's bedroom, checked everything was as it should be and walked out again, without the slightest hitch in her heart rate.

As she returned downstairs, a key scraped in the front door.

Tracy glanced at the clock, frowning. Ike had made better time than she'd expected.

Her pulse jumped when the front door began to open. Tracy told herself it was because she was anxious to see his response to everything she'd achieved. Just as she would be for any client using her services for the first time.

She plastered on a smile and prepared to be the solicitous housekeeper.

But it wasn't Ike who walked through the door. It was Karina and Rory, carrying a large shopping bag and a cooler. Something smelled delicious, reminding Tracy that she hadn't had a chance to eat anything since the power bar she'd had for breakfast.

Karina beamed. "I'm glad Ike came to his senses and hired you. He can't cope alone."

"No matter how much he believes otherwise." Tracy smiled, following them into the kitchen. "I suspect the first few days home will be a rude awakening for him."

Ike's mother started unpacking the shopping bag. "You'll set him straight."

"I don't know about that." Tracy opened the freezer and began filling it with the plastic containers Karina handed her. "At least he won't starve."

Ike's mother pushed aside the takeout menus, tutting. "As if I'd let my son eat that garbage. He needs good home cooking and lots of it."

Rory placed the cooler on the table, then unloaded foil-wrapped, labeled packages. "We brought enough food to feed the entire team for a month."

"I wasn't sure what he'd feel like eating, so I made all his favorites." Karina shrugged.

"I'm sure he'll be very grateful," Tracy said.

Karina tapped the side of her nose. "From what I can smell, you've made tonight's dinner for him."

"I thought a cottage pie would be easy to manage one-handed and filling after all that 'nutritionally balanced' hospital food."

"The smell reminds me of my ma's kitchen." Rory rubbed his stomach. "She used to make a fine cottage pie. And a fine shepherd's pie, come to that."

"There's a difference?" Karina looked confused.

"They're pretty much the same except cottage

pie is made with beef, while shepherd's pie is made with lamb," Rory explained.

"I learn new things every day with you." Karina smiled warmly at her husband.

He winked. "I do my best."

Karina giggled and fluttered her hand at him. "Get away with you."

Tracy looked away from the newlyweds and concentrated on fitting the last packages into the now-full freezer. The older couple were so sweet together and were clearly in love. It was nice that they'd found each other at this stage in their lives. They'd met through one of Karina's many community projects and it had taken a while for Rory to convince her that they weren't too old to get married.

Their happiness gave Tracy mixed feelings. Envy for what she didn't have, but also a tiny spark of hope. Perhaps there was someone out there for her.

"Making my boy dinner is very thoughtful." Karina nodded approvingly.

Tracy ignored the considering look in the older woman's eye. "All part of the Helping Hands service."

"It's still thoughtful. I can definitely take it easy about him being well looked after while we're away."

"I think you mean 'rest easy,' love," Rory said affectionately as he set the cooler down by the kitchen door.

"Eh, it means the same thing, no?"

"We understood what you meant," Tracy said politely. "When do you leave for Ireland?"

"Tomorrow night. We still have so much to do before we go. I don't know how I'll get all the packing done."

"When I convince you to leave the kitchen sink behind, you'll be fine." Rory laughed. "We do have shops over there, you know."

Karina shared a look with Tracy. "Men don't understand, do they?"

Tracy smiled. "They certainly don't."

"It'll be much better now that I know Ike won't be here alone and helpless."

She made him sound like a lost puppy, not a six-three, two-hundred-plus-pound man, who'd cut his arm off rather than admit he was helpless. Tracy winced at the analogy.

The doorbell rang, loud and long, as if someone were leaning on the bell.

"Sounds like Ike's home." Tracy went to the front door, donning a professional smile so he wouldn't see how much his arrival had unnerved her. But when she opened the door and heard him cursing, her smile faded. "Is there a problem?"

"Yeah." He leaned down to pick up the duffel bag at his feet. "Did you know it's impossible to unlock and open this door with only one arm?"

"Oh." She bit her lip, trying to hold back a giggle as he glared at the offending lock. His frustration was etched all over his face. "You could have asked your driver for help."

Ike scowled at her. "I didn't know I'd need it until I'd already sent him away."

More like he hadn't wanted to appear helpless in front of the other man. "You'll know for next time."

"Yeah." Ike stomped past her into the house like a bratty teenager.

Tracy stood for a moment, staring out at the tree-filled park across the street. It was days like today that she found it hard to remember why she'd thought a business providing services for temperamental professional athletes was such a great idea.

"Because you're bloody good at it," she said aloud to herself. "You can handle one out-of-sorts hockey player." Tracy headed inside. Though she did quickly cross her fingers before closing the door behind her.

"PERHAPS WE SHOULD cut our trip short."

Ike sighed. Though his mom was now excited about going to Ireland, her happiness had dimmed slightly when she'd remembered that the three-week trip meant she wouldn't be back in time for Thanksgiving. She'd somehow got into her head that he'd be stuck at home alone, eating takeout, instead of going to Jake's parents' annual party.

"I promise I'll go, so Aunt Tina can make sure I'm fed and watered," he reassured her. "Jake and Kenny will be around most of the day before they leave for Philly. I won't have time to feel lonely, though of course I'll miss you."

She looked long and hard into his eyes before pulling his head down to kiss his forehead. "We'll call or do Skype, so I can make sure you're okay."

He agreed, then helped Rory shoo her out the door to pack.

As pleased as Ike was that his mom finally had a good guy in her life to take care of her the way she deserved, it felt weird to think she wouldn't be around. She'd never not been there. No matter where he'd gone or what he'd done, she'd always been the constant in his life.

Times were certainly changing.

"I'll sort this out for you and get a wash on."

Ike turned to see Tracy hefting his duffel bag onto her shoulder. Damn it. He wasn't a total invalid. "I can manage that," he said through gritted teeth.

She smiled politely, ignoring his outstretched arm. "It's the housekeeper's responsibility to look after your things. Let me do my job."

Tracy was right. He'd made such a big deal about her helping him, he shouldn't give her grief when she did just that. "Knock yourself out."

As she continued up the stairs carrying his bag, Ike turned and strode back into the kitchen. Why didn't his mom's fussing bother him as much?

He didn't want to examine that too closely.

Still, just once, it would be great if he didn't have

to apologize to Tracy for acting like a jackass. Ike dropped onto a chair.

The problem was that the sight of Tracy at his front door this afternoon had speared him in the gut, winding him as effectively as the butt-end of a stick. How many nights, returning from a game or a road trip, had he imagined her welcoming him home? How many times had he swallowed his disappointment at the sight of his dark, empty house? The realization that she was only there because she had to be—because it was her *job*—not to mention the humiliation of being bested by a two-inch piece of metal and a door handle, and his happiness at being home had taken a nosedive.

"Get over it." Ike's words echoed around the kitchen.

Just because Tracy was here, in his house, just as he'd dreamed, didn't mean there was a chance for them. Just because her presence—her little homey touches, the hint of her perfume lingering in the air—had already made the place feel warmer, didn't mean things would turn out any better than last time. His feelings about having a fling hadn't changed. Sure, it would be amazing while it lasted, but if Tracy couldn't commit to him, at least as much as she committed to her business, then he wasn't interested.

One thing to come out of all those endless, boring days in the hospital was that Ike had started thinking seriously about what came after hockey. Sure, he probably had a good few years left before he hung up his skates, but what if he didn't? Another injury could sideline him permanently. And it didn't even need to be a playing injury. Guys had seriously hurt themselves getting out of a golf cart or even eating pancakes, for crying out loud.

Seeing Jake and then Tru so happy had made Ike long for his own family. After what had happened with Tracy, he'd put thoughts of settling down on the back burner. Now he knew it was crazy to wait until he retired. Once his arm had healed and he was back playing, Ike planned to turn his attention to finding the right woman. One who had the same priorities he did.

Tracy was only going to be in his life for a few days—a week, tops. Once his housekeeper started, things between him and Tracy would go back to the way they'd been before. And he'd be focusing on his healing arm and getting his body back into shape.

In the meantime, there had to be something he could do, other than sit on his ass while she waited on him hand and foot. Ike headed out into the hall, then upstairs.

Tracy was in his bathroom, sorting his dirty laundry. Ike leaned against the door frame, appreciating the way her brisk movements emphasized the way her black jeans fit her curvy butt and great legs. Maybe watching her work for him had some benefits after all.

"Do you have any preference for whether I wash darks or lights first?" she asked.

"Nope." He shrugged.

"There are more darks, so I'll do them."

A pair of black boxer shorts with Sexy Devil written in red across the front dropped to the floor. Before he could move, she'd bent down and picked them up. His groin tightened.

Man, he had it bad, if Tracy doing laundry turned him on.

As she walked past him into the bedroom, he stepped aside deliberately so they wouldn't touch.

"I think I've put your clean clothes away where they belong, but tell me if I haven't." Her calm voice told him she wasn't having the same problems dealing with his proximity.

He swore silently. "I'm sure it's okay."

He spotted a stack of clothing on the bed. "What's this?" He took an Ice Cats sweatshirt from the pile and noticed that one of the sleeves had been cut off.

"I got some tops from the team and doctored them. I figured they'd be easier for you to put on. There's also some sweatpants, so you don't have to struggle with buttons or zips."

He was touched by her thoughtfulness. "You've gone above and beyond for me." He grimaced. "And all I've done to show my appreciation is complain. For the umpteenth time, I'm..."

Tracy held up her hand. "Don't apologize again. Honestly, it's not necessary."

Ike frowned, confused. "It isn't?"

"It's not like I haven't dealt with cantankerous clients before."

Being classed as just another one of her clients stung. "It's still wrong for me to take out my frustrations on you."

"Yet you keep doing it," she said lightly. "Look, it'll be easier all around if we both accept that you're going to be difficult and I won't hit you over the head with a frying pan each time you are. It'll be a long week otherwise."

IKE LET OUT a surprised laugh. "Okay. Works for me. Though I'll try to be less of a pain in the ass."

Tracy's lips twitched. "Don't strain yourself."

"Some people think I'm charming."

"Uh-huh. I don't think *charming* is the word the nurses would use."

He followed her downstairs to the laundry room. "They were sad to see me go today."

"They probably threw a party when you left." She tossed the clothes into the washer.

"I wasn't that bad. After that first day, anyway."

"You keep believing that, if it makes you feel better." She programmed the wash before heading toward the kitchen.

He felt like a faithful puppy following after her.

"I'm just as glad to be home. I swear if I'd stayed any longer, the smell of disinfectant and institutional cooking would have been permanently ingrained in my skin."

She wrinkled her nose. "That smell does my head in, too. Speaking of which, I should heat up your dinner. You must be starving."

His stomach rumbled at the thought of home cooking. He grinned. "You could say."

"Sounds like I'd better make you an appetizer while the cottage pie is heating." She turned on the oven to preheat.

"Thanks, but I can wait for dinner." He opened the cutlery drawer. "While you do that, I'll set the table."

"There's no need. That's my—"

"I know," he interrupted. "It's your job. But I feel uncomfortable having you wait on me. At least let me do this."

She waved a hand in the direction of the table. "Go ahead."

As he reached for the knives and forks, he asked, "Are you joining me?"

The invitation seemed to surprise her, almost as much it did him. Though it wasn't clear whether it was a good surprise or a bad one.

"Oh. Well, I hadn't intended to. I was going to serve this and leave you in peace."

"I've had enough of peace and my own company for the past week." Besides, now that he'd asked, he wanted her to stay. Then he remembered it was Friday night. She probably had somewhere else to be. Crap. "I didn't think. You must have plans."

"Nothing important."

He perked up, then cursed himself for more puppylike behavior. He tried to act as though it didn't bother him either way. "You have to eat, and there's more than enough for both of us. It'll save you making a meal when you get home."

She put the cottage pie in the oven, then kept staring at the glass-fronted door for several moments, as if it held whatever answers she was looking for. Finally, she said carefully, "I don't think it's a good idea. A housekeeper shouldn't share the table with her boss."

"But you're not really my housekeeper and there's no way I'd ever call myself your boss. Not if I expect to keep my manhood intact."

Tracy looked up at him and smiled. "When you put it like that, how can I refuse?"

Ike did a mental fist-pump. "Score one for Mr. Charming."

"You're in negative figures, Mr. Grumpy. It'll take more than one measly score to erase that tally."

"Hey, every little bit helps." He set two places at the table, then added wineglasses. "I know you're driving, but one glass with dinner won't hurt."

"Are you allowed to drink with the meds you're taking?"

"Yeah. I'm not on the hard stuff anymore. I only

need to take painkillers when it aches and I'm trying not to do that because it makes me dopey."

She passed him a bottle of red wine. "I'm not rising to that comment, even though you handed it to me on a silver platter."

"You know what I mean."

"A small glass would be nice. Thank you." The sparkle in her eyes belied her prim tone.

He held up the bottle. "I won't even complain about how hard it is to use a corkscrew one-handed."

"Actually, it's a screw top."

"So it is." He trapped the bottle between his bandaged arm and his body and removed the cap with a flourish. "You've thought of everything."

"All part of the service."

He ignored the twinge in his chest at the reminder he was just a job, and poured the wine. "Thank you for your fine service."

She clinked her glass against his. "And here's to your speedy recovery."

As she lifted her glass to her lips, her gaze met his. The amber glow he saw in the dark brown depths caught him unawares. He hadn't seen that much warmth in her eyes since they'd split. Was she finally softening toward him?

He let his guard down just a little, so she could see that he had definitely softened toward her. The amber glow heated up and his body's reply was anything but soft.

He couldn't look away. Didn't want to. Was

pleased…hell, thrilled…that she didn't seem to want to, either.

Slowly, his gaze drifted lower. To her mouth.

His pulse jumped. He could practically taste her. He *wanted* to taste her.

Her lips parted slightly, inviting him closer.

He leaned toward her, his eyes firmly on the luscious prize awaiting him.

The dinging alert for a text message shattered the moment.

Tracy blinked, then stepped back and put her glass on the counter.

Ike cursed silently when she pulled out her phone to check the message. "I'm sorry, I have to deal with this."

Her flushed cheeks as she stepped out into the hall told him she wasn't as unaffected as she seemed. "No problem."

He wanted to puff out his chest and strut around the kitchen like a proud rooster. Instead, he sat at the kitchen table and drank some wine as he tried to figure out what the hell was going on. He groaned. *That* part was obvious. More important was what the hell he was going to do about it.

Ike had never been one to charge in without a plan. He was patient and methodical. He'd only acted impulsively once in his life—the first time he'd kissed Tracy. Here in this kitchen. If he was honest, that whole experience with Tracy had been out of character. And look how that had ended up.

Yeah, but it was one heck of a ride.

One almost-kiss and damned if he didn't want to do the same thing again.

He stopped himself. He was nuts to even think about it. That almost-kiss had been interrupted by business and where was Tracy now? That was all the reminder he needed that he was setting himself up to lose. Besides, hadn't he decided less than half an hour ago that a fling was out of the question? That he wanted commitment and marriage—the whole nine yards.

Why can't you have both? Not at the same time, obviously. But there was no reason he had to be a monk while he was waiting for a more suitable woman to come along. What harm could there be in a little no-strings fun with Tracy?

Get real. He was kidding himself if he believed he was a no-strings kind of guy where she was concerned.

Ike was no closer to working out what to do when Tracy came back into the kitchen.

"*Au revoir*, Lise." She ended the call. "Sorry about that." She headed over to the oven and checked the cottage pie. "Coming along nicely. Would you like peas or salad with dinner?"

"Peas would be great."

As she puttered about the kitchen, Ike watched carefully for any sign that she was even slightly affected by his presence. Nada.

He couldn't have imagined it—the heat, the invitation. It hadn't been wishful thinking.

It hadn't.

Yet she was behaving like nothing had happened… Almost happened.

By the time she served up dinner, Ike was frustrated and antsy. He wanted to prove she wasn't immune to him.

"This should hit the spot." Tracy leaned past him to put his plate on the table.

Her arm brushed his shoulder, sending a zing through his body. Her hair brushed against his cheek, amplifying that zing and directing it straight to his groin. Above the rich aroma of the steaming cottage pie, her light scent teased his nose.

His stomach rumbled again, but it wasn't the food that he was really hungry for.

"Ah, the hell with it," he muttered, before reaching up to cradle her neck and gently pull her mouth toward his.

CHAPTER EIGHT

OH, NO! IKE'S going to kiss me!

Thank God! Ike's going to kiss me!

Then Ike's lips touched Tracy's and the internal conflict stopped.

Kissing Ike was like slipping into her favorite Louboutins—a perfect fit, heavenly comfortable and sexy as hell. Just as her confidence was boosted when she wore her black suede Ron Rons, so it blossomed now as his mouth played with hers.

She reveled in the feel of his firm lips melding with hers. His taste—delicious and dark with a hint of danger—was even more intoxicating than she'd remembered. It was also as familiar as coming home. Their tongues danced in perfect harmony, as if they'd been partners only moments ago instead of several years.

The angle of their bodies, of Ike seated while she leaned over him, became awkward. She wanted to press closer, to feel his arms around her, his hard body against hers, from shoulder to ankle and every inch in between.

Ike must have had the same thought, because

without breaking the kiss, he surged upward out of his chair, pulling her to him. The weight of his bandaged arm against her back anchored her against him.

As if she needed anything to keep her there. Tracy lifted up onto her toes, winding her arms around his neck and threading her fingers through his hair.

His good hand stroked her back, then slipped under the hem of her sweater. He groaned when he encountered the silky barrier of her camisole. Tracy hardly had time to draw breath before his fingers bunched the fabric and tugged it free of her jeans.

She sighed against his mouth as the warmth of his hand caressed the arch of her spine and the curve of her hips. Her heart seemed to stutter when his fingers curled into her jeans, gripping tightly, as if he'd never let go.

The rocking beat of "Don't Stop Believin'" surrounded them.

Her phone. Not now. Not again. The first interruption had been bad enough.

Ike swore against her lips, echoing her thoughts. Then he deepened the kiss. His tongue challenged hers and the ringtone was drowned out by the sound of the blood thundering in her ears.

The music stopped, the sudden silence more jarring than when it had started. The thought that the call might have been important fluttered briefly through her brain, but she batted it away. She didn't care. She didn't want this moment, this kiss, to end.

The beep announcing a voice mail message was like permission to continue.

So she did.

Ike's hand journeyed northward. His fingers slid up to the band of her bra and undid the clasp.

Tracy knew what his next destination would be and she wanted it desperately. Her nipples were already hard, but the thought of his touch made them tighten almost painfully.

Her phone rang again. The tune that had always been an inspirational anthem for her suddenly sounded like a death knell, taking her out of the moment as effectively as the proverbial bucket of cold water.

The caller wasn't giving up. That meant an emergency, either business or personal. It also meant Tracy couldn't ignore it any longer.

"Leave it," Ike muttered against her mouth.

She wanted to. Really, she did. Because if she didn't, the connection between them would be lost. The spell would be broken and the magic gone.

"I can't." She dragged her lips away from his and stepped back, out of his arms.

She straightened her clothes and refastened her bra. The loss of his heat made her shiver and she rubbed her arms to take away the chill.

Ike turned away, running his hand through his dark hair. From his raspy breathing and the jagged rise and fall of his shoulders, she could tell he was struggling to get himself under control, too.

The music stopped and the kitchen was silent once again.

"I should see what fire I need to put out," she said as she pulled out her phone.

Ike waved a hand dismissively, then dropped into his chair and stared at the still-steaming dinner on his plate. From his stony expression, food was the last thing on his mind.

Tracy walked out into the hallway. Once she was hidden from Ike's view, she took several steadying breaths before checking her messages. Lise Chabal had called from Paris, panicking about the family's move. She'd worked herself into a state and was demanding Tracy phone immediately, even though it was after midnight in France.

As it turned out, there had been nothing to worry about. The Frenchwoman had misunderstood the wording in one of the documents she'd received from the removal company regarding the packing of valuable and precious items. Tracy explained what the formal language actually meant and reassured Lise that her collection of Japanese porcelain would be perfectly safe.

"I'm sorry to...trouble you," Lise said in her halting English.

"*Ce n'est rien.* Not a problem. Call me anytime. That's what I'm here for."

"I'm glad for your help, Tracy. *Merci beaucoup.*"

"My pleasure. *Au revoir.*"

Tracy delayed going back into the kitchen after

ending the call. She wanted to be in control before facing Ike again.

That kiss. She touched trembling fingers to her tender lips. She was surprised by how quickly, how urgently, she'd responded to Ike, after all this time and all that had happened between them. Tracy had realized in the hospital that the attraction between them wasn't as dead as either of them might have hoped. Still, she hadn't expected to be swept away by one kiss. Certainly not to the point where she'd been prepared to ignore her clients.

So much for putting her business first.

And that was the problem. With Ike, she seemed to lose the ability to balance both halves of her life. And the harder she strived to fix the balance, the more off-kilter she became. That was what had happened last time. She'd seen the signs, felt herself slipping into old habits and panicked when Ike had asked her to move in with him.

With the benefit of hindsight, she knew she'd overreacted.

Part of it had been down to bad timing. Her divorce had only recently been finalized, leaving her wary about commitment. At the same time, her business had started to take off. She'd been so determined to make it succeed. So scared of Hank's snide prediction—that she'd be broke before the year was out—coming true, that she hadn't been able to think seriously about anything else.

The other part of it was she was afraid of tying

herself to another man with the same old-fashioned attitudes about relationships and marriage. Ike believed women should be taken care of by the men in their life. It wasn't that he didn't think a woman should have her own interests or careers, but that they should take a backseat to her husband and family. Although Tracy understood now that his views were a reaction to his tough childhood and his mother's struggles when his father had left, at the time that kind of future had been her worst nightmare.

She'd tried to explain to Ike that she wasn't ready for such a big step, that she needed more time, but he hadn't been able to see past her refusal. He'd known where he wanted their relationship to go and hadn't wanted to wait. The more he'd dug his heels in, the more nervous she'd become. And the further she'd backed away. Until their relationship had imploded.

The chiming of the grandfather clock brought her back to the present. Time to go back into the kitchen. She had a job to do.

A job that would not involve kissing. No matter how much she was tempted—she couldn't lie to herself about that—she had to remember that nothing had really changed. They were still attracted to each other, but they were also still miles apart in what they wanted from a relationship. Only a fool would put herself through all that again.

Tracy ignored the twinge of disappointment and strode purposefully back to the kitchen.

Ike was putting his plate into the microwave

when she entered. She was surprised to see that he'd waited for her before eating. Good manners. There was that courtly side of him again.

"I would have served up your dinner, but I didn't want it to end up on the floor." He programmed the microwave and leaned against the counter to wait for it to reheat his food.

"Thanks for the thought." She thought briefly about forgoing dinner and the awkward conversation that was bound to occur. But she was hungry. And she wanted to establish some ground rules.

The microwave pinged as Tracy spooned cottage pie and peas onto her plate.

"Please start." Tracy stuck her plate in the microwave as Ike took his to the table. "Your dinner will go cold again otherwise."

He looked like he wanted to argue, but grabbed a fork. After his first mouthful, he moaned with pleasure. "Man, this is good."

She couldn't help her delighted smile. "There's enough for you to have seconds and another meal."

"Awesome."

Once her dinner was ready, she joined him at the table, sitting across from him. With the first mouthful, she realized she was famished. She seemed to eat half of her dinner without taking a breath.

They both concentrated on their food rather than conversation for a while. The silence was surprisingly companionable. Once Ike had finished, their argument about who should refill his plate—which she won—was good-natured. Slowly, they began talking. They discussed neutral things like the latest news from the NHL, what they'd both been reading and which TV shows they'd been watching.

As Tracy sipped her wine, she thought how nice it was to have a civil conversation again with Ike, one free from sniping. She'd enjoyed his company when they'd been together. It was one of the things she'd really missed.

Ike finished his food and laid his cutlery on his empty plate. "That was amazing. Who knew you were such a great cook?"

His compliment pleased her. She wasn't a domestic goddess by any stretch of the imagination, nor did she want to be. But she liked to think she was half-decent in the kitchen. "I have a few foolproof dishes that I make, but I'm no expert. Though I must admit my cheese scones are pretty special."

His pleading expression was worthy of a puppy. "They sound like the perfect thing for me to eat one-handed, don't you think?"

She laughed. "If you're good, I might make a batch for you."

"Trust me, I'll be *very* good."

Her pulse skittered at the double meaning in his words.

Oh, no. They were not going down that path again.

"Great," she said brightly, pushing back from the

table and gathering their plates. "Just what the doctor ordered."

She held up a hand to stop him from getting up. "I've got this. I'll clean up and be out of your hair. You must be getting tired. You don't want to overdo it on your first day home."

She bit her lip to stop the babbling, then darted about the kitchen, cleaning counters and loading the dishwasher. She was aware of Ike watching her.

Thank goodness she was nearly done. "Don't forget to take your clothes out of the dryer when they're done, or they'll be wrinkled. Ironing is not one of my favorite chores."

Ike stood. "I'm perfectly capable of managing my own laundry."

"I know, but it's—"

"Yeah, yeah. It's your *job*." He said it like it was a swearword.

Time to leave before things degenerated. She forced a smile. "If there's nothing else, I'll be off." She looked around for her bag.

Ike picked it up from the back of a chair and dangled it in front of her. "Are we going to talk about the kiss or not?"

She grabbed the bag from him and slung it over her shoulder, carefully avoiding his gaze. "There's nothing to talk about. It happened. It's over. It won't happen again."

"That's it?"

She shrugged. "What do you want me to say?"

"Hell, I don't know. But you're acting like it was a root canal. You were right there with me, kissing me back."

She didn't need the reminder. "Just because I enjoyed it doesn't mean I want to repeat it."

"Honey, you were all over me like white on rice. I bet I could prove you wrong in five seconds flat."

Tracy stepped back instinctively, even though he hadn't lifted a finger. His smirk told her she'd proved his point for him.

"I'm sure you could," she said primly. "But I don't see how that helps."

"Sure will help me feel better."

His innuendo only made her cheeks heat. "The chemistry… The whatever you want to call it—" she waved a hand back and forth between them "—was never the problem."

She didn't need to spell out what was.

"You want to ignore the kiss." Ike's tone said he didn't want to let it drop.

"I think that would be best. You're my client. It's not a good idea to mix business and…" Her voice trailed off. Hoist by her own petard.

Tracy snapped her mouth shut. She should leave before she made any more mistakes.

Ike looked at her long and hard. Finally, he scrubbed his hand over the back of his neck. "Whatever." He refilled his empty wineglass and stalked out of the kitchen.

Even though it was what she wanted, his rejection

stung. Tracy got her coat from the hall, then walked into the living room where Ike was sprawled on the sofa, flicking through the channels on the TV.

"I'll be back tomorrow. Will you want breakfast, or shall I come in at lunchtime?"

He didn't shift his gaze from the television. "I don't need you at all until Monday."

"Excuse me?" Her eyes widened with surprise.

"I can manage over the weekend. I have plenty of food, the house is clean and I can handle a dishwasher."

"Very well," she said coolly. "What time shall I be here on Monday? The housekeeper interview is scheduled for four."

"I have to be at the hospital in the morning to get this cast replaced with a splint. I've also got a physio appointment. How about three o'clock?"

"You're the client—whatever time you need me."

"Three it is."

"Okay. I'll see you then. Have a good weekend."

Ike raised a hand in farewell, but pretended absorption in a commercial for car insurance.

By the time Tracy got home, her temples were throbbing. She felt like she'd been through the wringer. She'd known today wouldn't be easy—nothing involving her and Ike ever could be—but she hadn't anticipated going through so many emotions. Maybe the low note the day had finished on was harder for her to take because there had been some unexpected high points. Including that bloody kiss.

"What are you so upset about?" she demanded as she got out of the car. "There's not a snowball's chance in hell of that happening again. You made it perfectly clear you wanted everything to be strictly business and that's what you'll get."

In truth, she admitted, if anyone had been rejected, it had been Ike. But he didn't need to give in so easily.

Tracy was grateful for the distraction of Poppet and Moppet, who scampered to meet her the minute she walked through the door, meowing for their dinner. She kicked off her shoes, then bowed to their demands. As she filled their bowls, Tracy contemplated the weekend ahead. It seemed pitifully empty and lonely. Oh, well. At least she'd be able to catch up on some of the work she'd pushed aside to help Ike.

Somehow that didn't make her feel better.

Enough. Tonight she would treat herself. No more work—she wasn't even going to step into her office. Tracy poured herself a glass of wine, then changed into her favorite brushed cotton pajamas. She clambered into bed and nestled into the pillows with the latest romantic suspense from one of her favorite authors. Moppet and Poppet jumped up and padded into their usual spots.

Perfect. What more could she want?

When the image of a certain green-eyed

goaltender flashed into her head, she dismissed it with the same ease with which he'd dismissed her earlier and opened her book.

THE RELIEF OF being home had worn off pretty quickly. After twenty-four hours, Ike had been restless and edgy. After forty-eight, he'd been bored out of his mind. Now, after seventy-two excruciatingly long hours, he was ready to climb the walls. Or would be, if he could do anything remotely like that with his useless arm. At one point last night, unable to sleep and in pain, he'd been ready to do that "coyote in a trap" thing and gnaw his damn arm off.

The inactivity was killing him. He'd never gone so long without exercise. He kept telling himself things would get better. It had only been bad this weekend because no one had been around. With his mom and Rory in Ireland, the Cats on the road and Linc at college, things had been unusually quiet. Even Maggie hadn't visited because baby Joe had a sniffle.

As for Tracy—that was his own damn fault. He shouldn't have pushed her away, but the way she'd shut down had stung. One minute she'd been kissing him as though her life depended on it and the next she'd grabbed that cell as though she'd been making the biggest deal in her career. Then she'd thrown that clichéd crap at him about not mixing business with pleasure. Tired, his arm aching, and fed up with the whole damn situation—as well as pissed at the sense of déjà vu—he'd lashed out.

And shot himself in the foot.

Now things were worse than ever between them. When Tracy had stopped by earlier for the housekeeper interview, she'd been cool and distant. Even though he'd agreed to hire the woman she'd recommended, Tracy had been so desperate to get away from him he'd practically seen the vapor trail behind her as she'd hurried out the door.

The perfect ending to a perfectly crappy couple of days.

His iPad jingled, alerting him to an incoming Facetime call.

With pathetic eagerness, he grabbed the tablet. His boredom lifted at the sight of Jake, Tru and Kenny crowding in front of the camera. "Your ugly faces are a sight for sore eyes."

"Back at you, bro." Tru grinned. "How're you doing?"

"Living the high life. Non-stop parties and fun, fun, fun."

"So, bored to death," Jake said.

Ike groaned. "Yeah. The highlight of my weekend was putting a waterproof sleeve around my cast so I could have a bath. Man, did that suck. I don't get why women like lying around in a bath."

Jake grimaced. "Me, neither. Especially not with all the smelly crap they use."

Kenny laughed. “You’re both doing it wrong. The idea is to have a woman *with you* in the bath.”

Naturally, his kid brother’s comment made Ike think of Tracy. The last thing he needed. “Nice idea, but I wouldn’t be much good with this.” Ike held up his bandaged arm.

“Still not got the hang of the woman doing all the work.” Tru shook his head. “Gotta be an age thing. Too stuck in your ways. Can’t give up the control.”

“Bite me.”

“That’s progress, net boy. Now, say it to a woman, and you might enjoy bath time more.”

A memory from when he’d first bought the place popped into Ike’s head. From when he and Tracy had christened the main bathroom. He could still see her flushed face, tendrils of dark hair curling around her face in the steamy air, water cascading over her curves as she rose up out of the water and straddled him. He could practically feel her lowering herself onto his hardness, sheathing him. Hot and tight and slick.

Fingers snapped, jolting him out of his reverie.

“Stay with us, bro,” Kenny teased. “Indulge in your bath-time fantasies later.”

“I’m still here. You guys cut out on me for a few seconds,” Ike lied smoothly. “Must have been a blip in the Wi-Fi connection.”

“Bullsh—” Kenny coughed as Tru cuffed him round the head.

"How was your trip to the hospital?" Jake asked. "Is everything okay?"

"Yeah. They removed my cast and put me in this splint. Doc Gibson said I'm progressing on schedule. Got a mean-looking scar."

"That'll impress the ladies."

"That's what the nurse said." Then she'd given him some cream to apply to help the scar fade. Not that he'd be sharing that information with his brothers.

"So what's the verdict? When will you be back?" Jake asked.

"Not soon enough. I had physio this morning and it looks like it'll be a long road."

Physio? Hah. More like baby exercises. He'd been pleased when Cheryl, his physiotherapist, had unwrapped his hand, freeing his fingers. *Now we're talking*, he'd thought. But that had been it. The only exercises he'd been allowed to do had been to "gently and slowly" bend one finger at a time. Not even the whole freaking hand at once.

"I can't hold or lift anything with this hand for at least a month, and I can't start working out until then."

"No running or the elliptical?" Tru asked.

"Nope. Nothing. In case I reinjure my arm." As if he was a numb-nuts who tripped over his own feet. "What do they think I'll do—bench-press a couple hundred pounds for fun?"

Kenny barked out a laugh. "You can't even do that when you're healthy."

"Sure, I can." Well, he had *once*.

"Easy to say, net boy, when you can't back it up."

"I'll prove it once I'm better." Hopefully Kenny would have forgotten by then. "In the meantime, I can't even ride a stationary bike. What the hell kind of damage could I do to myself on that?"

"Be patient and follow instructions," Jake said sternly. "It'll only be worse in the long run if you try to rush your recovery."

Jake had been in a similar position after he'd been badly injured in a tragic car accident a few years ago. He swore he could tell when a storm was coming now, from all the steel in his leg.

Suddenly Ike was tired of talking about his injury. This was his chance to shoot the breeze with the guys and he wasn't going to waste it whining about his waste-of-space arm.

"It's not like you need me back anyway. It's been a successful road trip so far."

"Yeah, Monty's been standing on his head to get us those wins," Jake said.

"Until tonight," Tru said. "Prepare to eat ice, pussycats."

"Prepare to melt under our hellfire, snowballs," Kenny retorted.

Ike joined in the trash talk. For the first time since his accident, he didn't feel so isolated.

Then someone off-screen called to them and they

had to go. With a heavy heart, he wished Jake and Kenny good luck for the game and Tru bad luck—injured or not, Ike was still an Ice Cat—which he promised to watch.

Once he'd signed off, the house seemed even quieter than before.

He had to get out of here or he'd go nuts. He had to *do* something. Surely he could take a long walk through the local park without risking injury.

An hour later, he was back. It had been good to be out of the house and get some fresh air. The brisk walk had taken some of the stiffness out of his limbs, but it hadn't raised his heart rate. He could almost feel his muscles atrophying.

Ike drained a bottle of water and looked at the clock. Still a couple of hours to go before dinner. He didn't want to watch TV. The thriller he'd started reading last night was good, but he'd be sitting on his ass all night.

What harm could a short stint on the stationary bike do?

Once he'd had the idea, he couldn't think about anything else. If he took care not to overdo things, it'd be okay. He didn't have to do his usual ten miles; even half that would make him feel better. He ignored the inner voice of caution that told him the medics had banned him from working out for a reason. That applied to ordinary people, not a professional athlete.

Having convinced himself it would be okay, Ike

walked upstairs and got changed. In his home gym, he programmed the plasma TV to show the latest episode of his favorite crime drama. He stuck a chilled water bottle in the bike's cup holder and a clean towel around his neck, then did a few leg stretches to warm up his dormant muscles. Grinning at how good it made him feel, he sat on the bike and started pedaling.

Even though the five miles was harder work than he'd expected, when Ike got to the end of the circuit, he'd barely broken a sweat. Perhaps he should do the other five miles, too. Since he couldn't lift weights or work on the machines, he wouldn't be overdoing it.

The second five miles was definitely more of a workout. Frustrated that it had taken so little to tire him, he was also pleased his body finally felt like it had done something.

Job done.

Getting off the bike, his legs were jellylike. He stumbled, catching himself at the last minute with his good hand. Whoa! Perhaps he'd overdone it, after all. A nice hot shower would fix him. It was easier slipping the waterproof sleeve over his splint than the cast, so he was soon standing under the pounding water.

"Man, that feels good," he moaned.

When he got out of the shower, Ike felt surprisingly weak. Worse than after that triple overtime game against the Flyers in the playoffs a few years back.

"Probably need to eat something," he muttered. "Low blood sugar."

He toweled off and got dressed before heading downstairs.

Halfway down, the light-headed feeling got even worse. Blinking and shaking his head to get rid of the weird sensation, he wondered what the hell was going on. It wasn't like he had a concussion. He'd be fine once he was downstairs. He'd grab a sandwich and chill out on the couch. Maybe even have dinner early—one of his mom's stews was already defrosting in the kitchen.

He snorted. Hell, no one was monitoring his schedule. He could eat what he wanted, whenever he damn well pleased. With that in mind, he started down the stairs.

His foot missed the step. Instinctively, he reached for the banister with his catching hand to stabilize himself.

In the split second that followed, it all went horribly wrong.

As his fingers closed around the varnished wood, the restriction of his splint reminded him that he shouldn't grab anything with that hand. He jerked it away and used his other hand. But he was still off-balance and the sudden movement destabilized him even more.

His foot was in no-man's-land in the air between two steps. Neither hand was holding on to anything.

Ike was falling and he couldn't stop himself.

Again, instinct took over. He threw his arms out in front of him to break his fall. Again, he realized he couldn't use his injured arm. More importantly, he needed to protect it. In a weird twisting motion, he tried to bring his arm back to his chest.

It was too late.

Ike landed on the wood floor at the bottom of the stairs with a sickening thud. Pain shot through his hip and lower back. Something tore in his arm.

He lay there for a few minutes, heart pounding, scared to move in case he made anything worse. Finally, he managed to propel himself into a sitting position. At least nothing was broken. Then his injured arm began to burn and throb. It felt like needles were jabbing into the scar line. He didn't have to undo the bandages to know he'd ruptured something.

He should call an ambulance or something. No. Someone might recognize his name and put it out in the media. Still, he couldn't just sit here until someone stopped by. Especially as no one would be stopping by until tomorrow. It didn't take a genius—which he wasn't or he wouldn't have put himself in this situation—to figure out who he had to call.

Gingerly, he reached into his pocket, pulled out his cell and dialed.

CHAPTER NINE

"THE ICE CATS are giving notice?"

Tracy's heart sank. Even though she'd had her suspicions and had even spent part of her unexpectedly free weekend looking at contingency plans for the company, the reality was still a shock. She certainly hadn't expected it to happen so soon.

Tracy struggled to mask her disappointment as she stared across the large glass-topped desk at Callum Hardshaw. When his assistant had called this morning asking her to come in for an unscheduled meeting this afternoon, Tracy hadn't had the impression there would be bad news. She'd actually harbored a small hope that Hardshaw might want to discuss Helping Hands. The idea that he'd end the contract altogether hadn't crossed her mind.

The general manager leaned back in his oversize leather chair. "In reviewing the organization's operations, I found that we were spending far too much on external suppliers—particularly for work we could manage more cost-effectively ourselves. Travel, relocation and player accommodation is one of the areas that will be brought in-house. Making this transition in the middle of the season isn't ideal, but I want to have our processes in place for the trade deadline."

"So this is with immediate effect, even though there is a three-month notice period in the contract?" She couldn't keep the shock from her voice. Even when she'd imagined the worst, she hadn't anticipated such a drastic turn of events.

"No. It will take time for the new Player Logistics Manager to get up to speed and we don't want any balls dropped in the meantime." Hardshaw's smile was overly hearty. "You'll finish your current projects, keeping the PLM fully informed, and hand over everything else as soon as possible. Naturally, we'd expect you to support Lois and ensure as smooth a transition as possible over the next three months."

"You already have someone in place?" How long had he been planning this?

"Under the circumstances, it seemed appropriate and expedient to recruit from within, rather than externally. Lois is one of our junior sales managers. She's very bright, so I'm confident she'll pick up her new responsibilities quickly. Especially with your support."

Tracy wasn't sure what pissed her off the most—that the GM seemed to think what she did was so easy that someone with no relevant experience could take over, or that Hardshaw expected her to train her replacement. Regardless, there was no point crying over spilled milk. She had to focus her energy on what she could control: her business. "I'll arrange for a handover in the next few days. Just to be clear, these are the projects I'm currently working on and will complete."

Tracy went through her active projects with him and was relieved that he agreed she should see them all through, even the most recent player trade completed only last week. She stood and stuck out her hand, determined to appear professional even though she wanted to smack him.

"It's been a pleasure working with the Ice Cats these past few years. If there is ever anything we can do for the organization, do let us know."

He shook her hand. "One thing I've learned in this game is never to say never."

Tracy strode out of the office with her head held high, though anyone looking closely would have seen her white-knuckled grip on her briefcase. She deliberately exchanged cheerful goodbyes with the receptionist and pressed the lift button casually, as if she hadn't a care in the world. If only. Tracy resisted the urge to tap her foot impatiently as she waited for the car to arrive. Instead, she focused on breathing steadily.

In and out. A few more minutes and she'd be in her car, away from prying eyes. Then she could give in to the emotions welling inside, tightening her throat.

In and out.

The elevator pinged. *Thank God. Hold it together just a bit longer.*

Once the metal doors had shut, she exhaled heavily and resisted the urge to dissolve into a miserable puddle by giving herself a stern talking-to.

Okay, so this was a major setback, but it wasn't the end of the world. Tracy had survived worse times; she'd survive this. She wasn't in immediate financial trouble, though she might have to find ways of tightening the business's belt if she hadn't replaced at least some of the revenue before the three months were up.

The obvious area was their intern. Even as the thought occurred, Tracy dismissed it. Carla was a godsend. She worked hard, had great initiative and common sense, and didn't need a lot of overseeing. Plus, she'd taken an enormous load off Tracy's plate on the admin side—which made her worth every penny of her small salary.

On top of that, Maggie wouldn't be back at work for several months at least, and then only part-time until Joe was older. Even without the Ice Cats contract, Tracy needed Carla's support to manage their other clients. Keeping her on would free Tracy to focus on finding new clients.

If it became necessary, Tracy would find the savings elsewhere. She would cut her own salary, as she'd done in the past when things had been tight.

The more she thought it through, the more her unhappiness got pushed aside in favor of forward thinking. The key was not to lose sight of her goal. She had plenty of ideas and had identified some potential opportunities; she just had to work on them sooner than she'd hoped.

Although she didn't want to stress out her sister, Tracy had to tell her about the termination. Maternity leave or not, Maggie was her partner and had a right to know. Tracy knew Maggie would support her decisions, but she'd stop by her sister's place tomorrow.

In the meantime, Tracy needed to get back to the office and turn her tentative ideas into a structured action plan. She unlocked her car, tossed her briefcase onto the backseat and slid behind the wheel.

Her phone rang just as she plugged it into the hands-free cradle. Tracy glanced at the caller ID on her dashboard screen and was surprised to see Ike's name.

Why was he calling?

Had she forgotten something? She cast her mind back to their earlier meeting. It had been stilted and uncomfortable, but as far as she could tell, she'd covered everything important. She pushed aside the twinge of guilt at having rushed away as soon as possible, and answered.

"Hello, Ike. What can I do for you?" she said, her tone polite but upbeat.

"I have a…bit of a problem. I need your help."

Tracy frowned. He sounded out of breath. "What's the matter?"

"I had...an accident." Pain edged his gruff voice. "I've hurt myself. I need you to come over."

Her stomach twisted. "Have you reinjured your arm?"

She didn't wait for his answer before pulling out of the parking space.

"I think so." He sounded miserable. "It's not good, for sure."

"Have you called an ambulance?"

"I was going to, but I didn't want to alert anyone in the media."

She rolled her eyes. He was acting as if he were Jon Bon Jovi, not a hockey player. As if the paparazzi hung on Ike's every move. Though she supposed if it was that bad, the sports media would be all over the story. She hoped it sounded worse than it was.

Tracy spoke calmly, trying to hide her concern. "I'm on my way. I can be with you in half an hour." If she pushed it. "Whatever you do, don't move."

"I won't."

His ready agreement told her all she needed to know. Ike was hurt badly.

She pressed her foot to the accelerator. Stuff the speed limit, Ike needed her help.

Idiot. Ike clenched his good fist and stared out of Tracy's car window at the scenery whipping past. His arm throbbed like an SOB. He hadn't dared look too closely at the bandage. Blood would be really bad news.

Why hadn't he followed the surgeon's instructions? Why hadn't he listened to Cheryl's advice? Hell, every damn person in his life had told him the same thing. *Be patient. Give your arm time to heal. Don't rush things.*

Ike had thought he knew better than any of them. *Stupid idiot.*

He'd sworn as he'd sat at the foot of his stairs, cradling his arm, that he'd do everything he was told without complaint, if the damage wasn't as bad as he suspected. If he could just play again this season.

He tried to tell himself it had only been a slight fall. He hadn't tumbled the full length of the stairs. And he'd done his best to protect his arm.

Who was he kidding? He knew his body well enough to tell when an injury was serious. He didn't need an examination or tests to know that it was bad. Blood or no blood, he was in trouble.

"We're almost at the hospital." Tracy flicked a concerned look at him. "How are you holding up?"

"Hanging in there," he lied.

Thank God for Tracy. Ike had never been so relieved to see anyone as he'd been when she'd burst through his front door. The panic in her dark eyes had had a strangely calming effect on him, as though she'd taken the worry from him. Warmed him, even as she'd blasted him for being a dumbass.

He'd been impressed by how quickly she'd turned

from worried to efficient. She'd sprung into action immediately. She'd helped him to his feet, ignoring his embarrassment, then bundled him into her SUV. She'd called ahead to the hospital and paged Dr. Gibson, so Ike wouldn't have to wait.

When they pulled up at the ER entrance, an orderly with a wheelchair awaited them.

Ike started to protest that he could walk, but Tracy's stern look silenced him. He stopped arguing because he was light-headed and the pain in his arm was making him nauseous. He sank into the chair with a sigh of relief.

"Would you like me to come in with you?" Tracy asked. "I can handle your paperwork."

"Yes, please." He felt better with her there and was in too much pain to worry about hiding it.

"All right." She squeezed his shoulder, then followed as the orderly wheeled him inside.

Dr. Gibson met them in a cubicle that had been set aside for Ike. "Let's take a look."

"I'll go and sort out the admin," Tracy said. "I'll be right outside if you need anything."

Suddenly, Ike wanted to delay her departure. "Could you let Jake know what's happened and where I am?"

"Of course. What about your brothers and your mum?"

"I'd rather wait until I have something concrete to tell them."

Her expression said she disagreed with him, but she nodded. “Okay.”

“You’d better call the Ice Cats, too.” Ike hated that they’d have to know what he’d done to himself, but there was no way around that.

“Why don’t I wait until we have something concrete to tell them?” She repeated his words with a smile, as if understanding his anxiety.

“Thanks.”

Once again, she’d gone above and beyond when he’d needed her. She’d been under no obligation to come and help him. Yet she had, without hesitation.

Ike had plenty of time to mull that over as Dr. Gibson examined his arm before sending him for an MRI.

Once he’d studied the results, the surgeon confirmed Ike’s worst fears. “You’ve re-torn one of the tendons completely and seriously damaged a second. The third looks to be intact, but I won’t know for sure until I get in and take a look.”

Ike swore. “But you can fix them again, right?”

“I can. However, there’s no guarantee that the new damage won’t have a cost. Healing and recovery will be far less predictable this time.”

Ike’s chest tightened. “Are you saying I won’t be able to use my arm properly again?”

“No. You should regain a reasonable amount of functionality. But I can’t promise how much. I certainly can’t guarantee that your arm will be strong enough for you to play hockey in the near future, if at all."

Ike ignored the last part. "'Near future' as in a few months, or a few years?"

"I don't know. We'll take it step-by-step and see how things go."

This time the nausea had nothing to do with the pain in his arm.

"Do whatever you have to, Doc. I promise I'll follow every instruction you give me to the letter."

The surgeon shook his head sadly. "I wish you players would make those promises before you cause me so many problems."

When the nurse came in to prep him for surgery, Ike asked for Tracy to join them.

"We're taking you down to the operating room shortly. Ms. Hayden can wait in your room."

No. He needed to see her now. He didn't know why it was important, only that it was.

"I need to see her before I go down." His firm tone told her this wasn't up for debate.

The nurse huffed, but when he was ready to go, she called Tracy into the cubicle. "You have five minutes."

"All set?" The anxious furrow in Tracy's brow belied her bright words.

"I guess." He tried to be stoic, but before he could help himself, the truth came tumbling out. "Not really." He told her what Dr. Gibson had said. "No guarantees. No promises. This could be it."

Putting his fears into words made them sharper, more real. Suddenly, he was terrified. Once he'd had the operation, there'd be no hiding from the truth. If it didn't work, he'd be out of options. "My career could be over."

"Don't borrow trouble. There's no guarantee your arm will be one hundred percent, but there's also no guarantee it won't be. Dr. Gibson is the best, so let him do his stuff."

Which meant if the surgeon couldn't fix him, no one could.

Tracy continued. "You won't know the outcome for weeks. Even if the initial prognosis isn't encouraging, I know you'll do everything you can to beat the odds."

Her words lifted the black cloud that had been hovering over his head. Yes, he would. He'd prove the surgeon wrong. He *would* play again. Hell, he'd be back for the playoffs.

Still, Ike didn't want to wake up alone. Just in case. "Any chance you can hang around until it's done?"

"Of course."

Her soft smile lifted his heart. He held out his good hand, palm up. "Promise?"

She laid her hand in his, then linked their fingers. "I promise."

"Okay. Let's get this done."

The nurse reappeared. "Ready?"

Ike took a deep breath and nodded. "Bring it on."

TO QUOTE THE famous former Yankee Yogi Berra, it was déjà vu all over again.

Tracy sat in Ike's hospital room again, watching his chest rise and fall steadily as the machines beeped and whirred around him. He'd been brought up from recovery a few minutes ago and the nurse had told her that Dr. Gibson would be by shortly to fill her in on how it had gone.

Though the operation hadn't taken as long as last time, Tracy had been more nervous and on edge. Perhaps because this *was* the second time. Though she'd tried not to let dark thoughts prey on her mind as she'd waited, those had been hard to ignore. Despite what she'd said to Ike, the likelihood was that he would miss at least the rest of the season. Maybe more. What if Dr. Gibson couldn't fix the damage? Or what if he could, but not enough for Ike to ever return to the ice? She'd seen how badly Ike had reacted when he was only looking at missing a few months. What would retirement do to him?

Tracy had alternated between cursing Ike for being such a stubborn fool and willing him to be okay. She'd even thought about how she could make sure he followed the bloody instructions this time. It wasn't really her business, but he clearly couldn't be trusted to stick to the rules on his own. Although maybe this second injury had scared him enough to make him toe the line.

Tracy moved the seat closer to Ike's bed. The bandage on Ike's arm was more substantial than before, covering every inch of his arm from fingertip to shoulder, but that was probably precautionary. His vital signs were good, but then he hadn't had the same blood loss or trauma as he'd had with his initial injury. She tried to tell herself that all her worrying wouldn't make the slightest difference, but it didn't ease her nerves. She didn't want to think about why she cared so much.

She laid her hand on Ike's. "You can wake up any time now," she said gently.

Ike didn't twitch a muscle. She sighed. Typical bloody stubborn man. "All right, then—in your own time."

The door swished open and Dr. Gibson walked into the room.

"How did it go?" Tracy's heart was pounding so hard she thought it would leap right out of her mouth. "Will he…his arm be all right?"

The surgeon wiped his hand across his jaw. "I think so. The surgery went as planned. The damage wasn't as bad as it appeared and I managed to reattach the tendons securely."

"I bet you wanted to triple-stitch them to make sure they couldn't come apart again."

"It'll all hold if he does what he's told this time."

"I'm sure you don't have to worry about that. Once he knows he had another lucky escape, he'll behave."

The surgeon smiled wryly. "I wish I believed that. Experience has proven otherwise. No matter how remorseful they are after things like this, professional athletes revert to type after a few weeks of boredom."

"I'll keep an eye on him. Make sure he stays out of trouble."

Tracy hadn't meant to make such a vow, let alone say it aloud. But she meant it. She couldn't give Ike the personal commitment he wanted, but she cared enough about him to make sure he didn't jeopardize his career. She'd make Ike behave if she had to handcuff him to the stair rail.

"That'll help, I'm sure." Dr. Gibson nodded. "He won't be happy to hear that this has set his recovery back by at least a month. All the progress he made has been wiped out and he'll need to start over with additional precautions."

"It's better than being told he's played his last game. So, you're cautiously optimistic?"

"Yes. The caveat being that I've done all I can and this is the best it'll be. It's now up to Ike. That's what I'll be telling him and the Ice Cats management."

Tracy knew Ike had to be dreading Callum Hardshaw's reaction to the news. Ike was too valuable an asset for the team to take any risks with his recovery. Any hint of uncertainty and they'd shut him down. Which would only rile Ike up even more.

An idea occurred to her. What if she could get Dr. Gibson to delay talking to the Ice Cats? Instead of focusing on the result of the surgery, they'd be worried about Ike coming through the operation successfully. Then they'd be so relieved to hear Ike was in better shape than they'd expected, they might not overreact. It was worth a shot.

She outlined her idea to the surgeon.

Dr. Gibson gave her a long, hard look. "I don't think it'll make much difference. The facts are the same, however you dress them up."

"I know, but I want to try and make common sense prevail."

He looked doubtful, but shrugged. "All right."

"Thank you. I'll call them now."

Tracy stepped out of Ike's room and headed for the dayroom. She wasn't looking forward to making this call. Not least because of her earlier meeting with Callum Hardshaw. The thought of speaking to him again so soon made her feel uncomfortable. The things she did for her frien— her clients.

She was put through to the GM's assistant initially, but Tracy insisted on speaking with him directly.

He came on the line shortly after. "What's so urgent that you'd interrupt an important meeting? We have nothing further to discuss regarding the contract and—"

Tracy interrupted, "Ike's fallen and reinjured his arm. He's in surgery and will be out shortly." She didn't feel guilty about the white lie after the way Hardshaw spoke to her.

His tone changed. "How badly is he hurt? What happened?"

She explained briefly, leaving out the part about Ike's workout. He could tell his GM that part himself. "Hopefully, Dr. Gibson can fix the damage."

"I'm coming down there."

The longer Hardshaw had to worry about Ike, the more likely he'd be relieved Ike was okay. "There's no rush. Ike won't be awake for a while, even once he's out of surgery."

He hesitated. "I do need to finish this meeting. I'll stop by as soon as it's done. Shouldn't be more than another hour."

"That'll work."

"Thanks for letting me know, and for looking after Ike." He sounded genuinely grateful.

"All part of the service." Her tongue wasn't in her cheek. Not really.

Now that she'd got the toughest call out of the way, she might as well get the rest done. First, she called Maggie—who was shocked, but not really surprised. If anyone knew about stubborn injured athletes, it was her sister. Then Tracy got ahold of Jake, who was pretty sanguine about the whole thing and promised to let Ike's brothers know.

Last, but definitely not least, Ike's mother. Given the time difference, Tracy figured that Karina and Rory would be asleep. If she called them now, they'd panic. Middle-of-the-night calls usually meant death or disaster. Better to call them in the morning. Maybe she'd suggest that Ike call them himself, so he could reassure his mum he was okay.

When she got back to Ike's room, Tracy was disappointed to see he was still asleep. She returned to the seat by his bed. Unsure how long it would be before he awoke, she wondered about doing some work in the dayroom while she waited. No. She'd promised Ike she'd be here for him. Besides, she knew she wouldn't be able to concentrate.

Ike had always slept like the dead; he'd be out cold as soon as his head hit the pillow. He claimed it was because he had a clear mind and a clean conscience. Tracy figured it was because, like most males, he was able to compartmentalize his life and close off his mind to whatever was stressing him.

That was an invaluable skill for a goaltender. They couldn't obsess about a goal they'd let in or a terrible clearance they'd made. Equally, they couldn't pat themselves on the back too hard after a fantastic save, in case the next shot got through.

Ike would need that ability in spades in the months ahead. Tracy agreed with Dr. Gibson that Ike's fervent vow—no matter how much he'd meant it in the heat of the moment—would be hard to live up to when February came around and things started heating up for the postseason. Especially if Monty was struggling or the Cats were on the bubble.

In that way, at least, Ike was very much like her. Perhaps that was part of their problem. There couldn't be two leaders in a dance. She sighed softly. Unfortunately, neither of them would ever be a follower.

Ignoring the twinge in her gut, Tracy focused on how she could help Ike. Despite what she'd said to Dr. Gibson, she had to admit that she couldn't see how she'd be able to save Ike from himself. Babysitting wasn't part of her Helping Hands remit. What's more, Ike wouldn't thank her for her interference.

Even so, she wanted to help him. Wanted to see him safely through to the other side and back onto the ice. There had to be a way she could make it work.

A guttural murmur broke into her thoughts. Like last time, Ike seemed to be having a nightmare. He was frowning and moving his head restlessly from side to side. His legs worked against the bedclothes, pulling them free, as if he couldn't stand to be constrained. Sweat beaded on his forehead and his breathing rasped.

As she had before, Tracy dampened a washcloth and wiped it over his forehead and down his cheeks, hoping to soothe him a little.

It seemed to do the trick, temporarily. He stopped thrashing and his breathing evened out. But the frown remained.

She laid her hand on top of his good one. Perhaps he'd sense he wasn't alone.

He calmed a little more.

Tracy was about to move her hand when suddenly he gripped it tightly, startling her.

His eyes snapped open. She could see confusion and panic in the dark green depths.

"It's okay, Ike," she soothed. "Everything's fine. You're all right."

His frown deepened, as if he couldn't understand what she was saying. His gaze flicked to his heavily bandaged arm, then away.

"The surgery went well. Your arm will be okay."

He looked at her. She could tell her words weren't really registering.

"My arm," he rasped.

"Looks worse than it is." She kept the soothing tone. "They've given your arm extra protection to be on the safe side."

He closed his eyes. He was quiet for so long, she thought he'd gone back to sleep. His grip on her hand remained tight. She stroked the back of his hand with her thumb and repeated the reassurances.

The next time he opened his eyes, his gaze was clearer. He coughed.

Tracy let go of his hand and reached for the glass of water, then held it for him so he could sip through the straw.

"Thanks." He nodded when he'd had enough. "The verdict?"

His gaze held hers before dropping nervously to his bandaged arm.

She should probably tell him gently, but she wanted Ike to get the message loud and clear. "You're bloody lucky. Dr. Gibson will fill you in on the details, but essentially he managed to fix your arm and it should be as good as new. *If* you do as you're told."

"I will." He ran his good hand through his dark hair. "Hell, I can't afford not to. This is too important to screw up."

"I'm glad to hear it."

His mouth twisted ruefully. "It was a rookie mistake, overdoing the exercise. I didn't count on how much my injury took out of me."

She softened her tone. "You didn't give your body a chance to recover from the trauma of the injury, let alone time to heal."

"I've always healed quickly before," he protested.

"You're not as young as you were," she teased. "I hear that can affect your healing rate."

"Thanks for that. As if I didn't already feel old and decrepit." Ike's expression sobered. "You're telling me the truth, aren't you? I will play again. You're not cushioning the blow." He searched her face. "Be straight with me. I want to know—even if it's bad news."

"I wouldn't lie to you. There are caveats, like last time, but you will play again."

"This season?"

She gave him a stern look. "Don't push your luck.

If you follow instructions to the letter, you may be able to take part in the postseason."

"I already said I'll do exactly as I'm told. I got it the first time."

"If you had, we wouldn't be having this conversation."

"Touché." He sighed. "I really don't want to miss another run at the Cup. Who knows how many more chances I'll get to hoist that baby over my head again."

"There's nothing wrong with setting yourself the goal of being back on the ice for the playoffs. But there are bound to be factors you can't control, which may cause setbacks. You'll have to be extra-patient with your arm and yourself."

"Easier said than done."

"You can do this. I have faith in you."

"Will you help me?" he asked earnestly.

"I've already said I would."

"I don't mean making sure I'm fed and watered and wearing clean clothes. I mean to work with me during my recovery. I'll pay you for your time. Call it part of your Helping Hands services. I know how important your business is to you..."

"Seriously?" Tracy bristled. "This again?"

Ike held up his hand. "Let me finish. I'm not stupid enough to make that mistake twice. What I was trying to say was, I know I have a tough journey ahead and I can't do this alone. I trust you. I need you to keep me on track. I'd prefer if you'd help me as a friend, but if that makes you uncomfortable, I'll take your help any way I can get it."

He reached out and caught hold of her hand. "Please."

His admission that he needed help was a huge step for Ike. She understood how much that acknowlegment had cost him. That he trusted her to help him when he was so vulnerable touched her deeply.

"All right. I'll help you. But not as a client, not as part of Helping Hands and certainly not for money." She lightened her tone. "You understand that means I don't have to be polite to you?"

"Have you ever been?" Ike's laugh was interrupted by a yawn. "Sorry. I'm really tired." His eyes were already drooping.

"Get some rest. I've got to go anyway."

"Thanks." He squeezed her hand. "For everything. I owe you big time."

"I'll add it to your bill." She smiled. "Just joking."

His lips quirked, then his eyes closed and he was asleep.

Tracy stood by the bed, looking down at their joined hands. This time, Ike looked peaceful as he slept. No frown. No restless movement. Her heart went out to him.

She started to slip her hand out of his, but he tightened his grip and shifted. The frown was back. "It'll be okay," she murmured. "You'll be okay."

Tracy didn't know why, but she leaned over and pressed a soft kiss to his forehead. Before she could pull away, he turned his face until their lips touched.

Her breath caught in her throat.

His fingers tightened around hers. Yet his eyes remained shut.

Their mouths fused.

She should draw back. Yet she lingered. Just for a moment.

It felt good…right.

But it was wrong.

She wished for a fleeting moment that it didn't have to be, then lifted her head and pulled her hand from his.

The corner of his mouth curved into a satisfied half smile as his breathing evened out.

Her lips curved briefly in response. Then she shook her head.

Friends was one thing. Friends with benefits was something else entirely. They weren't going down that route again, however pleasant it might be.

Pleasant? Hah! That was way too wishy-washy for what it'd be. And maybe that was the problem. It would blind her to why it was wrong until it was too late.

No. Definitely no. Definitely not going there.

Yet as she walked out of Ike's room, a little voice inside her asked, *Why not*?

CHAPTER TEN

"YOU'RE CHEATING!"

Tracy pointed to the winning hand Ike had just laid down with a flourish on his over-bed table. Cards he couldn't possibly have got without a crafty sleight of hand.

"I'm a Stanley Cup–winning goaltender. I don't need to cheat," he retorted loftily.

She leaned across and snatched a card from beneath his bandaged arm. "So this one just fell by accident?"

"How did that get there?" The twinkle in his eyes spoiled the too-innocent expression.

"And there was me thinking nothing sneaked past a Stanley Cup–winning goaltender."

"Even I'm not perfect."

Tracy laughed at his attempt at humility. "That's for sure."

It was great to see Ike in a good mood. Her strategy to stop him brooding about his situation was clearly working. For the past three days, Tracy had made sure that whenever she visited Ike, she did something to distract him. On Tuesday it had been a hard-fought duel of Battleship. He'd cheated then, too. Knowing Ike enjoyed logic problems as much as she did, she'd introduced him to Hanjie on Wednesday. He'd already worked through one book of the Japanese picture puzzles and had asked her to bring him more.

Today she'd brought a well-worn deck of cards from his den. It was the pack he'd had since he was a young boy and featured pictures of classic heroes of the game. He took the cards with him every time he traveled. It was the same deck they'd used back when they were together—only they hadn't played ordinary gin rummy.

Her cheeks heated at the memory.

"Maybe we should try another game. You might have more luck." His gruff tone and the heat in his look told her he was remembering the same evening.

"That was your argument the last time we played cards. I seem to remember you fiddled the dealing then, too."

His chuckle sent a delicious shiver through her. "And you removing an earring or a bracelet when you lost was fair?"

"The rules were that anything we were wearing counted as clothing." The huskiness in her voice spoiled the prim response she'd been going for.

He reached across and trailed a finger across her cheek to her ear, where he toyed with the dangling earring. "I was down to my shorts in a few hands and it was taking you forever to even take off your sweater. I did what I had to do."

Her pulse skipped. "Are you saying the wait wasn't worth it?"

"Hmm. I can't seem to remember too clearly. My brain must be fuzzy from the drugs." His finger followed her jawline to her chin, then up to her lips. "We could give it another shot and see if that jogs my memory."

Tracy stamped on the urge to say yes. Instead, she nipped his finger. "Even ignoring the fact that we're in a hospital room, with the door wide open and the nurses' station a few feet away—hardly the ideal venue for a game of strip gin—may I remind you that the only thing you're wearing is a hospital gown. I only need to win one hand and you're toast."

"I don't suppose you'd give an injured man a handicap, huh?" He gave her a pitiful look.

She removed her six bangles and laid them on the table. "How's that?"

"You're a wicked woman." He shook his head sadly.

"Takes one to know one."

"In that case, I'll have to settle for beating your ass at normal gin. Don't expect me to take it easy on you, either, after that little trick." He pushed the bracelets back toward her and picked up the deck of cards.

A nurse bustled into his room and checked his chart, then his arm. "Do you need a top-up of your pain medication?"

"Nah. I'm good, thanks. I'll need all my wits about me to beat this card shark."

"Uh-huh. So you're cheating again."

He sighed heavily. "What kind of hospital is this? I'm getting picked on by you, too?"

"You're not giving the nice nurses a hard time, are you, Ike?" JB flashed his charming grin at the nurse as he walked into the room, followed by Kenny.

"He wishes." The nurse made a note on Ike's chart and left.

"Welcome back, guys. Nice job on the road trip."

Despite his bright expression, Tracy heard the hint of wistfulness in Ike's voice.

The mood in the room changed as the two younger men exchanged barbed comments about their play over the past week with Ike. Why they couldn't just chat normally, Tracy had never understood. Anyway, now that they were here, she felt a little uncomfortable.

She got up from the bed. "I should probably get back to work. No rest for the wicked."

"We can continue the game tomorrow." Ike shot a heated look at her.

That was so much better than disapproval. Now that she thought about it, Ike hadn't made a snarky comment about her work since his accident. Go figure.

"Hey, what's this about the Cats bringing travel and relocation in-house?" Kenny asked.

Ike's surprised gaze shot to her. "Is that true?"

The time had never seemed right to tell him. Their new…whatever this was…had felt too fragile. She hadn't wanted to risk the information being used against her in some way. Now she felt a little guilty for not having trusted his reaction.

"I'm afraid so." She explained briefly what had happened and what it meant for her business. "I start training Lois and handing over ongoing work—like bringing that defenseman up from the AHL for the weekend's games—tomorrow."

"That's nuts," JB said. "Lois is way too inexperienced to be in charge of important team arrangements. She's barely been in Sales five minutes."

"You know her?" Tracy asked, surprised. Players didn't usually have much contact with the office staff.

"I know all the cute girls." JB frowned. "But I remember her particularly because I was warned off—she's related to Hardshaw in some way. Wife's niece or something."

"You're joking." Tracy hadn't thought the Cats' GM was the type to indulge in nepotism. That put a whole different spin on things.

"Will you be okay?" The concern in Ike's voice was unexpected. "That's a pretty big contract to lose."

"Maggie and I have already identified ways in which we can replace the lost business. It'll set us back a bit, but I'm sure we'll be on track again quickly." She'd make sure of it now she knew about the real reason behind Hardshaw's decision. No way would she let his unfair practice keep her from her goal.

Ike looked like he had more questions, but Tracy didn't want to get into a discussion about it now. Especially not in front of his brother and JB.

"On that note, I'd better get out of here. Lots to do." She grabbed her bag and waved goodbye to JB and Kenny. "See you tomorrow, Ike. I'll bring my iPad and show you that new adventure game I mentioned earlier."

"Can't wait."

The genuine warmth in his words made Tracy smile broadly all the way back to her car. She wasn't afraid to admit that she was already looking forward to tomorrow, too.

"I'M SHUTTING YOU down until next season."

Coach Macarty's words seemed to reverberate inside Ike's skull, sending a chill through his body.

No. This could not be happening.

It was like a scene from one of his nightmares, only Ike couldn't wake up. He stared at the three men standing around his bed—Coach, Callum Hardshaw and Dr. Gibson—and shook his head in disbelief. "You can't be serious."

"He can, and he is." Callum Hardshaw's expression was hard as granite and his tone matched. "We all agree that this decision is in our longer-term interest. The Ice Cats cannot afford to lose you permanently."

"But it's only been four days since my surgery." Ike pointed at Dr. Gibson. "You told me I was healing well and everything looked fine."

"Given the circumstances, it does. But I also said it was too early to make any predictions. Tearing those tendons again has complicated things."

"We know how committed you are, Ike," Macarty said, clearly playing the good cop to his boss's bad cop. "If we give you an opening, you'll push yourself to the limit and beyond to be able to play. If we said April, you'd want March. If we said May, you'd want April. We'll sacrifice this season to save your career."

"What happens if you need me for the playoffs? Assuming the team can actually get to the postseason with only their backup goaltender in net," Ike said, desperation clawing at him. "Monty has practically no postseason experience."

Hardshaw shot his cuffs, as if already bored with the discussion. "Monty was named the NHL's second star of the week for his performance on our recent road trip. Three wins and an overtime loss against the cream of the Western Conference is pretty darn good for 'only a backup.'"

As pleased as Ike was for his friend, the public recognition had stung. And made him wonder if it was a sign that there would soon be a changing of the guard. Even if Ike did get back, he might not be number one again.

"Sure," Ike said. "Monty did great out west, especially against the Kings. But the guys bailed him out by playing out of their skins against Anaheim and San Jose. Those games were crazy shoot-outs—twenty goals scored. Then Larocque saved Monty's bacon in Colorado with those two last-minute goals to get the game to overtime."

The GM shrugged. "Seven points is still seven points, and it keeps us in sight of the Penguins at the top of the Metropolitan division."

"What if things aren't looking so hot come March or April?"

"We'll deal with that if the time comes."

"That's nuts. There has to be some flexibility."

Macarty looked uncomfortable. "Maybe we can rev—"

Hardshaw cut off his coach. "Our decision is final. You're too valuable to this organization to take a risk. You can rejoin the team for training camp, not before."

It was November now. Training camp was next September. The dead time loomed ahead of Ike like a black hole. Physio first, then gradually getting back to working out at the gym. By himself. Then training to get back to fitness. By himself. Then off-ice and on-ice workouts with the trainer, but effectively by himself. In the normal scheme of things he'd eventually be back practicing with the guys, wearing the no-contact jersey. The way Hardshaw was talking, Ike wouldn't even be allowed to do that, let alone take part in a full practice.

Ike lay back against the pillows and stared at the ceiling. The walls seemed to close in on him, suffocating him. He clenched his jaw to stop himself from begging. Why had he been such an idiot? All he'd done was land himself back in the same freaking hospital, in the same freaking ward…hell, the same freaking bed.

"Come on, Doc. Help me out here."

"I'm sorry, but I agree with them. If you want to play next season, you need to give yourself time to heal properly."

Ike made one desperate, last-ditch effort. "I'll take this to the NHLPA."

Macarty shook his head. "The Players' Association fights for players' interests and yours are best served by keeping you off the ice until you're one hundred percent fit."

Ike hated to admit it, but his coach was right. While the NHLPA might sympathize with Ike's perspective—there wasn't a player alive who didn't bust a gut to come back from injury—they'd take the surgeon's advice and back the Ice Cats' position.

"That's your final word?" Ike stared down the three men in turn, hoping one of them would blink first and give him a glimmer of hope.

"Damn straight," Hardshaw said.

Macarty's expression was apologetic, but his agreement was firm.

Dr. Gibson met Ike's gaze without flinching. "If you reinjure this arm, your career will be over. You will be done. *Permanently.*"

"So, you're telling me to suck it up."

"It's only a few months. Is it really worth the rest of your career?" the surgeon said.

"But we're barely a third of the way through the season. I'll miss sixty-plus games."

"Better that than missing the next sixty-plus years," Dr. Gibson shot back. "You're a long time from retirement, Ike."

Acid burned the back of Ike's throat. "I get that. All I'm asking for is the possibility that if I heal well I could be activated."

"No." Hardshaw's jaw was set.

It was over. Ike was done. Shut down. Useless. Worthless.

The realization sent a sharp pain through him, so acute he had to fight to keep from catching his breath. "At least let me practice with the team as soon as I've been cleared for on-ice drills, even if it's no-contact."

Hardshaw started to refuse, but Macarty stepped in. "When Dr. Gibson clears you to skate, you're welcome to join us. Being with the team is as important to your recovery as physiotherapy and rest. But I expect you to follow instructions."

"Yeah, I know. To the letter." Relief flooded

through Ike. That small concession would have brought him to his knees if he hadn't been stuck in the damn bed. "So when can I get out of this place?"

Dr. Gibson smiled. "You know the drill. It's Friday today, so it'll probably be Monday. If you behave and everything looks good, I might release you a day early. Particularly since I know you have a good support system in place."

Ike forced himself to look relaxed. At least that was one thing he didn't need to worry about this time. "Great."

Once the men had gone, he allowed himself to release a deep breath. He felt like a dog on a chain, being yanked every which way by an impatient master. It was his own fault. The only person to blame for this was him. He'd let boredom and frustration get the better of him and made a stupid mistake. Now he was paying the price.

Much as Ike hated to admit it, both Tracy and Dr. Gibson were right. He was lucky. He grimaced at the word, but it was true. The situation could have been a hell of a lot worse. Ike was lucky the second injury hadn't been more serious. Lucky that the surgeon had been able to fix the damage. Lucky that this wasn't the end of his career. Missing the rest of the season was bad enough, but at least Ike would play again.

He'd learned his lesson. It all had to be different this time. He couldn't let anything get in the way of his recovery. Especially not himself. It wasn't going to be easy. He'd follow every instruction and do every finger exercise so he could get back on the ice ASAP.

What would he do if that wasn't enough?

Ike tried to push aside the terrifying thought. But once it had slipped into his mind, he couldn't shake it loose.

There were no guarantees. Dr. Gibson had been real clear about that. Come to think of it, the surgeon hadn't committed to anything specific. He'd been all caution and caveats and provisos. What if Ike's arm healed, but it wasn't strong enough to take the punishment of being a starting goaltender and playing sixty-plus games a season? What if Monty did such a great job the Cats didn't need Ike back as a starter?

He couldn't think like that. Couldn't worry about what he couldn't control, but focus on what he could. Those instructions and finger exercises. He *would* make it back—to the ice, to the Cats and to the starter's job.

But for the first time in his life and his career, Ike couldn't fully silence the little voice of doubt.

"ARE YOU AND Uncle Ike friends again?"

Not much got past Emily, Tracy thought. "Why do you ask?"

Her niece looked up from the mixing bowl. Flour dusted her ponytail and she had a smudge of batter on her cheek. “We’re making him your special cheese scones.”

“Well, Uncle Ike’s coming home from the hospital this afternoon. I thought a treat might cheer him up.”

“Is he okay?” Maggie asked, concerned. With Joe cradled against her shoulder, she was supervising the baking.

“I’m not sure,” Tracy admitted. “Since Hardshaw and Macarty told Ike they were shutting him down, he’s been subdued. He didn’t even react when Dr. Gibson signed his release a day early.”

Where before Ike had been determined to get up and get out, for the past couple of days, he’d acted as though he couldn’t be bothered. As though he was going through the motions. Nothing Tracy had done to distract him had worked. He’d claimed he was too tired to play games or his arm hurt.

“This whole situation has been miserable for him,” Maggie said, moving to place her sleeping son in his Moses basket. “I know he was silly to try to rush his recovery, but I can’t think of a hockey player—or any professional athlete—who wouldn’t have done the same thing. He’s unable to do even the most basic of workouts, when he’s spent so much of his life training to achieve peak fitness. If it was Jake, I’d have to duct-tape him to the bed.”

“It’s particularly difficult when you’re worried you’ll have to work twice as hard, for twice as long, to get back your shot or pass, or in Ike’s case, his catch." The way he snatched a puck out of the air so easily had always impressed Tracy.

"And you've got young guns coming up behind you, eager to take your roster spot. As sorry as Monty feels for Ike, he'll be relishing the chance to show he's got what it takes to be a starter, and you can't blame him."

It wasn't easy being backup to a player like Ike, who wanted to play every game and was both skilled enough and fit enough to handle the work. Ordinarily.

Tracy hadn't considered how the younger man's success might affect Ike mentally. "Surely Ike can't be worried that Monty will take over permanently."

"No way," Emily said hotly. "Uncle Ike's an elite goalie. Monty isn't."

"You're assuming Ike's thinking logically," Maggie said. "Under these circumstances, he can't possibly be. Bad enough that he has to start his recovery all over again, but to suddenly be told he can't work for the best part of a year, even if he does heal perfectly… Well, imagine how you'd feel."

Her sister's words gave Tracy pause. "You're right. I'd be a mess."

"And you have thirty-plus years of work still ahead of you. Ike's time is already limited—even fully healthy, he doesn't have many seasons left. To waste one because of an accident, made worse by his own stupidity, must be extremely hard for him to take."

"I hadn't thought about Ike's situation in quite that way." Tracy was chagrined. Even though she'd known everything Maggie had told her, somehow hearing it spelled out like that had opened her eyes to just how much he must be suffering. It would take more than a card game—even the strip version—to distract him from all that.

"Neither had I. Jake put it all into context for me by talking about how he struggled after his accident. Although his issues were driven more by misplaced guilt about Adam's death."

Jake had blamed himself for the fatal accident—even though Adam had been driving—because he'd thought he'd let his friend down when he'd ignored Adam's problems. What Jake hadn't known was that his teammate had been taking steroids and had set Jake up to take the fall by buying the drugs in Jake's name. It had nearly cost Jake his career until Maggie had found proof of Adam's deception.

Tracy couldn't guarantee Ike the same kind of happy ending, but now that she had a better understanding of what he was going through, hopefully she could find ways to keep him positive.

In the meantime, she did make bloody good cheese scones.

"OKAY. WHAT HAVE you done with the real Eisenhower Jelinek?"

Ike turned from staring out of the car window and frowned at Tracy. "Huh?"

"You were polite to the medical staff and haven't complained once since we left the hospital. Clearly Ike's body was snatched by aliens and you're a pod creature who looks like him."

His lips twitched, though the last thing he felt like doing was cracking a smile. "I did what I promised, so they'd let me out of there early."

"Right. That's why the nurse wanted to do a CAT scan on your brain to make sure you hadn't somehow got an aneurysm because your personality was so different."

He shrugged. "Arguing wouldn't make any difference, so why bother?"

Tracy flicked him a look, concern in her dark brown eyes. "If I didn't know better, I'd say you've given up."

The challenge in her words sparked a hint of anger inside him. Not enough to penetrate the thick gray fog that had descended on him over the past few days—blanketing him, weighing him down—as the reality of his situation had sunk in. He'd been unable to see beyond the misery of the months ahead and unable to fight his way out of the depression.

The spark flickered and died. What was the point of fighting? Of trying? Hardshaw wouldn't change his mind, even if Jesus laid hands on Ike and healed his arm instantly. "I haven't given up. I'm doing as I've been told. Nothing more, nothing less."

She arched an eyebrow, her expression disbelieving. "Definitely body snatchers. The Ike I know wouldn't let a small setback get to him. He'd tackle it head-on."

Irritation rekindled the spark. "A small setback? I'm done for the whole season."

"And you'll be back better and stronger for next season. This isn't like a concussion, where you could suffer again. Once you're healed, you'll be as good as new."

"You don't know that. Even the doc won't commit to me making a full recovery after the second injury." He pressed his lips together as he fought to keep the silent cursing that raged inside from escaping.

"The Ike I know wouldn't take this lying down like a meek lamb."

"I jeopardized my career by rushing things and trying to roar like a freaking lion. So, yeah, I'll baa, thanks very much."

She snorted. "You're acting like your career is over, not on hold *temporarily*."

"Potato, po-tahto." He shrugged again and turned back to the window.

"What happened to 'it ain't over till the fat lady sings'? I don't hear any arias."

"Maybe not, but the bitch is backstage warming up and waiting for her cue."

Tracy laughed, but sobered quickly. "Give yourself a break, Ike."

"No, thanks. This injury is more than enough."

"Now I'm really worried—you're cracking jokes."

Damn it. He didn't want to smile. This wasn't funny. "What do you expect?"

"Your 'never give up until the game's over' attitude." She flicked the turn signal with more force than necessary and turned right at the lights. "I know it's hard." Her voice softened. "But you *will* get better. It'll take time—longer than any of us would like—but you *will* be back to normal at the end of it."

"What if I'm not?" He hadn't meant for the question to slip out. Now that it had, he wanted to hear her answer.

"But you will. I have faith in you."

His throat tightened. He knew she meant what she said; she was a straight shooter. No games. Still, her plain answer humbled him.

And scared him to death.

Because he desperately wanted it to be true. As desperately as he wanted to believe her faith in him was enough.

He couldn't. He just couldn't.

The fear that had been rumbling inside him erupted. "But what if this is it? What if there is no way back? What if my arm won't ever be good enough or strong enough?" His voice cracked on the last word.

"You can't think like that." Tracy didn't hesitate. "Cross that bridge when…*if* you come to it. One shift at a time. Keep focused on the goal. You know this better than I do."

The uncertainty filling his mind was an unfamiliar emotion. One a goaltender couldn't afford to feel. One he'd never *let* himself feel. Yet it was so all-encompassing, he couldn't reach beyond it. "What if I do all that and the answer is still the same?" he asked quietly.

"You'll deal with it."

His head whipped round. "How the hell am I supposed to do that? Hockey is my life. If I can't play at the highest level, it's over."

Tracy pulled into his driveway and parked. She switched off the engine and turned to face him. Her clear gaze met his without flinching. "That'll be a terrible loss all round. But you don't have to lose hockey just because you can't play to the standard you want."

He sneered at her earnest words. "I won't be that fool in the AHL everyone laughs at. The one who rides the bus with the kids because he doesn't know when to give up."

Worse than the ridicule, he didn't want their pity.

"So take up coaching. Make a how-to video. I'm sure there are thousands of kids who'd love to know how the great Ike Jelinek did it. Or do more media work. The color commentaries you did a few years ago were well received. The point is there are options."

The thought of leaving the ice for good, that he might already have played his last professional game, hurt worse than the injury to his arm. He sucked in a breath through his clenched teeth, trying to ease the pain, but it didn't help. "It's not the same," he rasped.

"No, it isn't." Tracy's expression was serious, her voice calm.

What surprised him was that while there was understanding in her eyes, there was none of the pity he'd feared.

"It can't be the same. But that's a good thing." She laid her hand on his arm. "You don't want it to be the same. You *need* it to be different. You just have to accept that different doesn't mean worse."

"Yeah." Except, in his case, it *was* worse. Hockey was all-or-nothing for him. Play or walk away.

"You're borrowing trouble again, Ike." She rubbed her hand up and down his arm. Even through the layers of clothing, the warmth of her touch began to soothe his anxiety. "You don't need to think about any of this now. You certainly don't need to make any decisions straight away. Give it a few weeks at least before you consign yourself to immortal hell. You'll look like a bloody fool if you go off half-cocked and your arm turns out to be fine after all."

He knew she was trying to tease the darkness from him, but that damn fog pressed closer. "I doubt that'll happen. I've got a bad feeling that I screwed myself with what I did. I sensed something in Dr. Gibson's voice when he gave me the prognosis. He doesn't think I'll be one hundred percent."

"Surgeons are always overly cautious. The truth

is he doesn't know. He can only give you his best guess and his verdict was that you'd be fine."

"He danced around the truth. There's a big difference between 'fine' and 'good as new.'"

She rolled her eyes at him. "I think Dr. Gibson knows that. He's bound to act pessimistic if he thinks it'll make you be more cautious. He doesn't want to have to operate on you a third time."

"I guess." What she said made sense, but he didn't dare let himself be convinced.

"Concentrate on getting better and stronger. If I were you, I'd forget what Hardshaw said and have the goal of being ready for the postseason."

He frowned. "He made it clear that he won't change his mind."

"What happens if Monty gets injured? Especially after the trade deadline. Hardshaw will have another viable option. He can't go into the playoffs with an AHL goaltending tandem. If you're skating and fit, even if you're not a hundred percent, he'll have to activate you."

That spark of hope reignited and this time it seemed to glow a little brighter. "Okay," he allowed. "But the chances of that happening are pretty slim. Our boys on the D will be protecting Monty up the wazoo."

"You never know. Accidents happen. You're proof of that." She removed her hand.

As soon as she did, he missed her touch. "For sure."

"If worse comes to the worst, you could always play in the IIHF World Championships."

Ike hadn't considered that option. He'd never played in the tournament. Partly because he'd been involved in the postseason most years since he'd come up to the big leagues. Even when the Cats hadn't made the cut or had an early exit, he'd used the time to rest, both physically and mentally. Though it was more highly regarded in Europe, he—like other North Americans—had always viewed the International Ice Hockey Federation's competition as a consolation prize.

Perhaps it was a viable option. It wasn't the Olympics, but he'd still be representing his country. The important thing was that he'd be playing.

The glow brightened. There was nothing like game play to ensure his conditioning and fitness were prime. The games might not mean as much as fighting for the Cup, but they were better than nothing.

Assuming he'd be allowed to take part. Which was highly unlikely.

Damn it. Every time he started to get positive, he got a kick in the pants.

"Even if I was selected—which is doubtful, given I wouldn't have played all season—the Cats wouldn't let me take part."

"Why not? It's a great way for you to test your arm and for you to get back in the habit of real games before next season."

"The risk of injury is too high. They'd probably prefer to wait until the preseason."

Tracy shook her head. "Can they actually stop you? Surely they can't interfere with you representing your country."

"They pay my salary. They can do what they like."

"I suppose. On the other hand, they could give you the green light. You won't know until you get there. The point is moot if you're not fit."

"I guess you're right. It wouldn't hurt to be prepared."

Tracy clapped a hand to her chest. "Oh, my God, did you just agree with me? Maybe that nurse should have done a CAT scan on you after all."

He gave her a dry look. "Funny. Don't give up your day job."

"I won't. At least I'm trying hard not to. No thanks to your GM." She opened her door and got out of the car.

Ike fumbled with the door handle as she grabbed his bag from the backseat. He was relieved she didn't open the door for him, but waited patiently until he'd opened the damn thing himself.

"Callum Hardshaw isn't my favorite person right now, either," he said as they walked up the path to his front door. "What's he done now?"

"He's changed his mind and wants Lois to handle the Dennison trade, even though we agreed that would be one of the projects I'd keep. He thinks it will be 'good experience' for her. I've busted a gut to manage all the arrangements. It wasn't easy because Mrs. Dennison is expecting baby number three in January and wants her mother to come over from Lithuania so she won't be alone for the birth if the Cats are away when the happy event occurs. Plus she doesn't want the other two kids to miss any school because of the move, so I've been handling their enrollment. Nothing's finished, but I'm supposed to hand the whole lot over to Lois in a neat little package." The angrier she got, the faster her words came out and the crisper her accent became.

"You might want to breathe," Ike said. "I won't be able to catch you if you pass out."

She gave him a haughty look worthy of royalty, then opened the door and walked inside with her nose in the air.

Unfortunately, instead of cowing him, it turned him on. Damn it. This was not the time or place. What were they talking about? Oh, yes. Lois. Hardshaw. "Will he pay you for the work?"

"Of course. He has to. I'm under contract and I have the work he's committed to paying for in writing." She dropped Ike's bag at the foot of the stairs. "That's not the point."

"It isn't?" He could understand her being pissed because she'd lost money, but couldn't see the problem with handing over a pain-in-the-ass project for someone else to finish.

"There's more to this business than money. Our

reputation, for a start. I can't have my company associated with poor quality of service, which is what will happen in this case. Lois hasn't got the experience to handle the issues."

He still didn't get what she was so upset about, but then business wasn't his game. "You'll find a way to make sure that it all works out. You won't let Lois fail. And you won't let her tarnish your business's reputation. I have faith in you."

Her brown eyes widened with surprise at his deliberate echo of her earlier words to him. "I appreciate the vote of confidence."

"Right back at you."

"That's what friends are for."

Her easy words should have pleased him. That she could readily acknowledge the connection between them was a sign of how far he and Tracy had come in a few weeks.

Yet Ike was irritated. Really? That's all he was to her? A friend? After all the time they'd spent together this past week, he'd thought they'd begun to reestablish the deeper connection they'd once had. The arguments had given way to conversations. The sniping to teasing, even flirting. The attraction that had bubbled beneath the surface, even through the worst times, had finally broken through again.

Not that they'd acted on it. Not yet, anyway. Besides wanting to get out of the hospital, the chance to explore what had been building between them was a big reason Ike had been looking forward to getting home.

Friendship? That wasn't enough for him anymore.

CHAPTER ELEVEN

THE FLASH OF fire in Ike's green eyes was the only warning Tracy got that he was going to kiss her. Not that she was complaining. The man had amazing lips. She ran her tongue over them as his mouth came down on hers. A fizz of pleasure bubbled through her veins. Delicious. Not too full, not too thin.

She moaned deep in her throat as his tongue mimicked her actions and took a leisurely path across her lips. She wrapped her arms around his neck. Her fingers thrust through his hair, which was ridiculously soft for such a tough guy.

The rumble of his groan as he deepened the kiss echoed deep within her, making her throb. He pulled her closer still until her body was plastered against his. Her aching breasts pressed tight to his broad chest. His erection rocked hard and insistent between her legs. His bandaged arm, heavy against her back, bound her to him.

She'd stop. In a minute. Perhaps two. Just one more taste. And another.

Definitely not fair. He may not be the right man

for her, but holy moly, Ike could kiss. And it was a perfect kiss, damn it! The right level of firmness. He didn't dominate or devour her, but danced with her. They were equal partners; sometimes he took the lead, other times he'd let her take control.

He'd been the same when they'd made love. Her pulse jumped at the thought of giving in to the pleasure and letting the kiss take them to its natural conclusion. Her body cried out with need. A need she knew Ike could satisfy perfectly, too.

Just one more time.

But it wouldn't be just one more time. They—she—would never be able to stop at just one. And that's when the problems would start again.

They might be perfectly matched physically, but they certainly weren't when it came to the reality of everyday life. And no matter how wonderfully he kissed and how great they were together in bed, taking that path again would only lead to more heartache. She'd had enough of that to last a lifetime.

She forced the passion to cool.

Her heart heavy with regret, Tracy broke the kiss and pulled away.

It was silly to feel a twinge of disappointment that he let her go so easily. Just as it was ridiculous to wish she could return to the heady delights she'd been experiencing seconds ago. She blamed it on the chill that went through her at the loss of his heat. On the loneliness that crept into her body.

Worried that he'd read her emotions on her face,

she turned away and wrapped her arms around herself. Still, she couldn't resist running her tongue over her own lips to capture the taste of him one last time.

"We have to stop doing this," she croaked. "It won't work."

"Why the hell not?"

She tamped down the thrill that went through her at his hoarse words. "Because nothing has changed between us."

"That's for damn sure."

Now that they were back on familiar ground, she had the strength to turn around and face him. "Like I said before, the chemistry was never the problem. But the other thing that hasn't changed is that we want different things. Have different expectations. You want to settle down and I don't. If we got together again, the outcome would be the same."

"You're not even prepared to try?"

His incredulous tone made her angry. "What's the point?"

"Because this time we know the pitfalls and can work to overcome them. Attraction may not be enough, but it's a damn good brick in the foundation. And there's plenty more to add—like mutual respect. We have more in common than just great sex."

She couldn't deny that. "Maybe."

"Last time we didn't make the effort to solve our problems. We fell at the first hurdle and let things slip away. If we go into this with our eyes open, aware of the problems and prepared to work at them, we have a better chance of making it."

He made it sound so tempting. But no matter how much they worked at a relationship, Tracy couldn't give Ike the future, the commitment, he wanted. They might make it longer than last time, but they'd still be destined for failure.

"I know I rushed things before." He gave a self-deprecating half smile as he raised his bandaged arm. "Seems to be my problem all round. But I've learned my lesson. We'll take things at a pace you're comfortable with. One shift at a time."

Tracy should be pleased. He was saying all the right things. What's more, she believed he meant them.

Unfortunately, she was afraid that it was also too good to be true. Could he really be that patient? What if she was never ready to make the commitment he wanted? What if this new approach only delayed the inevitable and she still got sucked into that dependent relationship that terrified her? This time she might not be strong enough to make it out.

Still, despite her fear, there was a part of her that didn't want to shut the door completely. That wanted to believe in the tiny chance that this time it could work.

"There's a lot going on in both our lives right now," she hedged. "You have to focus on getting better. And my priority is to try to keep my company successful and growing."

To give Ike credit, he didn't flinch. "Sure, it's stressful, but I'd argue that this is the perfect time. Since I'm out of action for the season, the pressures of trying to balance a relationship with playing are gone—even if only temporarily. I appreciate your business situation isn't what you'd like, but on the other hand your schedule has freed up until you replace the Ice Cats' business."

He made it sound so easy. "I wish it was that straightforward."

"Why can't it be?" He puffed out a frustrated breath. "Look, we can't keep ignoring the attraction between us."

"Sure, we can. We're adults. We can control ourselves."

He gave her a chiding look. "Okay. I don't *want* to keep ignoring the attraction."

Since he'd been honest, she should be, too. "Me, neither. But, as I keep saying, that isn't the problem."

"I know. But you also said we shouldn't borrow trouble."

"Huh?" Tracy tilted her head to one side, confused.

"Why can't we agree just to enjoy what we've got? Nothing more. No commitment."

"No strings attached?"

He didn't seem to pick up on the sarcasm in her

voice. "I think we'd both want to be mutually exclusive."

Tracy couldn't believe it. The guy who'd blown up because she wouldn't live with him after a few months was proposing an affair? "So how would this work? We get together for sex whenever one of us gets an itch that needs scratching?"

"That's harsh." Anger flashed in his eyes.

"I'm sorry," she said quietly. "That was unfair. Your suggestion shocked me. Not what I'd expect you to suggest."

He inclined his head, accepting her apology. "Now that you're over the surprise, what do you think?"

She must be insane, because there was a part of her that actually wanted to give it a shot.

"I'm tempted. Obviously it suits my needs, but I'm not convinced it's really what you want. That it'll be enough for you."

"I can make up my own mind about what I want."

"I know it's what you think you want now, but you won't want it forever."

"Forever is a long time. How does either of us know what we'll want down the line?"

"I know that at some point you'll want to settle down."

"Doesn't everyone?"

Her heart twisted. "No. I don't want to get married again."

"Never?" Ike shook his head, like he couldn't believe it. "You don't want kids?"

"Maybe someday."

"I don't get it. Why don't you want to get married?"

"I don't want to be someone's wife again. I've seen too many marriages—including my own—where the wife starts out independent and slowly gets subsumed into her husband. She does what he wants and lives how he wants. I did it once and that was plenty."

"I am not your ex," he huffed.

"I know that."

And she did. Hank had never respected her enough to consider what she might want. He'd never really listened to her. He'd only cared about what he wanted to mold her into, not what she wanted.

Ike might not like what she had to say, but he didn't dismiss her out of hand. He might not like her priorities or her ambitions, but he was at least prepared to try to make things work between them. The problem was what happened when things went wrong. Or when they were no longer equal partners—like if she became his wife.

She wondered if it wasn't so much that she didn't trust Ike not to change, as she didn't trust herself not to slip back into old habits.

"There's such a thing as compromise," he said.

"Compromise becomes the thin end of the wedge. Eventually, one person does all the giving. That won't be me." She smiled sadly at him. "And we both know it would never be you."

"So that's it?" His green eyes bored into hers. "You're not even prepared to try?"

"I can't."

"You're throwing away what we could have because you want things your own way?"

His words lashed at her, making her feel small and petty. Yet, at the same time, they strengthened her determination when she'd feared it had been about to waver.

Tracy raised her chin and squared her shoulders. "I'm saving us both a lot of heartache, Ike. You think you'll be happy settling for what I can offer. But if you're honest, you'll know that one day it won't be enough."

Ike studied her for several long moments. His scrutiny made her courage tremble, like a muscle that has been worked too hard and too long. His jaw twitched as he clearly battled internally with himself. Slowly the sparks in his green eyes faded and dulled. His expression became shuttered.

Her heart mourned what she was losing, even though she knew he had never really been hers.

Finally, just when she thought she might crumble, Ike spun away. He went to jam his hands on hips, throwing his head back and cursing when his bandaged arm wouldn't comply.

She should go. Yet she couldn't make her feet

move. She couldn't even make her mouth work to tell him she was leaving.

"Have it your way," he said wearily.

Her throat tightened. She opened her mouth, but nothing came out. She didn't know what to say. Better to say nothing.

Tracy turned on her heel and walked the few steps to the front door.

"I assume your services will continue as agreed." His hard words echoed around the hall like ricocheting pucks.

She drew in a steadying breath, but didn't turn around. "Of course."

"Of course." His mocking repetition of her words followed her out the door.

Tracy had just reached her car when the front door slammed shut. She flinched. Tears burned her eyes, but she refused to let them fall. It was what she wanted. No, what she knew *had to be*. It still hurt like hell.

IKE LOVED THE HOLIDAYS, the traditions, the decorations and, of course, the food. But most of all, he loved spending time with the people he loved. Being surrounded by his family—whether blood, extended or of the ice—was truly special and he was always glad when the Cats' schedule allowed him to be home for Thanksgiving.

The team was in town this year, so many of the guys and their families had come to Jake's parents' place for the annual Badoletti-Jelinek Thanksgiving party. It was a smaller family group, though, with Tru and Jenny in Colorado, Linc playing for his college team and his mom and Rory in Ireland. Ike missed them, but thanks to modern technology, they'd all chatted on Skype earlier.

Right now, Ike and the guys were in the kitchen, taking part in the traditional male cleanup after another gut-busting Thanksgiving lunch. A small ancient TV blasted out the pre-game chatter for the Cowboys-Eagles game. The air was rich with the scent of turkey, sweetened by the cinnamon and vanilla of homemade pies. The women were watching classic movies in the living room, having prepared the food.

Not all the women, of course. Tracy had rushed off before they'd even had dessert to deal with a client emergency. What the hell kind of emergency could anyone have on Thanksgiving—an undercooked turkey? Apparently even on such an important family holiday, she couldn't switch off. Or wouldn't.

It wasn't as though she were scrabbling to save her company from going under. From what she and Maggie had said over lunch, they'd have more than enough new business to make up for losing the Ice Cats' contract. Maggie figured they might even hit the top three in the relocation market by Christmas, though Tracy had been more cautious.

Ike cast his mind back to the day she'd taken him

home from the hospital. He'd been a fool to push her to rekindle their relationship. To think she could ever be the right woman for him. He'd known better. But he'd been thinking with his other head, which had been fired up by that mind-blowing kiss. He'd had a lucky escape.

Ike hated to admit it, but Tracy was right. They did have different priorities and expectations. He couldn't be with a woman who put her clients ahead of family every time.

A wet sponge flew past his head.

"If I'd known I could get out of dish-washing duty, I'd have given myself a boo-boo on my arm, too," Kenny grumbled from the sink.

Ike flipped his younger brother the bird. "Be careful what you wish for," he growled. "I'd be happy to make your dream come true."

"You and what army, net boy?" Kenny laughed. "You don't have Tru defending your ass now, Jake's got the baby on board and I can handle JB."

Larocque, who was helping dry the dishes, snapped Kenny with a damp towel. "In your dreams, Kennedy."

Jake switched Joe to his other shoulder. "Watch yourself, kid. My son's full diaper is a lethal weapon."

"Gross." Kenny made the sign of the cross with his two forefingers as Jake carried Joe out of the kitchen. "Keep that toxic mess away from me."

Juergen Ingemar, the Cats' Swedish-born veteran forward, paused while stacking dried plates. "You told us you could deal with whatever crap was thrown at you, Kenny."

"I'd take any amount of chirping and dirty hits over a dirty diaper."

There was a heartfelt chorus of agreement.

JB coughed and muttered, "Chicken."

"Speak for yourself." Kenny elbowed his friend.

Larocque punched Kenny's arm in retaliation. Kenny then grabbed JB in a neck lock. The two scuffled, and name-calling ensued.

"Watch the china, bozos." Ike rose and stepped between them. "You break a plate and I'm cracking skulls."

"They're more scared of Jake's mom than they are of you," Juergen said calmly. "Besides, you're pretty harmless right now, Ike."

"Don't you mean armless," JB retorted.

Half the room groaned, the rest laughed, as everyone returned to their chores.

Man, he'd missed these guys. This was the first time since he'd injured himself that Ike had felt like he was still one of them. Not playing sucked, but being isolated from his teammates was worse. Ike was grateful to have even part of the day with them. They'd be bugging out of here in the next half hour to head down to Philly for tomorrow's game.

Ike wished he could go with them. Instead he'd be left behind with the women, kids and old men.

Crap. He'd better not get any invitations to play shuffleboard.

"If we're done in here, I'm going to grab some cuddle time with my woman. Remind her of what she'll be missing when I'm gone." JB flashed his lady-killer grin, the one that could melt the panties off any woman between the ages of sixteen and sixty. "Even if it means enduring that damn chick flick they're watching. The things we do for love."

"You mean the things you'll do to burn up the sheets with the hottest babe in town," Kenny retorted, unable to hide his envy.

JB's dates were always beautiful and famous, but he changed them as often as he changed his socks. His current arm candy was the star of the newest New York–based TV crime thriller. Even though the pair had been dating for almost a month—a record for the star forward—Ike didn't see a wedding in their future.

Larocque feigned a hurt expression. "I'm capable of love."

"Sure you are, JB," Juergen said. "With the face you see in the mirror every morning." He paused to let the hoots of laughter die down. "One of these days, some woman will knock you on your ass and then we'll see what you'll do for love."

"Never gonna happen." JB lifted his head arrogantly. "Just because you're gaga over your new girlfriend, don't toss that hearts and flowers crap at me."

Juergen just grinned in response.

What a difference a few months made. The Swede had gone through a rough time last season when his fiancée, a Norwegian soap star, was caught in bed with her costar. It had devastated Juergen. But lately, he'd been dating again. Despite a rocky start—his new girlfriend was also an actress—it looked like things were working out. He'd even brought her along today.

Another man down for the count.

Scotty Matthews poked his head into the kitchen. "Ten minutes, guys, and we need to hit the road."

In the flurry of goodbyes, Ike felt his mood darkening. Damn, he wanted to go with them. His mood was ripe for the kind of physical game the Flyers would give him.

The noise level in the house dropped once they'd all gone. Ike walked back into the now-empty kitchen and grabbed a beer. Though he could hear laughter and chatter from the living room, the silence in the kitchen was oppressive. The room was too warm. Too enclosed. Suffocating.

He had to get out of there. He longed for the crisp air of a rink. The need to feel the ice beneath his blades surged up within him, like a captured beast raging against its chains.

Hell, he couldn't even leave without help. He'd given his driver the day off. Maggie would give him a ride home later. But it would be a while yet before she'd be ready to go.

He hated that he couldn't do a damn thing for

himself. He hated being left behind yet again. He hated the whole situation. But then, that wasn't news to anyone. Least of all him. Still, he didn't have to hang out in the kitchen like some pathetic loser. He could use his legs, after all.

Ike grabbed his coat and headed outside onto the deck.

His arm ached. He should take a painkiller—even half a dose, just to take the edge off—but they made him feel dopey. He'd hold out until he got home, then the drugs could knock him out. That way, he might not dream.

He sighed, his breath forming a cloud in the chilly air. He was fed up with being down all the time.

Jake had warned him to find something else to think about, or he'd go nuts. "Put that famous focus of yours to good use. Study, take up a new interest, get your coaching credentials. Hell, write a book. Anything that isn't physiotherapy and exercise."

Ike needed a distraction. Maybe he should take his mom's advice and do something about his lack of a personal life. He hadn't dated—at least not seriously—in far too long.

He'd told himself it was because he needed to concentrate on his game. As each season passed, the game got a little tougher. It was harder to get ready for each battle and harder still to recover. To reach peak fitness and maintain it while grinding out eighty-two games took pretty much everything he had; there wasn't much left over for anything else.

He felt too old and too jaded to do the club and party scene. Even if he did make the effort, the chances of finding the right kind of woman were near zero. The only women available were either starry-eyed girls who were empty-headed and clingy, or jaded older women aggressively looking for a wealthy second husband.

Perhaps that said more about him than them.

A burst of laughter from the living room had Ike turning his head. The warm glow from the windows reinforced his feeling of loneliness and isolation. He shivered even though he wasn't cold. Everyone looked so cozy and happy inside.

It occurred to Ike that this was a preview of what was to come when he retired. He'd always assumed that not playing—especially around the holidays—wouldn't bother him so much, because he'd have his own family by then. A wife to cuddle up to and kids to make a fuss over.

As things stood, all he'd be was alone. On the outside looking in.

If today had taught him anything it was that maybe it was time for him to get his ass in gear and start finding the right woman to have that family with.

"Hey, Uncle Ike." Emily bounded out onto the deck. "What are you doing out here? It's freezing."

It was hard to be miserable around Maggie's daughter. "Better the cold than suffering through that sappy movie you ladies were watching."

"Not me. I had to go along with it because I'm 'one of the girls.'" She added air quotes with the finesse of a teenager, though she still had a few years to go.

He knew she'd much rather have been in the kitchen with the Ice Cats. Especially if it meant she could watch the game. She preferred hockey to football, but both were better than anything remotely girly.

"Anyway, it's over. The guy got the girl and everyone lived happily ever after." Emily rolled her eyes. "I was the only one who didn't get teary-eyed over the kissy-face bits."

Ike grinned. "Good for you, Em. So, what brings you out here?"

"I didn't want you to be lonely now that all your friends have gone."

The imp's earnest words touched him. She then spoiled the moment by adding, "And I thought you might want to have seconds of pie and ice cream with me."

"Your mom said no, huh?"

Emily shifted from foot to foot. "She said I could have some if I found a nice, kind adult to have some, too."

He'd bet that wasn't really what Maggie had said, but what the hell—it was a holiday and given the dearth of females desperate for his company, he'd take what he could get. "Okay. Let's see what we can find."

They were sitting in the kitchen tucking into a chocolate pie when Tracy walked in.

Damn, she looked good in her snug-fitting red sweater and swirling black skirt that ended just above her knees. Her spike-heeled black shoes emphasized her gorgeous legs. Despite Ike's efforts to be nonchalant, his mouth went dry.

Other than a brief hitch in her stride, Tracy showed no sign of being bothered by his presence. "I missed out on pie earlier, so I came to get some."

"Yay. You're back." Emily jumped up to get her aunt a plate. "You were gone for ages."

"I'm sorry. It couldn't be avoided. One of my clients needed help." Tracy's gaze flicked to Ike, as if bracing for his reaction.

"On Thanksgiving?" He was proud that his voice sounded casual. Almost disinterested.

"Household problems can happen on a holiday, just like any other day," she said crisply.

"That's a shame."

"That's my job."

He chose not to meet her gaze, knowing what he'd see in her eyes. He wasn't in the mood for an "I told you so."

"You will be able to make my game on Saturday, won't you, Auntie Tracy?" Emily's question broke the tense moment.

"Of course. Assuming you'll still be able to play after all the pie you've eaten."

Emily grinned. "I'm a growing girl."

Tracy's affectionate laugh sent a tingle down his spine. Jeez, he had it bad.

"Well, make sure you don't grow too much." She ruffled her niece's hair. "Now I'm going to put my feet up and enjoy this pie before my phone rings again."

Once she'd gone, Ike slowly released a breath.

Only to have it catch when Emily asked, "Is Auntie Tracy mad at you again?"

"Uh, no. Why?"

"She had her sniffy voice on, which she only uses when she's mad."

Out of the mouths of babes. "It's okay. We're good."

Emily didn't look convinced, but her mind skipped onto another topic. "How come you don't have a girlfriend?"

It was a good thing he wasn't eating, or he'd have choked. It was also a good thing he'd thought about this topic earlier, because he could use the same excuses on Emily.

She listened to him intently, shaking her head sadly when he'd finished. "It's a shame you're a boy, because you need a matchmaker."

"A what?"

"You know, like in that film about the fiddler we watched earlier." She began to sing, "'Matchmaker, matchmaker, make me a match…'"

He recognized the tune from *Fiddler on the Roof*. "Oh. Well, that's different."

"Why?"

Ike cursed the fact that she was too old to be satisfied with "because I said so." "That's an old film, about a time long ago."

"I bet they still have matchmakers these days. Auntie Tracy says you can find almost anything on the internet if you know how to look."

When she pulled out her cell, Ike put his hand over it to stop her. The last thing he needed was her doing that kind of Google search. He dreaded to think what she'd find. "That's okay. I'm good. If I need help, I'll know what to do."

But Emily wasn't deterred. "I bet Auntie Tracy could help. She can find anything."

"I…uh…"

"Emily," Jake's dad called from the doorway. "The game's starting. Nonna said we can watch it in the basement."

Saved by the bell. Or at least the Cowboys-Eagles game.

Matchmaking forgotten, Emily dashed after Gio.

Ike laughed softly. He could imagine Tracy's reaction if he asked her to find him the perfect match. Forget being ready to play in April. Once she got done with him, he'd be lucky to walk upright again.

As he chewed a mouthful of pie, Ike went back to what he'd been thinking about earlier. The distraction. Dating. Finding someone to settle down with. The time was definitely right; it wasn't as if he had a lot else on his plate for the next few months. The more he thought about it, the more he realized that was what he wanted to do. He still wasn't sure how he'd go about it, but it couldn't be that hard. Just like he did when he had to face a new player, he'd do his research, work out a strategy and come up with an action plan. Piece of cake.

I bet Auntie Tracy could help.

Emily's words echoed in his head. Maybe she had a point.

Tracy *had* offered to help any way she could. And it *was* her job to help him find, evaluate and hire the services he needed. As far as Helping Hands was concerned, was a dating agency really so different from a yard company?

It wasn't like he could approach a dating agency himself anyway. He couldn't risk word getting out. The media would have a field day with that story. Ike would never live it down, on or off the ice. He could trust Tracy to be discreet.

But did he really want to go down that road with her?

He couldn't think of an alternative. Perhaps it was because now he'd got the idea in his head, nothing else seemed like it would work as well.

Still, it was *Tracy*.

Ike pulled himself up short. His problem was he was acting as though there were still something between him and Tracy. There wasn't. She'd made that very clear. Hadn't he realized she was right only a short while ago?

This wasn't personal, it was business.

So it all boiled down to a simple fact—Ike needed help and Tracy was the best person for the job.

The problem was how to make sure she didn't turn down his request. Or castrate him.

He had to make her an offer she couldn't refuse. But what could he possibly give her that she couldn't get for herself?

His cell chirped with a text message. Ike laughed when he saw that Kenny had sent a selfie of the guys on the team bus. They were all pulling faces to look sad that he wasn't there. He'd have to take a photo of himself, grinning, surrounded by all the women, and send it back to them.

For the first time, Ike didn't feel a black cloud hovering over him at the thought of not being with the team. That wasn't to say it wouldn't return—probably tomorrow, during the game—but tonight, he was surprisingly okay. He had something else to think about and plan.

But first, payback for his brother.

Ike swiped his phone screen to get to the camera. He paused at the sight of his wallpaper—a photo of him hoisting the Stanley Cup. That picture was both an incentive to win again and a reminder that he'd achieved his dream once before, so he could do it again. Now the photo sparked an idea. He knew exactly what he had to offer to get Tracy to help him.

A way to achieve her goal.

CHAPTER TWELVE

"YOU WANT ME to do *what*?" Tracy's jaw dropped. "You cannot be serious."

Ike's earnest expression didn't change. "I'm not getting any younger and this—" he held up his bandaged arm "—has made me realize how precarious my career is. Life after hockey might be closer than I'd like. As you said, this is the perfect opportunity to get some building blocks in place for the future."

"But you… I can't," Tracy spluttered. He couldn't ask *that* of her. What kind of person did he think she was?

"Why not?" His innocent tone sparked her temper.

"I'm not a pimp or a madam."

When Ike had called this morning saying he needed to discuss an important project, she'd assumed he had something else he needed her help with while he was recuperating. After his disapproving look when she'd had to duck out of the Thanksgiving party yesterday, she'd been tempted to refuse. But professionalism had won out, so she'd come over to his house and was now sitting in his living room.

After all, things between them were back to normal. Whatever bridges they'd been building had been blown apart by her refusal to have a relationship with him. That saddened her almost as much as it annoyed her.

Which was why she hadn't explained that it really had been an emergency yesterday. A pipe had burst in the rented house where the Chabals were staying, flooding the children's bedrooms. Besides getting someone to fix the problem, she'd had to find alternative accommodation for the family. Not easy on a holiday.

Not that Ike would have listened anyway. To him, it would have been another example of her business coming first. And she refused to defend herself to him.

"I'm not asking you to set me up with a hooker." Ike's eyes glittered dangerously. "If all I wanted was sex, there are plenty of puck bunnies who'd be glad to have my notch on their bedpost."

"Well, that's what your 'important' project sounded like to me," she said coolly.

"Asking you to find some women for me to date is nothing like hiring me a prostitute. I'm talking about the kind of woman I could have a future with."

His words shouldn't have affected her—she'd pushed him away with both hands—yet they caused a sharp pang in her chest. "There are plenty of dating agencies around. Call one of them."

"I can't risk the information leaking. Hockey may

not be as popular around here as other sports, but it would still make for uncomfortable headlines. 'Star goaltender can't catch a woman' would be a social media hit. I wouldn't be able to go anywhere without a paparazzi tail and endless media speculation. If I talked to a woman, the pictures would go viral before I'd finished saying hello."

He had a point. But still… "There are a number of local exclusive introduction services who specialize in finding suitable dates for men in your situation."

"Please. You think I'd sign up with one of those skinny bleached-blonde barracudas? I've seen the ads in the airline magazines." He gave an exaggerated shudder. "I'd rather face the Rangers naked than discuss my personal life with any of those so-called exclusive introduction bureaus."

She wiped the image from her mind and tamped down her skittering pulse. The last thing she needed right now was to think about Ike naked. "Some of those women do look predatory."

"Plus, I can't see myself wanting to get serious and settle down with the kind of people they'd suggest. I've already dated my share of models, actresses, trust-fund babies and high-flying career women whose bank accounts probably outstrip mine by several zeroes."

Tracy wasn't sure how that made her feel. She didn't fit into any of those categories. Not that she wanted to, but she couldn't help wondering where that put her. "I still don't see how I can help. I don't know anything about matchmaking."

"All you'd have to do is work with me to figure out my requirements—like you did when I bought this house—then you'd introduce me to some women and I'd take it from there. It isn't rocket science."

He wasn't seriously expecting her to fix him up with her friends? "Matching you to a future wife is not a service we offer. However I know a woman who runs a small high-end introduction agency locally, whom I can guarantee would be discreet. You'll like Layla—she's very down-to-earth. I'm sure she could put you in touch with some suitable women."

"If you want her to help you, fine. But I've explained why I'm not signing up with a dating agency." He leaned back in his chair, crossing his arms. "I thought Helping Hands was supposed to provide the services your clients needed."

Trust him to nail the perfect jibe. "We're not a dating agency."

"I didn't realize you only provided the services you wanted to."

He was twisting her words. "That's not fair."

"Isn't it? I need your help and you're refusing to give it."

Tracy squared her shoulders. "I'm sorry, but as I said, this isn't my field of expertise. I don't have the contacts I would need and I couldn't provide the high quality of service that clients like yourself are entitled to expect," she said frostily, hoping he'd give up his crazy quest.

"Even if I pay the going rate plus twenty percent?"

Her jaw dropped. "You do know how much that is?"

He shrugged nonchalantly as he named a generous six-figure fee.

Did he really think she was that shallow? "Money isn't the issue."

His knowing smile was almost feral. "So what terms would be favorable?"

"This isn't a negotiation," she protested. "I've already said I won't do it. No amount of money would make me play matchmaker for you."

"What if I could give you something else you really wanted?"

Confident that there was no bait he could dangle that would convince her to say yes, she mimicked his earlier nonchalant shrug. "Nothing you can give me would change my mind."

"Not even the number-one spot in the market?"

"What?" Her heart thudded against her ribs. "You can't guarantee that." Could he?

She hated that she'd nibbled at the bloody bait after all.

He leaned forward. "There were complaints from the guys yesterday that they're not getting the support they used to have from you. If you help me, I'll stir up the team to demand the Cats change back to Making Your Move."

"Callum Hardshaw's determined to streamline and consolidate to make the Ice Cats more profitable." She wasn't weakening, she was merely pointing out why his offer wasn't viable. "A few complaints from the players won't be enough to sway him."

Ike looked as if he were going to argue, but all he did was sigh. "You're right. I probably don't have that kind of influence with him, either. Especially right now." For a moment he looked vulnerable. "Who knows what other measures Hardshaw will put in place in the name of cost-saving."

His comment surprised her. "What do you mean?"

"From what I hear, the changes aren't limited to suppliers. He's also turning the entire front office upside-down. Who's to say he won't do the same with the team? Especially if we don't make the cut for the playoffs again this season. Look at how he let Tru and a couple of other veterans go in the summer. No one's safe."

"Surely you don't include yourself in that."

"Why not? My salary is among the highest in the NHL and there are more top-class goaltenders than jobs. Plus, there's no guarantee my arm will be strong enough for me to play at the level I did before."

She didn't want to get into another discussion

about his arm, so she tried another angle. "You have a no-trade clause."

"You can be made to waive them, under the right circumstances. Like if you find your position untenable—only playing backup, for example. Even if Hardshaw didn't go that route, my contract is up for renewal shortly. He may decide to force my hand, rather than let me go for nothing."

How had the conversation turned around so quickly? From finding him a possible future wife to his career being in dire straits and being made to leave the Ice Cats. "Are we back to me telling you not to borrow trouble?"

Ike didn't respond for a moment. Then he shook his head, as if clearing it of those miserable thoughts. "I'm not. Just being practical. And that's why I shouldn't keep my personal life on the back burner any longer. Why this project I'm asking you to help me with is so important."

He really was the most infuriating… Tracy sucked in a deep breath before she told him exactly what she thought of him. She wouldn't let him goad her into losing her professionalism. Two could play at that game. "Even if you could influence the Ice Cats' contract—which we both agree you can't—regaining it wouldn't be enough to deliver what you promised."

She wasn't disappointed; she couldn't lose what she'd never had. But it made rejecting his matchmaking idea a lot easier.

Ike wasn't deterred. "That was only one part of my plan. Obviously, it would have been nicer if that would have worked, but the rest of it's still doable."

"The rest being...?"

"I'll be the face of Helping Hands. You can use me as the centerpiece of your marketing and advertising campaigns. I'm also prepared to be on hand to personally support your pitches to organizations, at least until I'm back playing next season."

Tracy hadn't thought Ike could shock her anymore. Yet this morning he'd managed to catch her out twice. First with his outrageous request, and now with his unbelievable offer.

In her business, references were gold, but endorsements were rare diamonds. A professional athlete who lent his name to a service gave it credibility as well as cachet. Sure, some sports stars would push anything in return for big bucks. But everyone knew who they were. Ike wasn't one of those guys. His support could make sports franchises listen more carefully to what she had to say. It was a game changer.

Companies paid millions for Ike's endorsement and he was offering to give it to her free of charge.

Not free. Tracy stopped herself before she got carried away. There was a pretty hefty price tag on his endorsement.

One she couldn't pay.

She was about to tell him that when she stopped. Was she really prepared to throw away this chance to achieve the goal she'd dreamed of for so long, simply because her nose was out of joint?

Her heart screamed *yes*. She couldn't fix up Ike with other women. Watch him date them, maybe even fall in love with them? Even though they were finished, that didn't mean she wanted a ringside seat to him finding a woman who could give him what he wanted—a family, a future. She certainly didn't want to gift wrap said perfect woman and put her in Ike's Christmas stocking.

As if he sensed her indecision, Ike asked, "What have you got to lose?"

She didn't want to think about that. "And if I say no?"

Ike sighed heavily. "I'd go to your competition." He rested his arms on his knees. "That's not what I want, but you're either with me or you're not. And if you're not, then…" He let his words trail off.

Tracy tried one last time to appeal to that courtly side of him. "I'm not sure I can do this, Ike. It's a lot to ask of me."

"It's going to happen anyway." His tone softened. "You're not going to change your mind about us, are you?"

For a moment, she thought she saw a plea in his green eyes.

In that same moment, she wondered if there was a chance a relationship with Ike could work. Certainly there was more chance of one working with him than with anyone else.

No sooner had the thought entered her mind than she dismissed it sharply. She couldn't give herself up to a man like that again. She couldn't lose herself. She couldn't take the risk. Even for Ike. She had to walk her own path. Even if it was a lonely one.

She shook her head, unable to say the words.

"Then this is the way it has to be."

Tracy refused to give in there and then. "I can't give you an answer right now. I'll need to discuss it with Maggie." Maybe her sister could see a way out.

"Okay. Let me know when you've made your decision."

Though his voice was even, the hint of satisfaction in his eyes poked at her frustration. He thought… no, he *knew* he'd won.

Not so fast.

She stood, enjoying the advantage of looking down on him. "If we agree to this deal, I'd want it clearly outlined, specifics and details, in black and white. Signed and sealed. How many introductions and what we'll receive in return. In particular, what your endorsement will entail."

"Not a problem. I'd expect nothing less. Get me the paperwork whenever you're ready and I'll run it past my agent and lawyer. Then we'll both be covered."

When Ike started to get up, she held up her hand to stop him. "I can see myself out."

Tracy kept up the cool facade until she was in her car. It started to waver as, driving home, she found herself imagining Ike dating a series of perfect women. Blonde, brunette, redhead. Tall, slim, beautiful. Successful, accomplished and willing to be Mrs. Ike Jelinek.

She shook her head to clear the mental images, then changed direction and drove to her sister's house.

Her facade weakened further when Maggie opened her door. "This is a nice surprise. Come in."

Swallowing the lump in her throat, Tracy blinked to keep the tears at bay. When she didn't move, Maggie's smile faded.

She studied Tracy's face, then, without saying a word, folded her into a hug.

"WHEN ARE YOU going to tell me what's wrong?" Maggie's expression was understanding but intractable.

Maggie had provided the age-old English pick-me-up of a pot of tea and chocolate biscuits, then listened quietly as Tracy wittered on about various frustrating but admittedly minor issues that had arisen recently in their business. Tracy deliberately hadn't mentioned the situation with Ike. She figured the longer she delayed, the more likely she'd be able to discuss it rationally.

Clearly, Maggie hadn't been fooled by her stalling tactics.

Tracy gave it one last shot. "That's what I've been telling you about for the past hour."

"No, it isn't," her sister said firmly. "All those problems combined are not why you were close to tears when you arrived."

When Tracy started to protest, Maggie cut her off with a reproving look. "Business issues don't get you down—they challenge you."

Tracy's laugh was a little shaky, but she couldn't deny the truth.

"The point is, you always find a solution and everyone involved is better off than they were before."

Ike's proposition would certainly leave Making Your Move far better off. If Tracy was prepared to put aside her own feelings about what he wanted her to do. All the time she and Maggie had been talking, Tracy had been going over her options in her head. No matter how she looked at the problem, it still boiled down to one simple question—did she agree to Ike's request or not?

If only the answer was as simple. Could she achieve her goal without Ike's help? Of course. It might take longer, but she was already well on track. Would it be easier with his endorsement? Absolutely. So, from that perspective, saying no wasn't a major hardship.

On the other hand, she'd lose Ike's friendship and support. Permanently. She had no doubt that he'd cut her out of his life completely and once he'd made up his mind to do that, it would take a miracle to get him to change it.

Did she really want to cross that line? No. Even

if the alternative was to see Ike happy with someone else.

She couldn't be what Ike wanted. As much as she cared for him—which was more than she had or ever could care for another man—maybe the best solution was to give him what he wanted.

Knowing what she had to do and going through with it were two different things, though.

"I can see your brain working. And you're upset again. You're worrying me. What's going on?" Maggie demanded.

Tracy didn't know why she was hesitating. She could tell her sister anything without fear of judgment and she could trust her advice. Plus, Maggie would be objective—something Tracy had no hope of being. Still, it was tough to know where to start.

"Perhaps a little moral support will loosen those lips." Maggie stood and went over to where Joe lay in his Moses basket. She picked him up and brought him to Tracy. "Cuddle your nephew. He loves you unconditionally. He won't understand what you tell me, so he'll still coo at you. Actually, he'll drool all over you, but it's done with love."

The warm bundle snuggled against her, easing the tightness in Tracy's chest. "We, or rather I, have had an interesting business proposition."

"The way you said that makes me think there's something wrong with it. Don't tell me—the Rangers want your services."

Tracy laughed, startling Joe. "That would put the cat amongst the pigeons."

"Not the Blue Shirts, then. How about the Islanders? The Flyers?"

"None of the above. Right sport, wrong team."

Maggie frowned, clearly stumped. "Don't keep me in suspense. Who?"

"Ike."

"Your Ike?"

"He's not 'my' Ike." Her heart hitched. "But yes, that Ike."

"He's come up with a way to get the Ice Cats' contract back? Good man! For a guy with a stick up his bum, he's okay."

"That's exactly where I want to shove a stick right now." Tracy explained Ike's request and the conclusion she'd come to.

Maggie's eyes widened. "You're thinking of agreeing?"

"It's a neat solution all round. Everyone gets what they want." The words burned her mouth.

"Sweetie, we don't need his help *that* badly. Frankly, we don't need his help at all. We're doing well enough without his precious endorsement, thank you very much. Tell him to shove his bloody proposition where the sun doesn't shine—along with that stick."

Tracy smiled. She could always rely on her sister to have her back. "But I think the long-term benefit would outweigh the short-term pain."

"Would it?" Maggie sounded doubtful.

"I admit, setting the whole thing up will be tough initially, but I reckon if we limit the number of introductions—say, to three or four—I could get this over and done with quite quickly." She was pleased with how convincing her answer sounded.

Her sister's snort said it wasn't convincing enough. "You'd still have to interview the women. Plus, you'd have to go through some kind of questionnaire with Ike, so you'd know exactly what he's looking for. Then you'd have to discuss prospective candidates with him. Are you sure you're up for that? I know I wouldn't have been with Jake."

Tracy couldn't lie to Maggie. "Probably not."

"I thought we agreed that you'd give Ike a second chance if one came up. If you had, this whole discussion would be moot. Then again, Ike wouldn't have come up with this ludicrous idea, either."

"A chance hasn't come up." Tracy's cheeks flushed as she recalled the kiss the previous weekend. "Well, not really." Her heart pounded, as if calling out her lie. "We kissed. But when it came to taking things further, I couldn't do it."

"Wait. Back up a minute. You and Ike kissed?"

"It's not Victorian times. I'm not ruined. There don't have to be duels at dawn."

"Funny. So how was it?"

"Nice." At her sister's glare, she added, "Fantastic."

"And you weren't tempted to...?" Maggie broke

off and nodded at her son. She waved her finger in a circle, wordlessly finishing the sentence.

"Of course I was. He even suggested we have that hot fling you pushed for."

"You refused a chance to tear up the sheets with him, no strings attached?" Maggie's voice rose in pitch until she almost squeaked the last word.

"I had to."

"Why on earth did you *have* to? He offered you exactly what you wanted."

"Nothing's changed. He's still who he is and I'm who I am."

Maggie rolled her eyes. "You can do better than that psychological claptrap."

"But it's true. He and I want different things and that's never going to change." Tracy sighed. "If he could have guaranteed that a fling was all he'd ever want, I'd have gladly 'torn up the sheets' with him. But that's not his endgame. At some point he'd want to take things further and we'd go through the same arguments again. He wants a wife and a family. I can't...won't be that for him."

"Why not?"

"You know why not."

Her sister dismissed that with a wave of her hand. "So you'd rather set Ike up with another woman than take the risk that things might not work out?"

Tracy shrugged one shoulder. "It gives us both what we want."

"Rubbish. What you want is each other."

"But being together won't work."

"How do you know if you won't even try?"

"Because I know Ike. And I know myself."

Her sister gave her a long look. "You won't turn into Mum just because you get serious about a man."

"I wish that was true, but I already know it isn't. Look what happened when I was married to Hank. And I saw the same signs after only being with Ike a short time. Perhaps it's in the genes."

"If it was, I'd have the same problem. I can't deny we've both made mistakes when it came to our first marriages. Lee was an extreme version of Dad." Their father might have been controlling, even emotionally abusive, but he wasn't the physically abusive monster that Maggie's ex was. "You encouraged me to give Jake a chance. To have faith that he was different. That the fault lay with them, not me."

"You're the exception. Ike and I are a lost cause." The admission was so painful, Tracy could hardly say the words. Was the truth that everyone else had been able to escape the past and *she* was the exception?

"Rubbish. You're making it a lost cause because you're scared of getting hurt again. And I understand that. But, sweetie, you're throwing away a chance for happiness. It could work out this time. You're both older and wiser and you know what the pitfalls are. You're not the person you were when you guys dated and neither, I suspect, is Ike."

Tracy wanted to believe her sister, but a little

demon of fear deep inside her wouldn't release its viselike grip.

"I give up." Maggie threw up her hands in despair. "This is a mistake, but if you really think you can handle it, go ahead. Are you sure you won't be jealous when you send Ike off on dates with those wonder-women?"

Tracy's hesitation gave her away. "I'll deal with it. It's not like he hasn't dated other women since I've known him."

"But he wasn't serious about them."

"It's a small price to pay for what we'll gain for Making Your Move."

"Just remember, even the number-one-ranked business won't keep you warm at night."

"Maybe not, but it will help me sleep easier."

"Well, I'll be here to pick up the pieces when it goes belly-up."

"I appreciate the thought, but I'll be okay. All I have to do is keep my eye on the prize. This will all be done and dusted in a few weeks. Maybe even by Christmas. Then we can look forward to a successful new year."

Joe endeared himself forever to his aunt as he let out a robust cry, forcing his mother to drop the subject in favor of feeding him.

Keep your eye on the prize. Tracy repeated those words like a mantra as she drove home a short while later. It was business, just as it had been when she'd found Ike his house and helped him after his accident. Only she'd never be jealous of his house or his driver.

Enough! She'd made her decision. Now she had to be constructive and form a plan of action. The best way to do that was to get some advice. Luckily, she had an expert on hand to provide her with the necessary expertise.

Tracy told her phone to call Layla and waited for it to connect.

THE SMELL OF an ice rink was as reminiscent of home for Ike as his mom's baklava.

After his father had walked out on the family, the ice had provided a refuge from the responsibilities thrust onto Ike's young shoulders. Aunt Tina and Uncle Gio had done their best—raising Karina's four boys along with Jake—but as the oldest, Ike had worried that it wouldn't be enough to keep his family together. In their neighborhood, tales of well-meaning social workers taking children from parents who couldn't cope were commonplace.

Ten-year-old Ike had stepped into the role of man of the house, particularly when his mom had been at work. He'd made sure his brothers were always clean and presentable and that they all—barring Linc, who'd still been a baby—went to school. He'd packed lunches, overseen homework, listened to their reading and tested their spelling and math.

Hockey had been a chance for Ike to be a kid again. All he had to focus on was the game and keeping the puck out of his net. Since then, no matter where the rink was or how badly his team needed to win, Ike felt at home when he set foot inside.

This time, though, he wasn't the one playing. He'd come with the rest of the family to see Emily's Squirt Ice Cats team take on the neighboring town's Squirt Phantoms. It was a shame Jake and Kenny couldn't be here, but the guys had moved on to Pittsburgh after their 3–2 defeat of the Flyers. Still, Emily would have a good cheering section. Together with Ike, she'd have Maggie, Tracy and Jake's parents.

Of course, Tracy wasn't at the rink yet. She'd been called away to another client emergency. That was how it would always be with her. He understood better now that it wasn't because she didn't care about the people she loved, but that she gave so much to caring about her clients. They were priority 1 and 1A.

Unfortunately that wasn't enough for him.

While he regretted that his future didn't include Tracy, he didn't want to compete with travel arrangements and house-hunting and the countless different services her agency had on offer. He appreciated that her job wasn't a nine-to-five deal and he'd seen how much her business relied on quality of service. Hell, he'd benefitted enormously from it. Especially from Tracy's personal touch. And that was the point—if they were together, he wanted to be the only one who got the benefit of her personal touch.

That might be selfish, but his job was killer enough on relationships. To have both of them here, there and everywhere wouldn't work. Not for the two of them and not for their kids. His family wouldn't grow up with the same instability he'd had. Someone had to be the anchor. Since it couldn't be him, it would have to be his wife.

That didn't mean his heart didn't want Tracy. Even as he'd outlined his idea to her the day before yesterday, there'd been that tiny lingering hope that she'd change her mind and give them a chance. But she hadn't.

He'd felt a twinge of guilt, especially when he'd seen how much his proposition had upset her. Hope had grown momentarily, too. But both the hope and the guilt had vanished when she'd laid down her terms for any potential agreement.

Though Tracy had yet to confirm her acceptance, he knew she wouldn't refuse. He expected her answer today, after the game. Then his path would be set and there'd be no going back.

Ike sat on the cold metal bleachers and watched the young players warming up on the ice. Emily waved at him before joining her teammates in a circle around their coach. After a quick team talk, they were dispatched to begin drills.

How sad was it that he was jealous of the gangly ten-year-old with the too-small pads roughing up his crease? The kid was obviously going through a growth spurt and his parents had decided to wait it out before buying him new gear. He remembered that all too well—except in his case, his mom hadn't been able to afford new equipment. Uncle Gio had done his best to find good-quality secondhand gear, but Ike had often made do with equipment that didn't fit. Ike hadn't cared, as long as he could play.

Now, seeing the boy tugging at his pads reinforced how much Ike wanted to play. He'd give anything, even his old too-short pads, to be able to skate into that crease.

His mind was caught between past and present when Maggie sat next to him. She handed him the tiny well-wrapped bundle that was Joe before turning her attention to the ice. She let Ike play with Joe for a few minutes before starting her inquisition.

"I didn't take you for a man who gave up easily."

He turned to her, confused. "What have I given up on?"

"Not what—who. My sister."

"There's no point fighting a battle you can't win."

"Really? I thought the motto was 'fight until the whistle blows.'"

"It's been blowing long and hard for a while now."

"Uh-huh. Seems to me that's just an excuse."

How had he turned into the bad guy? "Your sister's the one with the whistle in her mouth. I've tried to get her to have a relationship with me, but she's made it clear she's not interested."

"So you've given up." It was a statement, not a question.

"Give me a break, Maggie. If there was the slightest chance, I'd hang in there. No amount of fight or heart or will is going to make it happen for us."

"I wouldn't be so sure."

Ike frowned. "Tracy's changed her mind?"

"It's not that simple. She… We both carry a lot of baggage. From our parents, from our ex-husbands."

"I knew her ex was a jerk, but he didn't…"

Maggie interrupted, "No, he wasn't violent like Lee. But his behavior was just as damaging. The point is Tracy's never had a healthy relationship. She's certainly never had an equal partnership." She gave him a wry look. "Including with you."

"Me? I never expected her to—" how had Tracy put it? "—be subsumed into me."

"Maybe not, but you also didn't give her room to be herself."

"How do you figure?"

"The way you act about her business."

"I've been incredibly supportive of her business. Look at all the stuff she's been doing for me. And what I've offered her in return for her help."

"How about the way you behaved when she had to leave on Thanksgiving? I bet you're all sniffy because she's not here yet."

"I don't get 'sniffy.'" He hoped his lofty tone hid guilt that Maggie had nailed it.

"Do you know why she left on Thursday? Or why she's late today?"

"I'm sure the reason was important both times. But that doesn't take away from the fact that she always lets Making Your Move interfere with family."

"And hockey doesn't interfere?"

Ike shifted uncomfortably. "That's different."

"Is it? I don't see Jake here for Emily's big game."

"We don't get a choice about which games we play or when."

"Just like Tracy doesn't get a choice about when her clients need her." Maggie punched him in the arm. She then told him about the Chabals' problems on Thanksgiving. "And right now, she's helping a basketball player whose household shipment got delivered to Dallas, West Virginia, instead of Dallas, Texas. The player isn't even a current client. His new team used one of our competitors, who've left him in this mess because they can't do anything on a weekend. He begged Tracy to help him."

"That's nice of her, but it doesn't change anything with regards to us."

"I can't decide who I'm most cross with—you for holding her to ransom, or her for bloody paying up."

Ike sighed. "I care a lot for Tracy. If there was the slightest chance we'd have a future together, I'd drop this dating thing in a heartbeat. But there isn't, so it's time to move on."

"You can't hold on just a little longer? I know your request has shaken her. She might yet come around."

He hated the way Maggie could get his hopes up all over again. "I can't spend the rest of my life waiting for something that probably won't happen."

"What'll you do if she can't find you 'the one'?"

"I'll keep looking. I won't settle for almost good enough."

"What if your perfect woman is right under your nose?"

"If we can't have the future I want, then I guess I'll end up alone."

Maggie huffed, then dusted her hands against her thighs. "Well, you're both old enough to do as you please."

Ike handed her son back. "Sorry to disappoint you."

"Me, too." She fixed him with a stern look. "One more thing. If you hurt her, I'll hurt you." Without giving him a chance to reply, she stalked off.

How could Maggie think he'd deliberately hurt Tracy? Hadn't she listened? Tracy was the one to blame, not him.

He turned his gaze back to the ice but his mind was still on their conversation. No matter what Maggie said, Ike had to believe he was doing the right thing. He'd put an end to a relationship with Tracy. Now he had to reinforce that.

It wouldn't be fair to any other woman if he didn't. He couldn't date someone else, knowing his heart wasn't in it. Like he did before a game, he mentally put his emotions about Tracy in a box and slammed the lid shut.

Then, as if Fate was laughing her ass off at him, Tracy appeared next to him. She didn't waste time on small talk.

"Making Your Move will take your job. I suggest we meet on Tuesday afternoon, at my home office, to finalize terms. I'll take you through how I propose to tackle your project and also take your dating requirements then. Shall we say two o'clock?"

If she were upset about his "project," it sure as hell didn't show. If anything, she seemed eager to rise to the challenge. Her words were the nails that sealed that mental box.

"Fine." He made his voice as cool as hers. "I look forward to seeing your proposal then."

He didn't watch her as she walked away. Instead he focused on the kids practicing their shots against the gangly goaltender. For once in his life, Ike didn't want to be in goal. He wanted to be the one banging pucks into the net.

CHAPTER THIRTEEN

POWER-DRESSING FOR a meeting that was taking place in your own home was *not* overkill.

Tracy needed every advantage she could get. Besides, it was more like donning armor for battle—just with more style. She attached the opal brooch—a present to herself to celebrate her first year in business—to the jacket of her red suit to remind her of everything she'd achieved. She then considered the shoes in her closet. She needed heels—for height, to make her legs look great and to make her feel like a million bucks.

Straps or bows? Black or red? Louboutins or Zanottis?

Her gaze landed on a box in the middle of the pile. Black patent, triple straps with buttons, red soles. Perfect.

One last check in the mirror. She touched the opal earrings—the first "frivolous" thing she'd bought with her own money after her divorce was final—to boost her strength. Then she freshened her lipstick. She snapped the lid back on the tube, like a knight pulling down his visor, as a sign she was ready for battle.

She headed down one level to her empty office. Carla had popped out to post checks and invoices, so there was no one to distract her. Tracy sat at her desk and tried to let the quiet permeate her tense body.

The clock downstairs chimed two, making her jump and undoing all the good.

"Keep your eye on the bloody prize," she muttered to herself.

Since she wouldn't be able to relax until Ike arrived, she might as well double-check she had everything she needed. She opened his file and flipped through the documents within.

A few minutes later, Carla knocked on the door frame. "You look dressed to kill."

"Thank you." Tracy managed a half smile. "But if I killed my clients, I wouldn't be in business very long."

"That's true." The intern laughed. "In that case, you'll knock your next appointment on his very nice butt."

Tracy's smile faded. "Ike's just a client."

"Of course he is," Carla said wryly. "He's also a man, and there isn't a man alive who wouldn't be bowled over by you in that outfit. Especially those shoes."

Tracy tilted an ankle. "Aren't they fabulous?"

"One of these days, I'm going to sneak into your closet and have a shoe party."

"Feel free to play with them anytime."

Carla sighed happily. "You'd never get me out of

there." Then she shook her head, as if to rid herself of her daydream. "I wanted to let you know that Ike's arrived. He's waiting in the living room."

Tracy's body tensed. "I didn't hear the doorbell."

"We came up the front steps at the same time, so I let him in."

Tracy tried not to let on how much the lack of warning had thrown her. "Thank you."

"I've given him a drink—water—and put out a plate of those shortbread cookies we love from the local bakery."

"Perfect." Tracy rose and grabbed Ike's file, a pen and her iPad. "You really are becoming indispensable."

"Anytime you feel like giving me a raise, feel free."

"If this project pays off like I'm expecting, you'll get that raise." Tracy hadn't told Carla exactly what the new project entailed, just that she was doing some extra work for Ike.

"Fantastic. Then maybe I can afford a cool pair of shoes of my own." The younger woman sat at her desk. "Note to self—check if I can afford a knock-off of those beauties."

As Tracy walked downstairs, she mentally revisited the checklist she'd made after her chat with Layla. Her friend had been very helpful. After Tracy's initial call, they'd met to discuss the situation in more depth. She'd offered to pay Layla a consulting fee, but her friend had asked for payment in kind—relocation to a new office.

Tracy hadn't told Layla who her client was, but had given enough information for her to work with. They'd then spent several hours devising a questionnaire that Tracy could use with Ike. In addition, Layla had searched her database and provided a list of possible candidates. They'd agreed to meet again, after Tracy had seen Ike, to go over his answers and fine-tune the list.

Tracy had been surprised by the number of women Layla had on her database.

"I never believed I'd get so many clients," her friend had said. "Especially with the number of exclusive agencies in the area. I wanted to provide genuine help for genuine people, so I tried to make my service more approachable and less like a cattle market for the rich and famous."

It had clearly worked; Layla's success rate was impressive.

Her friend was confident there'd be several women in her database who'd meet Ike's requirements. Which was great. Really.

Keep your eye on the prize.

Tracy squared her shoulders and walked into the living room.

Ike stood as she entered. "Hey. How's it going?"

He looked good. Too good. He was wearing a dark green collarless shirt that emphasized both his broad chest and his eyes. One sleeve had been pinned above his cast. His black jeans were faded and fit his strong legs to perfection. His wind-tousled dark hair was longer than normal, making her fingers itch to run through the silky strands.

Tracy stamped down on the attraction, as if with her spiked heels, and went over to where he stood. She didn't offer her hand, even though it would have put the meeting on an unequivocally professional footing, because she couldn't rely on maintaining her control if they touched.

"Fine, thanks. I hope you don't mind meeting in here. Given what we'll be discussing, I want you to be relaxed." She indicated for Ike to sit.

Once he had, she took the armchair across from him. "Let's get the administrative stuff out of the way."

"I've read your proposal and think it's fine." He handed her a large manila envelope, then sat back. "My lawyer and my agent went through everything and saw no problems, so I've signed the papers. You'll find a check in there for the agreed amount."

He was certainly keen; she'd only emailed them yesterday. Still, the sooner they got started, the sooner it would be over. Tracy ignored the pang she felt at the thought that he couldn't wait to move on, too.

"Let's get cracking." She passed him the questionnaire she and Layla had devised. "This is the easiest way to get to the heart of your requirements."

She winced inwardly at the word *heart*.

Keep your eye on the prize.

"It's based on what Layla uses, but we've tailored it to your specifications," she said crisply, as if discussing the features of a potential house. "I've filled in the basic information already, to save time."

Ike scanned the first page. "Yeah. Fine. Looks straightforward."

"I'll leave you to fill in physical details at your leisure. For today, I think it's important that we cover the essential elements of personality, values and interests."

"Whatever works. You're the expert." His cool tone matched hers.

Her withering look seemed to bounce off him like a puck off his pads. "Apparently this works best if you give answers that are phrased positively—what you want, rather than what you don't want."

The temperature in the room seemed to drop by several degrees.

"A woman who wants me and the things I want. Who has the same ideals and traditional values. Who wants a future that includes marriage and kids."

Tracy had known this session would be uncomfortable, but hearing him spell it out hit her hard. It wasn't what he'd said that hurt. It's what he *hadn't* said. He wanted someone who wasn't her. Her fingers shook as she concentrated on writing his answer neatly on the page.

She sipped her water. "Okay, good. Does it matter if the woman already has children?"

"Nope."

"What about pets?"

"Nope."

"Do you have a problem with a divorcee?"

"At our age, everyone has a history. As long as she's not in a relationship right now, the past is the past."

"Do you mind if she works?"

"Most women do. My mom did. She shouldn't have had to work as hard as she did, but she had no choice. She had to support herself and us." He crossed his arms. "The important thing is that the right woman won't see her work as her life. Or to put it *positively*, she must be capable of achieving balance in her life."

That zinger caught Tracy right in the breastbone, stealing her breath. They'd barely started and she wasn't sure how much more of this she could take.

She steeled herself to continue. "Any professions you wouldn't want her to work in?"

"Other than the oldest?" The humor in his voice didn't reach his eyes. "I try not to prejudge people based on their jobs because I don't want them to be prejudiced about me because of mine."

No—he only judged after the fact. "What if the woman works shifts or travels a lot?"

"Again, as long as she's willing to compromise, it should be okay. If she can't or won't..." He shrugged.

Breathe in, breathe out. Another sip of water. "I assume you'd like someone who's interested in sports."

He shrugged. "I guess as long as she doesn't hate sports, and especially doesn't hate hockey, that should be enough."

Finally something that didn't make her feel like the worst woman in the world.

Thankfully, the next batch of questions was about educational level, religion, politics, hobbies and interests, so she got through those relatively unscathed. She even managed to smile at his response to the question about dietary habits. He was right; he and a vegan had no chance together.

Halfway there. All she had to do was stick it out for another couple of pages and she'd be done. "For the second part, we need to focus on you."

Ike shifted uncomfortably. "Why? You already know me."

"It's part of the process of building a fuller picture, so I can make the best matches for you." She forced a reassuring smile. "The first set isn't too taxing. Favorite book, favorite film, that kind of thing."

"Okay. Shoot."

Despite his misgivings, Ike answered the questions honestly and cheerfully. He was thoughtful and often surprisingly expansive about his choices.

The tension in the room seemed to dissipate, along with the formality. The question-and-answer session became less of a brittle back-and-forth and more of a conversation. At the same time, Tracy's body began to relax, the tightness in her shoulders easing. The whole thing became almost pleasant. Even their debates were good-natured.

She wondered if Ike was the first man in her life who'd listened to her opinions, let alone respected them. What did that say about her?

As she filled the pages with her handwritten notes, Tracy couldn't ignore how much she and Ike had in common. Their tastes were similar in many ways. They might disagree about their musical preferences—he liked his rock hard and heavy, while she preferred hers soft and glam—or what they liked to read—his non-fiction and detective fiction versus her romance novels and dark thrillers—or watch—he wanted action, action, action, while she insisted on a happy ending. But the crucial thing was that they both loved music, reading and movies. And they were both addicted to computer adventure games, with the same classic *King's Quest* as their all-time favorite.

Interestingly, Tracy learned a lot about Ike that she hadn't known. Before today, she couldn't have said what his preferences were for anything, except in bed. She felt as if she'd barely scratched the surface before. Perhaps they hadn't been together long enough to discover those little tidbits about each other. She certainly never remembered them talking like this.

Would things have turned out differently if they

had? Would their commonalities have drawn them closer, making their differences less obvious?

Unfortunately that ship had already sailed. That's why they were sitting here, having this conversation. A pang of regret tugged at her chest, but she continued.

Keep your eye on the prize.

The final batch of questions was more searching, more personal. What would Ike do in certain situations? What did he think about certain actions? Which words and phrases described him, his personality and his values?

Tracy began to feel awkward, as if she were stepping into forbidden territory. Ike must have felt it, too, as his answers became shorter and more abrupt. The relaxed feeling had gone; stiff formality had returned.

They both sighed together as Tracy jotted down the notes for the final question.

"You now know everything about me, except my inseam measurement." Irritation edged Ike's words.

"I know it was hard work, but it'll be worth it in the end."

"Let's hope so."

She slid the completed questionnaire into his file. "I'll input your responses this afternoon. That'll generate a list of candidates for you to look over, which I'll email to you tomorrow. You should be able to have your first date this weekend."

Once again the words left a bitter taste in her

mouth. He'd better deliver his side of the deal with knobs on, given what she was putting herself through.

Ike got to his feet. "I look forward to hearing from you."

Once he'd gone, Tracy headed upstairs to her office. She dropped into her chair and swiveled slowly from side to side. She should be pleased; it had gone better than expected.

"That's the problem," she muttered.

She'd seen Ike in a different light. What's more, she liked this Ike. The whole meeting had somehow put his old-fashioned views into context. She had new insight into the influence his childhood had had on his perspective on women. Being part of the extended family group, Tracy had heard many times of the responsibilities Ike and Tru had taken on when their father had left. But for the first time, she understood that while Ike saw his role as protector and provider, it wasn't as dominator and king of all he owned. She could no longer fit him into the same category as her father and Hank.

Having a relationship together didn't seem as awful as she'd once thought.

She could even see herself falling in love with him.

Her heart gave a heavy thud.

Unfortunately, it was too late. Tracy had burned a bridge that couldn't be rebuilt. Ike had moved on and she had committed to helping him find the woman of his dreams. No matter how she felt, she had to fulfill the terms of their agreement. Business really did have to come first.

What a terrible time to realize that her fear of repeating the errors of the past had caused her to make a terrible mistake for her own future. And in keeping her eye on the prize, she'd missed the most important thing of all. The prize she'd once held in her hands and thrown away with both hands.

"SHOULDN'T YOU BE getting ready for your next date?"

Kenny's question amped up Ike's guilt. What did it say about Ike that he was considering staying in to watch Edmonton play Florida instead of heading out for dinner with the next woman on his list?

Macarty had given the team a rest day after their brutal schedule over the past couple of weeks since Thanksgiving, so Kenny had stopped by. The two of them were slumped on Ike's couch. Open soda cans and a half-empty box of their mom's Christmas cookies littered his coffee table.

"I've got time." Ike didn't move. "I don't have to meet bachelorette number four until seven-thirty."

"You sound like you'd rather have a root canal."

"Nah, it's not that bad."

"I'm bowled over by your enthusiasm. Were the women all hounds? Did you at least get some mattress time?"

"No and no."

Kenny shook his head sadly. "Jeez, I'm almost

embarrassed to be your brother. Those women are desperate for it and you don't get any bang for your bucks."

"I'm not doing this for sex." Why did everyone think that was the only thing that mattered? For that matter, why did everyone think he needed help getting laid?

"You can't get serious about someone you're not compatible with. You gotta test the merchandise before you buy."

"I figured I'd leave that until after the first date. No point 'testing the merchandise' if it's not what you want anyway."

"I guess. But my way, you get something out of an otherwise wasted evening." His brother grinned. "At your age, you can't afford to be too fussy."

"Some women prefer a mature man over a horny kid."

"I've got one word for you, bro. Cougar. *Rowr*!"

Ike laughed at Kenny's big-cat impression, complete with scratching claws. "Whatever floats your boat."

"The question is why these women aren't floating yours. I thought Tracy was doing some kind of magic to find the woman of your dreams." He added in a singsong falsetto, "That you can marry and have cute babies and live in the happy land of rainbows forever."

"Mock all you like, kid. Your day will come sooner than you think."

"Please. I'll retain my youthful good looks and prime physique long after I've hung up my skates."

Ike had once had similar illusions. "Yeah. Look what happened to me."

"You were never this good-looking, bro." Kenny sobered. He nodded at Ike's arm in its lightweight cast. "I pray to the hockey gods that never happens to me. You'll be okay, right?"

"Doc says I'm healing better than expected and Cheryl's pleased with my progress at physio."

"Any word on when you'll be back skating?"

"Not yet. But I should be cleared for light workouts in the new year."

"Cool." Kenny brightened. "So tell me about the not-hounds."

Not much kept his brother serious for long. Ike suspected it had a lot to do with effectively being the youngest child—Linc had still been a baby—when their father had left. Ike and Tru had been the ones with all the responsibility, so Kenny had become the light relief, the sunshine in an otherwise grim situation. He still was.

"They were attractive. We just didn't connect for a variety of reasons."

Kenny feigned shock. "Hard to believe, you being such a sociable, fun-loving guy."

Ike cuffed him across the back of the head. "I leave the clown stuff to you."

"Yeah, yeah. You've been out with three women and didn't hit it off with any of them?"

"Not enough to want a second date."

He filled his brother in on the women. All three had seemed great on paper and had made a decent first impression. They were all attractive and good company. But beyond that, none had lived up to expectations.

The first one had seemed nice. She was a school librarian, loved kids, big into craft projects and enjoyed watching sport. Unfortunately, she'd wanted a guy who worked nine-to-five, was home for dinner promptly every night and at weekends, was willing to work on his "honey do" list. For the right woman, he'd have made a case for the future. But she'd seemed...inflexible. Everything in its place or done to schedule. To the point that she'd had to get home after their dinner to watch her favorite show and work on her latest crochet project. Hell, she'd made him feel spontaneous!

Dream girl number two had looked like a model and worked in finance for one of the local car dealers. She *loved* hockey and hockey players. It had become clear early on in the evening that she had her sights set on marrying a famous hockey player and living the glamorous life. The parties, the famous people, the paparazzi—so not his scene.

He'd really thought the third woman, Darla, had hit it out of the park. Smart, sexy, funny and liked sports. She had a career in advertising and was financially independent, but eager to marry and start a family. Ike had been congratulating Tracy on finding a woman who checked all the right boxes, until he'd asked if she planned to give up work or go back part-time when she had children. She'd looked at him as if he were nuts and said, "That's what nannies are for." Things had cooled pretty rapidly between them after that.

"Finding Ms. Perfect is more complicated than you thought, huh?" Kenny said. "How many more dates do you get?"

"One more after this one, if I want it."

"What does Tracy say about you striking out so far?"

Something else that had Ike ready to toss in the towel. Not only was the search not working out, but Tracy's cheerful attitude was bugging the hell out of him. She'd encouraged him after each failed date, then talked up the next candidate. He knew that's what she was supposed to do, but couldn't she be a little unhappy about introducing him to other women? Their friendship had stalled, too. They barely spoke about anything other than the damn project. The whole exercise was an unmitigated disaster.

At least she'd get something positive out of it. Even though he'd known it might not work, Ike had been true to his word and stirred up unrest among the players about the problems they'd had since the switch from Tracy's company to Lois. From what he'd heard, the front office was taking a lot of heat and there'd been several closed-door meetings with player reps. He wouldn't be surprised if Hardshaw didn't change his mind any day now.

Plus, he'd been booked for the photo shoot after Christmas for Tracy's advertising and promotional materials. He'd already submitted quotes for his endorsement and was waiting to hear back on whether she needed anything more.

Looked like she'd got the better end of the deal after all.

"Tracy gave me the standard bull. These things take time. Can't expect to score on your first shot. She's confident about the woman I'm supposed to meet tonight. Becca. Single mom, runs her own part-time craft business from home while her kid's at school. The girl plays hockey with Emily."

"Sounds like your kind of woman." Kenny frowned. "Why aren't you more excited?"

Ike shrugged. "So I won't be disappointed if it doesn't work out again."

"For sure it won't work out if you sit on your ass all night." Kenny slapped him on the back, then got to his feet. "I'm out of here. I have my own hot date later, with 'Misty from Minnesota.' She *loves* hockey players with dark hair and green eyes."

"Since when did puck bunnies become choosy?"

"Who cares? She can wrap those long, *long* legs around me and I'll be happy."

Ike envied his brother's easy attitude. Had he ever been that laidback about women—or anything else, for that matter?

Once Kenny had gone, Ike went upstairs to shower. He didn't hold out much hope for the evening, but it was too late to back out now. If this woman was a bust, too, Ike would pull the plug. No point putting himself through this anymore.

An hour later, his driver, Frankie, pulled up in front of the fancy steak restaurant in Weehawken, where Ike and Becca were due to meet.

Frankie got out to open Ike's door. "Have a nice evening."

"Yeah, thanks," Ike said as he got out of the car. "I'll call you when I'm done."

"Sure thing." Frankie touched his cap.

Ike watched Frankie drive off. His last chance to renege on the evening had vanished. He inhaled deeply, then reached for the brass handle and opened the door. He might as well get this over with. At least he knew the steak here was excellent.

Becca was standing by the window, staring out across the Hudson at the city lights, so Ike got a chance to observe her unnoticed. He recognized her from the photograph on her profile, though the picture hadn't done her justice. She was pretty, rather than stunningly beautiful, with dark, shoulder-length hair. She wasn't over-dressed or under-dressed; her blue sweaterdress was the perfect choice for the restaurant.

All in all, he had a good feeling about her.

Then she turned toward him and Ike realized she was on her phone. He couldn't help being disappointed. Not another woman who couldn't switch off from work.

Don't be dumb, he told himself. She could have been speaking to anyone. It wasn't fair to judge her based on Tracy's actions.

Becca spotted him as she hung up and walked over to meet him. "I'm sorry. I didn't realize you'd arrived." She smiled warmly. "I was checking in with my daughter. Jade likes to know I'm okay when I'm out. Since it's just the two of us, she's a bit of a worrier."

Ike's disappointment vanished. He remembered all the times he'd worried about his mom and was impressed that Becca had taken the time to reassure her daughter. "No problem. I only just got here. Shall we get seated?"

"Yes, please. I'm starving. I don't often go out for fancy dinners, so I deliberately didn't eat much today. I want to be able to enjoy every mouthful."

It was a nice change to have a date who wouldn't be fussing about what she ate. Tracy had always enjoyed her food, too. He shoved down that thought before it got any further. No more thinking about Tracy. There would only be two people on this date. "I know what you mean. There's a monster rib-eye with my name on it."

By the time they'd been shown to their table, consulted the menus and placed their order, Ike was relaxed and enjoying himself. He was glad he hadn't canceled the evening.

Over appetizers, they talked generally, getting to know each other. Becca admitted to loving hockey, but she wasn't an Ice Cats' fan. "My late husband introduced me to hockey when we lived in Denver, so I'm afraid I bleed burgundy and blue."

"You're lucky," Ike said with mock seriousness. "The Avs are the only other acceptable team to support, because my brother plays for them."

"Believe it or not, Jade got Tru's jersey for her birthday from her grandparents."

"Hmm. Maybe she needs to have a sweater from the more skillful Jelinek brother."

"What number does Kenny wear?"

He laughed. Sharp. A sense of humor. Things were definitely looking up.

The conversation turned more personal as they dug into their steaks. She asked how he was coping with his injury and he found himself admitting how difficult it had been. The excruciatingly slow progress with physiotherapy. Sticking to his promise to do exactly as he was told, even though he was sure his muscles were atrophying from lack of use. Crossing off the days until he could start working out. Missing the ice. Missing his teammates. Dealing with the isolation.

Becca was easy to talk to and a good listener.

In return, she told Ike about how tough it had been losing her husband when her daughter had only been a year old. He'd been an adrenaline junkie who'd competed in extreme sports and had died extreme-skiing. Although she'd been left comfortably off, she'd decided to move back home to New Jersey, where she'd have her family's support.

"So, you run your own business." Everything was going so well, Ike hated to raise the subject. But he wanted to deal with that thorny issue up front. The past had taught him that much.

"Yes, but it's more for fun than a serious career. Once Jade was in school, I found I needed something for me. To get me out of the house and occupy my time. Even if I loved housework—which I'll tell you right now, I don't—there are only so many hours you can spend cleaning and washing. We won't mention ironing." She gave an exaggerated shudder, then leaned forward, lowering her voice conspiratorially. "I love my daughter dearly, but I needed adult company and adult conversation that didn't revolve around children."

By dessert, Ike knew for sure that this date was a success and that he'd be seeing Becca again. She was good company and he felt comfortable with her. She more than checked all the boxes. To paraphrase the baby bear in the book he used to read to his brothers, Becca was "just right." They agreed to go out again, there and then.

In the car on the way home, one minor thing occurred to Ike. Despite the great evening, there hadn't been much of a spark between him and Becca. He hadn't expected to have the same instant, hot attraction as he'd had with Tracy—he'd never responded to any other woman that way. Anyway, he knew lust was no good without love. But he'd thought Becca might arouse something more than a warm feeling.

Perhaps this was another example of him borrowing trouble. It was only a first date, after all. Everything else was right, so the heat was bound to come.

Ike pushed the thought to the back of his mind and pulled out his phone to check the scores. All the Cats' rival teams were losing. Yeah, definitely a great night.

CHAPTER FOURTEEN

TWELVE O'CLOCK AND Ike still hadn't called to update Tracy on last night's dinner.

He usually called first thing the following morning. It had been hell listening to him go through each date in detail: where they'd gone, what they'd done and what he'd thought of the woman. She didn't know how she'd kept sane through those calls.

Though privately she'd been a teensy bit pleased when none of the women had panned out, she'd calmly reassured Ike that his next date would be "the one" and objectively discussed what refinements he needed to make to the profile of his ideal woman. That part had been particularly tough. Especially when the profile that evolved had made it clear that Tracy couldn't be that woman.

She knew Ike's comments hadn't been targeted at her, but they had highlighted how unsuitable she was for him. She'd hung up from each successive call feeling more and more miserable. Reminding herself that this was what she'd wanted—that her goal would finally be achieved because of their deal—hadn't helped.

While it had been torture having to hear about his dates, not hearing from him was far worse. Sitting in her office, staring at the silent phone, made that previous hell seem like a walk in the park.

Was the reason he hadn't phoned because last night's dinner with Becca had been a success? Her heart hitched. Was he late calling because the date had taken a passionate turn—the way it had when she and Ike had gone out that first time? Were Ike and Becca having breakfast in bed together?

She tried to clear her mind of the images that flashed up as if on one of those old film projectors. Images that were a sickening combination of memory and imagination—with Becca's face superimposed over her own.

Suddenly, Tracy didn't want the phone to ring at all. She did *not* need a blow-by-blow account of how perfect this woman was for him.

Focus on the upside. On that bloody prize.

Tracy had succeeded. Despite her misgivings about Ike's crazy proposition and her own emotional upheaval, she'd delivered as promised. She'd upheld her end of the deal.

To be fair, so had Ike. Once he'd done the photo shoot, Tracy could produce the new materials she and Maggie had developed. But even without the glossy brochures and advertorials, Ike's verbal endorsement was already paying dividends. Interest in Making Your Move and Helping Hands, in particular, had skyrocketed.

Now that her job on this dating project was done, she also wouldn't be dealing with Ike so regularly anymore. She could manage the rest of her work for him from a distance and, over time, she'd heal—as she had before.

On the other hand, she couldn't avoid seeing Ike at family events. Not just Ike—Becca, too. Tracy didn't need the happy couple to remind her of what it had been like for her before she'd messed things up with her insecurities.

Tracy sighed heavily. She'd have to minimize their interactions, which wouldn't be easy with Christmas coming up. Not the time of year to avoid family events.

The phone rang. Tracy's heart leaped into her mouth.

She was relieved when she saw Maggie's number. Still, Tracy's fingers weren't quite steady as she picked up the receiver. "Hey, sis."

"I just wanted to check that you know what you're making for the Badoletti-Hayden-Jelinek Christmas Day party? Obviously, we'll roast a turkey, but with everyone having different traditions of Christmas food, we'll have a nice variety. This is what we have so far."

Maggie bubbled with enthusiasm as she listed what people were bringing.

Since the Cats had a home-stand between Christmas and New Year's, Maggie and Jake had decided to host the celebration at their house. To ensure her sister didn't overdo things, Tracy had offered to co-host the party with them.

Not the best way to avoid contact with Ike. This was exactly the kind of family get-together she'd been worried about. Worse, as one of the hosts, she couldn't duck out.

But as much as she was now dreading the party, Tracy couldn't rain on Maggie's parade. "Per your instructions, I'll be bringing enough roast potatoes to feed the five thousand and also bread sauce," she said finally, when her sister finally wound down enough to get a word in edgeways. "Plus, just for you, a Christmas pudding." Tracy couldn't stand the traditional English dessert, but she always tried to get one from the UK for her sister, who loved it.

"Have I told you recently that you're the best?"

"I'm not sure, but feel free to say it again."

"You're the best."

By the time she hung up, Tracy's head was pounding from the strain of being upbeat. She rubbed her temples, then leaned back in her chair and closed her eyes.

The phone rang again, startling her. She jerked upright, her heart thumping heavily. Caller ID showed Ike's home number.

Tracy was tempted not to pick up.

"Don't be soft," she reprimanded herself. "You've never been a coward." At least, not in her professional life. No matter how bad the business situation had been, she'd always faced her problems head-on and confidently, even if that confidence had only been for show. "Don't start now. You can do this."

Willing her voice to be cool and steady, she answered. "Making Your Move, Tracy Hayden speaking."

"It's Ike. How's it going?" His cheerful tone set her teeth on edge.

"Oh, hello." She feigned surprise, as if he'd broken her concentration. "Goodness, where has the time gone this morning? The last thing I remember I was sitting at my desk with my morning tea and it's now… What time is it?"

"Twelve-fifteen. Are you too busy to talk?"

She wished desperately she could use the out he'd given her, but it would only be delaying the inevitable. "Just give me a second to get your file." As if it weren't already sitting open on her desk.

She shuffled some papers to sound busy. "Now, let me see…" She hummed and flicked the page a couple of times, as if reading through her notes. "That's right. You were seeing Becca last night. How did it go?" Her deliberately perky tone made her cringe. Next she'd be putting her hair in a high ponytail and popping her gum.

"We had a really good time. Everything went well. I liked her a lot."

Great. Super. "That's nice." Tracy hoped he couldn't hear the brittle edge that underlined her words. "Success at last."

"Yeah. I have to admit, I was skeptical going in,

but you were right. It was only a matter of time before the perfect woman showed up."

Thank God she was on the phone and didn't have to do more than murmur the occasional platitude as Ike raved about how *wonderful* Becca was, how *wonderful* the evening had been and how *wonderfully* she met all his requirements.

Wonderful.

"So, how would you like to proceed?" she asked brightly, as if this were the best news ever. "Would you still like to meet the final candidate?"

"No. I'd like to give this a chance and see where it'll lead. I've already arranged to see Becca again."

"Oh." She tried to mask her surprise. "You don't want to hold the last introduction in reserve, just in case?"

"Nope. If this doesn't work out, I'll give up on the dating thing for a while."

Clearly the evening with Becca really had been *wonderful*. For the first time, instead of being happy about meeting a client's requirements, Tracy cursed her success.

"I should get that in writing, Ike, so I can close off the file and Carla can send out the final invoice. I'm sure Layla will be delighted to chalk up another win."

"Thank her for me. Clearly that crazy questionnaire works."

More's the pity. "Of course it does. Layla wouldn't be as successful as she is without a proven process."

"I guess." Ike sounded confused by her snippy reply. "So, it's all good then?"

"Absolutely."

"Great. For a moment there you sounded...off."

"Nope. I'm fine. Pleased to have another satisfied customer." Mentally she groaned. She didn't need to think about Ike's satisfaction.

"Then we should discuss your part of the deal. I'm all yours, now that the dating thing seems settled. What else do you need me to do on the endorsement front?"

His cheerful tone made Tracy want to toss her mug of cold tea all over him. "I think we have everything we need for the time being. The pieces you wrote were great and we plan to use them all. You hit the right tone and maintained a good balance between constructive information and superlative-laced praise. Potential clients will definitely be impressed. Thank you."

"My pleasure. Oh, and just so you know, poor Lois is really struggling to keep up with her new job. From what I've heard, there hasn't been a single project that hasn't had unresolved issues or problems that needed extra work."

Finally, something to make Tracy smile. Karma was doing her thing. "That's a shame."

"Isn't it?" His deep chuckle sent a tingle through Tracy's body.

An unwanted, totally inappropriate tingle.

She bit her lip, hoping the pain would distract

her. "Jake mentioned a room mix-up in Pittsburgh on that road trip over Thanksgiving."

"Some guys were assigned rooms with only a king bed and the hotel was full because of a major convention in town. There's getting on with your roommate, and being a little too close, you know?"

Tracy covered her mouth, trying not to laugh out loud. She could imagine how pissed off the affected Cats would've been. "Callum Hardshaw can't have been happy."

"Coach Macarty wasn't, for sure. It won't take too many more mistakes like that for the players to revolt. I'm making sure they voice their complaints loudly."

"I can't deny that it would give me a certain satisfaction to have your GM have to come crawling back to me. Thank you."

"Looks like this deal worked out well all around. We both got what we wanted."

"Yes, we did." *Wonderful.*

There wasn't much else to say. After their goodbyes, Tracy hung up, then sat swiveling slowly in her chair. She should update Ike's client file, call Layla or send an email to Carla about the invoice. All of that could wait. For the moment, she didn't have the energy. Or the will.

She should be celebrating. This was a major achievement for her personally and for her company. As impossible as Ike's request had seemed, Tracy had provided exactly what he'd asked for. Of course, she couldn't spell out the details of what she'd done, but there were ways to blur the specifics in marketing copy, while ensuring the key message was clear. Potential clients would understand that no matter what their requirements, her company could deliver. Ike's whole-hearted endorsement would ensure that new business flooded in.

With the top spot so close, she'd proved, for once and for all, that she could succeed without a man directing her on what to do. She'd have made her mark and no one could take that away from her. Her future would be secure and she would never again need to be dependent on anyone else. Success would prove that she wasn't weak like her mother. That she was strong enough to stand on her own.

So why did her success seem hollow? Empty.

Because Tracy had also just proved the truth in that old adage her mother loved to quote—be careful what you wish for because you just might get it. Doris Hayden always had seen the glass as half-full, with the glass being cracked and the liquid being poison. But in this case, her pessimism was justified. Now that Tracy pretty much had what she thought she wanted, she knew she'd been wishing for the wrong thing.

She should have wished for a way to have it all—both business success and a relationship with Ike. Now that he was finally out of her reach, she realized she'd been hoping that this stupid dating project would fail, so she could have one more chance to try to make things work with him.

Ironically, the stupid dating process had helped her see that there were ways to compromise without giving up what she wanted. Especially as Ike wasn't as inflexible as she'd thought. Few things seemed to be so firmly set in stone anymore, for either of them.

Maybe they had both changed a little, after all.

Unfortunately, none of that mattered. It was too late. She'd let that last chance slip away and Ike had found his perfect woman.

USUALLY IKE CONSIDERED it a good thing when a woman sighed as he was kissing her. Unfortunately, this wasn't that kind of sigh.

He lifted his head. "This isn't working, is it?"

"I'm sorry." Becca smiled sadly and shook her head. "I wanted it to. I really did."

"Yeah. Me, too." Relief filled Ike. It wasn't just him.

They were cuddling on the sofa at her house, having been out to a movie and dinner. Though they'd been on a few dates in the past couple of weeks, this was the first time she'd invited him in after an evening out. Come to that, it was the first time he'd suggested being invited in. It was definitely the first time they'd really kissed. Previously, he'd given her a peck on the cheek or a buss of the lips before saying goodnight, but nothing more.

That should have told him something. It *had* told

him something, but he hadn't been listening. Or maybe he hadn't wanted to hear.

"I kept thinking the passion…the heat…something would come with time. Everything else is so perfect," Becca said earnestly. "But there's nothing there. No fireworks. At least not for me. And I don't think it's there for you, either."

"Nope." This time, Ike was the one who sighed. He dropped his arms and she moved back out of his embrace. "It was nice, but nothing more. No offence, but it actually felt kind of weird kissing you."

"I felt that way, too." He could see his relief mirrored in her blue eyes. "Like I was kissing a brother or a friend. But not a boyfriend."

"Right. Though for the record, I would *never* kiss any of my brothers like that."

"Good to know." Becca's grin eased some of the tension in him. "The thing is I settled for nice with my late husband and I promised myself I wouldn't settle again. Next time, I want skyrockets, weak knees and the whole shebang."

Like he'd had with Tracy. No matter how hard Ike tried to avoid thinking about her, it always came back to Tracy. Damn it. She'd ruined him for anyone else. No other woman could ever match up. "You're right. We shouldn't settle for anything less."

"Hopefully, there's someone out there for both of us."

There is, but... He didn't want to go there. Not in his head or with Becca. "You'll find someone perfect. Hey, maybe there's someone on the Avs I can set you up with. Tru's taken, but there are some good guys in Colorado. They can't play as well as me, obviously, but they might manage skyrockets."

"I'll keep my fingers crossed." Becca laughed. "I really like you, Ike. You're a special man and I hope we can be friends."

"For sure." He tried to keep the disappointment from his voice. Much as he liked Becca—and he did—he hadn't been looking for another friend. What was wrong with him that the mere thought of getting serious with him sent women running the other way?

There was no point prolonging the discussion. There was nothing else to say. He pushed to his feet. "Will you be okay?"

"I'll be fine. I'm glad we were honest about this before we went any further." She gave him a penetrating look. "How about you?"

"I'm good." He grabbed his jacket from the back of the armchair. "The offer to get you and Jade tickets to see the Cats play the Avs still stands. But tell your daughter the only Jelinek jersey she's allowed to wear is mine."

"We'd both like that, even with the totally unfair restriction."

"I'll arrange it and be in touch." He leaned over and brushed a brief kiss on her cheek. "I'll see myself out."

"Are you sure you don't want me to call you a cab? You sent your driver away."

"Frankie won't be too far." Thankfully, Ike hadn't dismissed him for the night. Maybe he'd known subconsciously things wouldn't work out.

"Take care, Ike."

"You, too."

Frankie didn't take long to arrive once Ike phoned him.

Ike sank into the plush leather seat and stared out of the window. The scenery did little to improve his mood. It looked like everyone had gone mad with the Christmas lights and decorations—every house seemed to be covered in flashing and sparkling crap. And nothing quite captured the festive spirit like an inflatable Santa playing poker with his reindeer. Ho-freaking-ho.

He'd been looking forward to Christmas. Had even thought about taking Becca and Jade along to the annual Badoletti-Jelinek celebration, but had decided it might be too soon. He didn't want to rush things. At least he hadn't mentioned it to anyone, so wouldn't have to answer any awkward questions. Though once they found out he and Becca were finished before they'd even really started, he might get quizzed about what he planned to do next.

Ike wasn't sure what his next move would be. He hadn't changed his mind about not wanting any more introductions through Tracy. While it hadn't been a wholly unpleasant experience, it had been awkward and uncomfortable. Not something Ike wanted to continue. Especially as he knew it wouldn't work anyway. This thing with Becca had shown that pretty damn clearly. How could it work, when the woman he wanted was the one setting him up with those dates? And he had as much chance of convincing her to give them another shot as he had of hoisting the Stanley Cup over his head. Hell, hoisting anything heavier than a puck right now.

Frankie dropped him at home a short while later. As Ike walked up the front path, his footsteps crunching on the cleared and salted paving stones, he noticed that his house was the only one on the block that wasn't lit up or festive. He didn't usually decorate, mainly because he was so busy training or playing or traveling that he didn't have time to mess with lights, a tree and all the other crap. Besides, over the holidays, he was always at his mom's or Jake's parents' place, and they decorated enough for everyone.

Normally, the lack of decoration didn't bother him. But tonight, the house seemed like an uncomfortable metaphor for his life. Dark, empty, cold. Separated from the others, like he was from his teammates. Alone.

Ike's morose feelings only deepened as he fought the urge to go for a run to clear his head. He wasn't dumb enough to risk slipping on ice. He wasn't even going to risk using the elliptical, though he'd finally been cleared for light workouts after Christmas. It was only a few more days. He'd come this far, he couldn't screw it up just because he felt down. He should focus instead on the fact that the holidays marked the beginning of him getting that part of his life back under control.

Unfortunately, that also meant he'd have fewer reasons to see or talk to Tracy. He tried to tell himself that was a good thing as he walked into his house, but he wasn't very convincing. Out of sight, out of mind worked both ways.

As he shrugged out of his jacket, Ike realized he should probably tell Tracy about things not working out with Becca. Nah. She'd find out soon enough. They'd already closed the books on the dating project. Why bring it up again, only to tell her he'd bombed out on what he'd told her was a sure thing? Okay, so he also didn't want her encouraging him to take that extra introduction he'd said he didn't need.

He slumped onto his couch and closed his eyes. He imagined the ice beneath his blades and the crisp air in his lungs as he skated around a rink. Even that didn't help much. He was still at least a month away from doing that for real.

February couldn't come soon enough.

ESCAPING OUTSIDE AT holiday parties was beginning to be a habit.

It was Christmas Day this time, and Ike was standing on Jake and Maggie's back deck overlooking the snow-covered yard. The noise and the heat of all the bodies packed into the house, which was kept extrawarm for baby Joe, had become claustrophobic. If he was honest, so had all the holiday togetherness. Ike loved everyone in that house—family, friends and teammates—but for the first time, he'd understood how it was possible to feel lonely in a crowd.

Especially when that crowd was made up of two distinct groups—the happily paired off and the happily single. He didn't belong to either group. He sure as hell wasn't happy to be single. So, first chance he'd got, he'd slipped outside.

Ike took a long drink of his beer, then sighed, his breath misting in the frigid air. The light was fading fast as evening approached, lengthening the shadows and turning everything gray. Wind blew through the trees, rattling the bare limbs. Despite his heavy down jacket, Ike shivered.

"So this is where you're hiding." Jake came to stand next to him.

"Hardly hiding. I'm in full view of everyone in the kitchen."

"You know what I mean." Jake gave him a serious look. "I've been where you are. I know how hard it is to be injured. The isolation, the boredom and frustration."

"Yeah. It sucks, for sure." He didn't want his friend to dig any deeper, so he said, "But things are looking up. My arm's responded well to therapy and is healing faster than expected. I can start exercising in the new year, though I'll have to take it cautiously for a bit. I'm supposed to hold off on the treadmill until I've built some strength back up, and I'm not allowed to run outside until this snow has cleared." He held up his splinted arm. "This is coming off, too. I only have to wear it for support when I'm doing what they call 'heavier activity.'"

Jake slapped Ike on the back. "Awesome. Any word on when you can start skating?"

"If I keep improving at this rate, mid- to late January."

"So you could be practicing with us by the mid- to end of February?"

"Dr. Gibson won't make any promises beyond getting me back skating. He wants to see how I make out with various levels of exercise before letting me back on the ice." Ike grinned. "My goal is to be ready for non-contact practice way before the end of February, and full practice not long after that."

"Then Hardshaw and Macarty will have to let you rejoin the team."

"Coach will want me back for sure, but Hardshaw was adamant I'm done until October. I doubt he'll change his mind, no matter how fit and ready I am." He didn't voice the niggling worry he had that his GM might not want him back at all.

"Sure, he will. The Cats are sitting pretty right now—we've had a nice run since that trip out West—but things can change fast. If we're in danger of missing the cut, he'll get you back between the pipes pronto. Truth is, as good as Monty's been playing, he's not you. We'll need your expertise if we're going to make a decent run at the Cup. Hardshaw knows that as well as anyone. They'll need to get you playing time before the season ends, so you're at peak game fitness for the first round."

Ike desperately wanted that to be true, but he'd learned one thing since his accident—just because he wanted something badly didn't mean it would happen. All he could do was his freaking best and hope the team's management changed their minds. "We'll see. I'll be busting my ass to be ready, then it's up to them."

"As long as you don't bust your arm again."

"I don't plan to. Hell, I don't plan to ever get injured again. This sucks."

"I hear you. Got that freaking T-shirt." Jake nodded, his expression sympathetic. "In the meantime, I'm freezing my ass off out here. You coming back inside?"

Ike wasn't ready to put on his happy face and be sociable. "I'll hang out here for a while longer, thanks."

"Don't leave it too long. Frostbite won't help."

When Jake had gone, Ike scrubbed his hand over his jaw. Maybe he should get out of here before someone else came to cheer him up.

A burst of laughter drew his attention to the large leaded windows. Compared to the gray hues outside, the kitchen had a warm yellow glow. The picture within the icicle-edged windows was of happiness, family, people enjoying themselves, like a Norman Rockwell painting. As he had the other night after leaving Becca's house, Ike felt left out. The kid outside the candy store. Not quite "bah, humbug," but close.

Everyone was gathered in the kitchen, trying out the various dishes. Ike's stomach rumbled at the delicious smells wafting through the opened vent-windows. He watched his mom and Rory feeding each other spoonfuls of different foods and debating with Jake's parents about what they wanted to sample next. Kenny and Emily tussled over bread sticks, while Jake stood with his arm around Maggie, who was holding Joe, looking proud and content.

His heart jumped as his gaze was drawn to Tracy standing alone on the far side of the kitchen. She held a full plate, but wasn't eating. Despite her cheery red dress, her pensive expression suggested she felt as removed from the festivities as he did.

The need to go inside and replace that sad expression with a smile surged inside him. He even stepped toward the back door, but he was already too late. Ike ground his teeth as JB casually slung his arm over Tracy's shoulder and said something to make her blush. She laughed and shook her head. She set her plate down as JB handed her a champagne flute. Ike cursed under his breath as the two clinked glasses.

Damn it. Why couldn't that have been him?

Ike turned away and drained his beer. So much for shutting off his feelings for Tracy. That box in his brain refused to stay closed. If only he'd felt the same intense desire with Becca.

He had to get out of there.

Ike slammed his empty bottle on the deck railing and stomped toward the steps leading down into the yard. It was the coward's way out. He should go inside and say goodbye, but he couldn't face it.

At the bottom of the steps, he remembered he had to call Frankie to pick him up. Not being able to drive was another frustration in a long line of them. Ike pulled out his cell and made the call. He'd just hung up when he heard the screen door open and someone come outside. Not wanting to explain, Ike moved into the shadow of a large, thick-trunked tree and waited.

His breath caught when he saw Tracy standing where he'd been a minute earlier.

She picked up his discarded bottle, then peered out into the yard.

Ike shifted farther into the shadows. He should go, but his feet were rooted to the spot.

Until Tracy shivered and wrapped her arms around herself. She'd come outside without a coat. Ike shook his head. She'd freeze to death.

Before he could stop himself, Ike moved out of the shadows and headed for the steps.

"WHAT IDIOT GOES outside without a coat in New Jersey in December?" Tracy muttered as she rubbed her hands up and down her arms.

Her red wool dress was no match for the weather. Then again, she hadn't worn it for warmth. The dress, with its round neck and pencil skirt, flattered her figure. And it had always gotten a reaction from Ike.

Still, with night falling and the temperatures dropping, she should've stopped to put on her coat and change back into the fur-lined boots she'd arrived in. Instead, she'd rushed outside in her red Jimmy Choos and left her coat hanging in the hall cupboard. Thankfully the deck had been shoveled, leaving only a light dusting, or she'd have probably slipped and gone head over heels.

The reason for her crazy dash into the freezing temperatures was right in front of her. The lone beer bottle planted in the snow on the deck railing. Unfortunately, it looked like she was too late and Ike had already left. She puffed out a breath, watching the frosty cloud swirl in front of her before disappearing—rather like Ike had just done.

He'd been standing on the deck, looking lost and lonely, and it had tugged at her heartstrings. Was there trouble in paradise? Was that why Becca wasn't with him?

Tracy had to admit she was relieved. She'd been dreading the party and had steeled herself to face the pair and their happiness. She'd considered faking the flu, but hadn't wanted to let Maggie down. Plus, she was damned if she'd be that pathetic.

Heavy footsteps coming up to the deck startled her. Heart pounding, she whirled round.

The light spilling from the kitchen window illuminated Ike's face as he came into view.

"I thought you'd gone." Bloody hell. Now he knew she'd been watching him.

"I *was* leaving." He walked slowly toward her, unzipping his padded jacket. "Then I saw this crazy Brit standing outside without a coat in temperatures cold enough to freeze the nuts off a brass monkey, and decided to do her a favor before she died from exposure." He shrugged out of his coat and wrapped it around her shoulders.

Warmth from his body surrounded her, seeping into her chilled arms. The jacket smelled of him—that heady mix of clean, fresh male and a hint of spice.

"Uh, thanks," she stuttered. "But now you'll freeze."

"I'm good for a few minutes. I think I can survive the cold." He cocked a thumb at his chest. "Hockey player."

Tracy rolled her eyes. "As well as not feeling pain, you hardy men don't feel the cold, either. I'm amazed you cover up the superhero logo on your chest with a shirt."

"Don't want the other guys to feel inferior." His modest expression made her laugh. "Anyway, what's wrong with being a superhero? You get cool toys and wicked cars."

"I'm with you there. Though in my case, it's the rocking boots."

"It's always about the shoes with you women." Ike shook his head, as if unable to understand the fuss.

"Give a girl the right pair of shoes and she can conquer the world."

"I thought you just wore them to make your legs look better."

Tracy's cheeks heated. Trust Ike to hit that nail on the head. "Who says the two things are mutually exclusive?"

"I'll plead the fifth. I've already got one injury and that spiked heel looks lethal."

"Smart man." She turned to look at the bottle and wondered how to ask about Becca.

Ike seemed content to stand next to her, saying nothing, staring out into the shadowed yard. The silence stretched out between them, companionable rather than awkward. If it weren't for the fact that it was bloody freezing, Tracy could happily have hung out there with him all night. Ugh. She had it worse than she'd thought.

"You didn't bring Becca with you today?"

"Nope," he said curtly.

Touchy. That shouldn't make her happy, but it did. "I'm sorry." She tried to sound sincere, but knew she failed. "Last time we spoke, it sounded so promising."

Ike sighed heavily. "Things didn't work out the way I thought they would."

Ignoring the way her heart leaped at his words, Tracy tried to analyze his tone. He sounded disappointed, rather than heartbroken. Had he been the one to end things? "I thought you were getting on really well."

"We were, but as friends rather than anything more."

As Ike explained what had happened and how there hadn't been any physical spark between them, Tracy felt her chest lighten.

She told herself to calm down. Just because things hadn't worked out with Becca didn't mean Tracy got another chance. Ike had probably had enough of women and dating after the past few weeks. Anyway, she still owed him one more introduction, according to their agreement.

Stuff that. "That's a shame."

Ike shrugged. "It is what it is."

"That's profound." Tracy nudged him teasingly with her elbow.

"It's a goaltender thing." He nudged her back. "We're deep thinkers—philosophers of the ice."

"Is that what they call it? I thought it was a two-syllable word beginning with *bull*."

"If the manure fits..." Ike's laugh sounded rusty.

"So why are you leaving early?"

"I'm tired. You can have too much of a good thing."

Tracy understood. "It can get a little intense over the holidays."

A gust of wind cut through the open jacket, chilling her. As nice as this was, she had to go somewhere warmer.

"Thanks for the loan." She slipped his coat off her shoulders and handed it back to him. "Put this on, tough guy, before you catch your death of cold. It's no good following the rules about your arm if you catch pneumonia."

"Yes, ma'am." He put on the coat, but didn't zip it up. "Enjoy the rest of the party."

"I will." Only a little lie.

Ike walked her to the back door, then reached past her to hold the screen door open. "I'll see you on New Year's Eve at Mom's."

She couldn't wait. "I'll be there. In the meantime, merry Christmas."

As she turned to go, Ike stopped her. "Hold up. You've forgotten something."

"What's that?"

He nodded to something above her head. "A Christmas tradition. It would be bad luck to ignore it."

Her heart skipped as she looked up and saw the bunch of mistletoe attached to the lamp. "Oh. Yes." She swallowed. "Neither of us needs to start the new year with bad luck."

She reached up, only planning to kiss him lightly.

But what started as a simple buss became more as his lips lingered against hers.

She drew back slightly, her gaze lifting to meet his. The passion burning in his green eyes made her catch her breath.

He wanted her. *Really* wanted her.

As much as she wanted him.

Ike shut the screen door firmly, without breaking the connection.

Tracy watched his head move lower as his lips descended inch by inch to meet hers. Her eyelids fluttered shut as she waited for his kiss.

At the first touch, fire shot through her.

As his tongue parted her lips, her nipples hardened but her knees turned to jelly.

She wound her arms around his neck, her fingers threading through his hair, pressing his head, his mouth, closer still. A half step forward and her body was against his.

Ike pulled the sides of the jacket around her, then wrapped his arms around her back. Even through their clothes, his heat seared her skin. He deepened the kiss until every cell in her body tingled.

She wasn't cold anymore. The opposite. Too warm.

She didn't care. She was where she wanted to be. In Ike's arms.

A burst of laughter cut through the haze of passion.

A moan of complaint rumbled deep in Ike's chest,

vibrating against her already sensitized breasts. A matching whimper escaped her lips as she tried to maintain the intensity of their kiss.

But the spell had been broken.

Ike eased his mouth away from hers with a regretful sigh.

Tracy's pulse jumped when, instead of letting her go, his arms tightened around her. "Let's get out of here and continue this where we won't be interrupted."

His gruff voice sent a shiver through Tracy that had nothing to do with the cold.

This was the moment of truth. The point of no return.

She licked her lips, relishing the lingering taste of him. "Yes." Her voice was barely above a whisper.

Ike caressed her face, trailing his fingertips along her cheekbone and down to her jaw.

"Yes," she repeated more strongly. "Let me get my things."

"If we go back inside, we'll get caught and distracted. People will want to talk to us." He ran his thumb over her swollen lower lip. "Especially when they see this." He smiled fondly. "Who knows when we'll make it out of there again. I don't want to lose the moment."

"Me, neither," she said huskily. She wasn't going to let this gift of another chance with Ike slip away.

Unfortunately, a quick getaway wasn't possible. "I'd love to sneak out the back way, but I need to let Maggie know I'm leaving." She nodded at her feet. "Besides, these shoes weren't made for walking through the snow."

"This is the part where I should sweep you off your feet and carry you to my car." Ike grimaced at his bandaged arm. "Not going to happen. I can't even drive you home myself."

Tracy smiled, her heart warmed. Always the gentleman. For the first time, that didn't seem such a bad thing. "Thanks for the thought."

"I could give you a piggyback."

She laughed and pointed at the pencil skirt of her dress. "In this? I don't think so. I'd have to hitch it up so far, your driver would get a view he wasn't expecting."

Ike waggled his eyebrows. "It would give him some Christmas cheer, for sure. But you're right, that's a view I want to keep for myself."

The desire that had begun to cool spiked again as his voice deepened. "Give me five minutes. I'll meet you round the front."

Ike pressed a quick, hard kiss to her lips before stepping away. He opened the screen door again, but this time he also opened the back door. "I'll be waiting."

Tracy walked sedately into the house; she didn't want to draw attention to herself. Inside, her heart was pounding wildly and her body was willing her to hurry.

She found her purse, boots and coat. She was

about to go in search of her sister when she saw Maggie coming out of Joe's bedroom. Tracy dashed upstairs to meet her.

"Are you all right?" Maggie asked. "You look a little flushed."

"I'm fine. I'm going to duck out of here, though, and go home."

Her sister arched a knowing eyebrow. "Alone?"

"No."

"With Ike?"

"Yes."

"Good. Have fun."

"That's it?"

"How about 'it's about time'?"

Her sister's wry tone caused Tracy a moment of concern. "I don't know if this is going to work out. The problems we had haven't gone away, and…"

Maggie put her finger on Tracy's lips, silencing her. "Don't overanalyze it. For once, just enjoy. You both deserve some happiness in your lives. Worry about what comes next later." She grinned. "I'm the big sister. You have to do as I say."

Tracy laughed and hugged her. "Just this once, I'll listen."

"I'm recording the date for posterity." Maggie shooed her away. "Now get out of here before someone notices you're leaving. I'll cover for you. I'll get Jake to drop your car off tomorrow sometime. Not too early."

"Thanks. You're the best."

Tracy made it outside without interruption. Ike's driver was already there with the engine running. Ike was leaning against the car, arms folded, waiting for her. He opened her door, waited for her to slip inside, then closed it and went around to the other side.

"Five minutes exactly. I'm impressed," he said as the car pulled away. "No problems getting away?"

"None."

"Good." He reached for her hand, lacing his fingers with hers. "No second thoughts?"

"None."

"Very good."

Tracy leaned over and whispered in his ear, "Can't wait."

Ike's grin was wicked. "Wonderful."

CHAPTER FIFTEEN

THE MOMENT TRACY'S front door closed, Ike's mouth captured hers.

Hard. Fast. Deep. Hungry.

She was a willing captive. Her back was pressed against the solid oak, while his hard body pressed against her front from her breasts to her thighs. Desire thundered through her veins. She reveled in the flames that licked out from her core, making every extremity sizzle and burn. Fingers, toes, the tips of her ears, the soles of her feet and everywhere in between.

It wasn't enough to merely be receptive to Ike's passion, to let him drive her wild with his hand and mouth. She wanted to take as well as receive. To taste and tease and touch. To make him lose control. To overwhelm him with need.

As the balance of power changed, he chuckled and shifted slightly to let her have her way with him.

They weren't going to make it upstairs. They weren't going to make it out of the front hall. Hands explored. Fingers fumbled with clothing, removed layer after layer, then caressed the bare skin revealed.

Even though it had been a few years, they slipped back into a rhythm born of familiarity. He knew where to nibble to make her gasp with pleasure. How hard to suckle her nipples to make her wet and ready for him. She knew where to scrape her fingernails to make him moan with need.

She hooked one leg around him, pulling him tighter against her, and wound her arms around his neck.

He responded by caressing his hand down her side, over her hip, following the curve of her bottom.

He gripped the back of her thigh as if to lift her, then swore. "This won't work. My arm. I can't hold you."

"You don't need to." Her smile was inviting and full of sexy promise. "We can take this…lower." She nipped at his bottom lip. "Much lower. Horizontal."

He grinned. "I like the way you think," he murmured against her mouth, before letting his tongue dance with hers.

They slid down the door, slowly, until they lay side-by-side on the hall runner. Though the thickness of the rug protected them from the wood floor, the coolness of the pile was almost icy against her heated skin.

Tracy shivered.

Ike rolled and covered her body with his, warming her. Always the gentleman.

She knew he couldn't stay like that for long, though, because of his injured arm, so she quickly reversed their positions and rose above him, her knees beside his hips.

"I like the way you think," Ike moaned again, as her slick, wet core settled against his hardness. "But if you do that, this won't last very long."

"Oh, dear." Tracy leaned over to press her lips to his, deliberately rubbing herself against his length. "That would be a shame."

His breath hissed through his teeth. "You can't…"

"I can't?" She widened her eyes in mock innocence. "What about this?"

She leaned forward again, nibbling at his earlobe, then swiping her tongue along his jaw. His erection throbbed against her.

"Tracy. I'm warning you…"

"Hmm. Not that either?" She slowly slid backward over him before lowering her head to kiss her way down the corded muscles of his neck and along the ridge of his collarbone.

The delicious friction of his hardness between her legs fueled her own desire, making her hotter and wetter. Back and forth she went, until they were both panting and desperate.

Suddenly, it wasn't enough. She wanted to feel him deep within her.

"Protection?" she gasped.

"Don't move." He reached out and grabbed his pants, shaking the wallet free. "In there."

Once he was covered, Tracy lifted herself above him. As his tip nudged her entrance, he surged up against her, but she refused to be rushed. She slid slowly down his smooth, hard length, inch by tantalizing inch.

Ike's jaw clenched and the tendons in his neck stood out as he tried desperately to hold on to his control. "Payback is a bitch," he gritted out.

Her laugh sounded sultry in the silent hall. "I look forward to it."

She hadn't expected that payback to be instant. Ike had other ideas.

He reached between them and began to rub the swollen bud where their bodies joined. Using his other hand, his fingertips trailed a teasing path from one breast to another, circling her nipples, but not quite touching them.

Need clawed at her. God, how she wanted him. Wanted this.

Completion was within her reach, but she stopped herself from tumbling over the edge.

A bead of sweat trickled down her back. Two could play at that game. She wasn't coming without him.

Tracy began to ride him. Raising herself slowly until he almost slipped out of her, then plunging down again.

Ike retaliated by cupping, then squeezing her breast and flicking his thumb over the taut nipple.

His other thumb rubbed harder at the core of her desire.

That familiar rhythm took over, turning the game into something far more serious. They moved as one. Harder, faster. Pounding, straining, reaching.

She experienced a momentary thrill as he tensed beneath her, then poured into her with a guttural shout. The sensation of him pulsing deep inside drove her to her own completion. She cried out as wave after wave of pleasure crashed over her. The sensation was so great that her limbs went numb and she collapsed breathlessly on top of Ike.

Victory had never felt so sweet.

TRACY WAS BACK in Ike's arms and back in his bed. If this was a dream, Ike was happy to stay asleep.

Okay, technically, *he* was back in *her* bed, but he wasn't quibbling over that minor detail. Not when he was curled around her delicious, warm body. She still fit perfectly against him; her breast filled the palm of his hand and her bottom pressed against his stirring erection. He breathed in her scent, which tempted him to flick his tongue over that sensitive spot just below her ear.

Tracy hummed with pleasure, though she didn't wake up. She wriggled, settling herself more tightly against him. His body hardened further. He shifted, trying to ease the ache in his groin. Nothing doing. Only Tracy would be enough.

How could he still have anything left in the tank

after last night? After the quickie in the front hall, they'd dashed upstairs to her bedroom, where he'd taken things much, much more slowly. He grinned. Oh, yeah. Payback was one delicious bitch.

When they'd recovered enough to move, they'd realized it was already midnight and they were both starving. They'd had snacks at the kitchen table before they'd snacked on each other on the kitchen table. Back in bed, the curves and planes of her body shimmering in the moonlight had reignited his hunger.

Ike nibbled the back of Tracy's neck. No other woman had ever affected him this much. He couldn't get enough of her. The taste of her, the smell of her, the feel of her.

He moaned softly.

"Is your arm hurting you?" Tracy asked sleepily.

His arm? Nope. Not a twinge. "It's fine," he murmured.

"Hmm. Not your arm. I wonder what else is paining you."

Ike chuckled. "Really? You can't tell?"

She reached back, sliding her hand between their bodies, and wrapped her fingers around his aching length. "Well, I did have this little hint..."

"Little?"

"Large hint?"

"Better."

"I can make *this* better. If you'd like. If it would

help." Her hand started to move up and down. Slowly. Deliberately.

He moaned again. "Is this what you call Helping Hands?"

"I do like to provide a personal service, uniquely tailored to your needs." Her low, sexy laugh hardened him further. Her grip tightened, her actions gathering speed. "Who knew that talking business had such an impressive effect on you?"

A strangled laugh escaped as his nerve endings sizzled. He strained, trying desperately not to explode. Knowing it was only a matter of seconds, he covered her hand with his, stilling her motion. "Not yet. Not without you."

"That can be arranged," she said huskily, guiding his erection to meet her hot, slick wetness. "I've done my part, now it's up to you to do yours."

"With pleasure." Resisting the urge to plunge inside her, he removed his hand from hers and trailed it over her hip and between her legs.

When he found her sweet spot, she gasped, then sighed. Her butt pressed harder against him, in response to his fondling, and the tip of him slipped inside her.

Her body language and her moaned words of encouragement told him she was ready.

Suddenly he couldn't wait any longer. He plunged inside and she clenched around him, doing the job her hand had done only moments before.

They moved together in perfect sync, in a dance

they'd done many times before. Deep, hard stroke after stroke.

His release built in him. Desire raged out of control. He fought to hold on, but it was a lost cause. He felt her contractions ripple tightly along his length.

Her release was the final encouragement for his own and he erupted within her.

AN INSISTENT PADDING on her chest woke Tracy the second time.

She opened her eyes to see Poppet working on the bedcovers. Finally, as she did most mornings, the little tuxedo cat turned full circle a couple of times, then settled down. Her green eyes watched expectantly, in case anyone might be thinking of replenishing the empty food bowls.

Glancing at the clock, Tracy saw it was still early, so she stroked Poppet's head until the cat's eyes drooped. She turned her head slightly to see Ike lying on his side, facing her. His deep, even breathing told her he hadn't been disturbed by her cats, even though Moppet was curled up in the crook of his knees. His hand cradled Tracy's hip firmly, as if even in sleep he didn't want to let her go.

Surprisingly, that didn't bother Tracy as much as it once had. She wasn't restless, eager to slip out from his possessive touch. In fact, she felt…contented. As if this was where she belonged. More importantly, as if this was where Ike belonged.

This felt right.

A little niggle of unease tugged at her breastbone. The problems between them hadn't been resolved. They'd got this far last time.

This time would be different. She wouldn't let her fear of the future overwhelm her. They'd work on their relationship together. They'd find a way. They'd compromise. It wouldn't be easy, but then, she'd learned from her business that nothing worthwhile ever was. She and Ike would probably fight—they were both too strong-willed and stubborn to avoid that—but they'd also make up. Her lips curved.

"I'm a recuperating man. I'm not sure I can manage whatever wicked idea is making you smile like that for at least a few more hours," Ike said sleepily.

"Who knew an injured arm could affect your stamina?" Her smile widened. "Luckily for you, I don't want to disturb the cats."

"Yeah, yeah. You don't fool me. You're as worn out as I am."

"Well, I did have to do all the work to protect your arm."

He nipped her shoulder. "I seem to remember doing more than just lying here. Especially the third time."

"Hmm." She tapped her lips with her finger as if thinking. "I'm not sure I recall that one specifically. You might need to refresh my memory."

"It'll be my pleasure." He yawned. "As soon as I get my energy back."

"How about I fix some breakfast?" Tracy sat up carefully, trying not to disturb Poppet.

"Should I be flattered by how keen you are to abuse my body again?"

"Don't flatter yourself, net boy." She smacked his chest. "I was thinking that you might be as hungry as I am, since neither of us ate much at the party."

"Now you mention it, I'm starving."

She slipped out of bed and pulled on her dressing gown. "Feel free to take it easy and recharge those batteries. I'll bring breakfast back up here."

"Don't be too long." His eyes were already closing. "I'll keep the bed warm for you."

Tracy practically skipped downstairs, with Moppet and Poppet scampering after her. She hummed to herself as she fed the cats, then prepared a breakfast tray.

She was defrosting some cheese scones in the microwave when she wondered whether her sudden burst of domesticity—dashing around, making Ike breakfast, deliberately including his favorite things—was a step onto that slippery slope.

A vision of her mother doing the same thing for her father popped into her head.

Tracy slashed her hand through the air, wiping that image from her mind. There was an important difference between the two situations. She wasn't doing this because she had to or because Ike had ordered her to. She was doing it because she wanted to. What's more, she knew that under different circumstances, he'd do the same thing for her.

She thought back to when she'd been married to Hank. With the benefit of hindsight, Tracy realized she'd been repeating patterns of behavior she'd learned from her mother. Her ex-husband had expected certain behavior and she hadn't questioned it—partly because she hadn't been strong enough, but also because she simply hadn't thought she could.

The last time she and Ike had been together, she'd been scared she was falling into those same patterns. When she'd panicked about moving in with him, not only had she not given him a chance to prove he wasn't like her ex, but she hadn't given herself a chance, either.

Yes, this time would be different. She'd make sure of it.

Ike didn't wake when she placed the tray on the bed, so she leaned over and kissed him.

"I could get used to this," he murmured, snagging an arm around her neck and pulling her closer. He pressed a firm kiss to her lips. "But first, coffee."

"Good to know where your priorities are," she teased.

"Just so you know, I'm keeping score for later."

"I hope so." She ducked back out of his reach and passed him a steaming mug.

They made quick work of breakfast, then snuggled together under the covers. The weather outside looked blustery and cold, but it was warm and cozy in bed. They talked about the party and baby Joe and the Ice Cats. They were talking about what they'd got and given for Christmas, when Ike suddenly stopped midsentence.

"I wanted to get you a present. I'm sorry I didn't."

Her heart warmed that he'd been thinking of her that way, even before last night. "I didn't get you anything, either, though I thought about it, too." She stroked his face, tracing her fingertips along his rugged jaw. "This…us…is our present to each other."

"I like that. A lot. So, no second thoughts?" Despite his seemingly casual tone, she could feel the tension in his body.

Tracy met his gaze squarely. "Definitely not."

"Are you sure?" His thumb caressed her cheek. "Nothing's changed between us."

The hint of vulnerability underlining his words strengthened her resolve. "We need to give this a proper try. We can take it slowly. We have a decent foundation to build on. If we both want this to work, we'll find a way to make it happen."

"What about wanting different things? Having different expectations."

"We're reasonably intelligent people. It can't be beyond us to find common ground. Besides, we don't need to solve all our problems right here, right now, do we?"

"I guess not."

"Then let's move forward."

Ike said nothing for several moments, clearly mulling over what she'd said.

Though she understood his reticence, his silence made her nervous. It wasn't too late, was it? "It's worth a shot, isn't it?"

"Hell, yes. That's all I've ever wanted."

Tracy released a silent breath of relief. "Then what's the problem?"

"No problem. I'm just surprised. You've been so adamant it wouldn't work. What changed your mind?"

She hesitated, then realized she had to start as she meant to go on.

"Helping you with the dates," she admitted ruefully.

His expression brightened. "You were jealous."

"In your dreams." Then she remembered she was supposed to be honest. "Maybe a little."

"I hoped you might be. Even though I thought we were done, I couldn't help comparing everyone to you. They never stood a chance."

His admissions sent a warm glow through her. "Going through those questions made me realize I never took the time to get to know you. Or to let our relationship develop properly."

Ike laid his fingers across her lips. "Uh-uh. No dreaded *R* word."

She smiled. "Okay."

"Then let's do this."

He wrapped her tightly in his arms. His chin

rested on the top of her head. Her head lay against his chest. The strong, steady beat of his heart beneath her ear seemed the perfect accompaniment to their agreement.

This time it would work. They'd both make sure of it.

LATER THAT EVENING, Tracy reflected that it had been one of the best Boxing Days she'd ever had. And not just because Ike's energy had been restored very quickly by breakfast. Amazing what cheese scones could do for his stamina.

She and Ike had spent a lazy day together, watching old Christmas movies and snacking on the party leftovers Jake had brought over when he'd dropped off Tracy's car. Obviously, her brother-in-law hadn't been surprised to see them together, but it had been nice that he'd made a point of saying he was happy for them.

"You've snagged a good one there, bro."

Ike had slung his arm across Tracy's shoulder and said. "Yeah, I made a perfect catch and I plan to hang on to her."

She'd acted offended at being compared to a puck, but really she'd been thrilled.

Now they were relaxing in her living room. Tracy sat on the sofa, reading, her legs stretched out along the cushions, while Ike sat on the floor, his back against her thigh, playing a game on his iPad. The lights on the tree twinkled and Christmas music—a selection of Bing, Frank, Doris and Nat they'd both agreed on—played softly in the background.

"I can't find the freaking thing." Ike swore. He thrust his iPad up to Tracy. "Can you see a hammer or a mallet or anything to break open that box?"

She studied the screen for a few seconds, then zoomed in before spotting a crowbar up against a tree. "How about that?" She passed the tablet back.

"Yeah. That's it." He groaned. "I always forget I can zoom. Thanks."

"Glad to help." She ruffled his hair, then returned to her book to find out how the hero and heroine were going to escape the warped killer.

The phone rang, startling her. She looked at the caller ID and prayed for strength before answering. "Hi, Mum. Happy Boxing Day."

"It's not a happy time for me. Christmas isn't the same without your father."

Tracy bit her lip to keep from saying it was better. "I thought you were at your sister's until New Year's Day."

"I am."

"She always has a full house, which is fun."

"But it's not *my* family and you know I prefer to be at home. I don't see why you and Maggie couldn't come here."

Her mother knew perfectly well—they'd had this conversation countless times in recent weeks—but Tracy played along. "Joe is far too young to travel and this is a very busy time of year for my business. I can't get away."

"Your father always said—"

"We have the same bloody argument over and over." Tracy lost it at that point and the conversation degenerated from there. By the time she hung up, she was wrung out and close to tears. "Why do I let her get to me? Why can't I just let it all go over my head?"

Ike moved up onto the sofa and pulled her close. "Families—can't live with them, can't shoot them."

She gave him a half smile. "It's all right for you. You have a nice family."

"I'm lucky, for sure. But don't forget my dad is a complete jackass."

Tracy had been at the Badolettis' Fourth of July party when Radek Jelinek had showed up unannounced. He'd made a big show about wanting to reconnect with his sons, when what he'd really wanted was their money. Luckily, he'd shown his true colors and been exiled for good.

"Mine was a bully and a tyrant," she said. "His house, his rules. Women were helpless, useless, worthless creatures, who knew nothing and did as they were told. God forbid they should think for themselves, or worse, disagree with him. I don't know if it was bad enough to be classed as emotional abuse, but it got close."

Ike hugged her tighter, pressing a kiss to her temple. "Your mom went along with him?"

"His word was gospel. Everything she did was his way. His words came out of her mouth. It's no bloody wonder Maggie and I left home as soon as we could."

"It says a lot about you both that you turned out as great as you did."

"We made mistakes, especially with the men we then married. Thankfully we both got out and we're okay now." She gave a self-deprecating smile. "At least Maggie is. I'm still a work in progress."

"Seems to me you're doing okay, too." Ike paused. "I know what Maggie's bastard of an ex was like." A muscle in his jaw jerked. "Do you want to tell me about yours?"

They'd avoided such serious topics when they were together before, too focused on enjoying the moment. Tracy had still been too raw to be able to talk about Hank rationally, so that had suited her fine. Now she realized it might have been a mistake. How could Ike understand her fears when he didn't know the background?

Admitting what she'd been like—what she'd allowed herself to be like—was embarrassing. But if they were to make their rela— whatever this was called work, she had to be open about her past.

She let out a long breath and dived straight in. "Hank was just like my father. More charming, better educated and much wealthier, but beneath it all, he was the same. I fell for a pretty face and an American accent. I was so eager to please, I turned into my mother before I realized what was happening."

Ike said very little, prompting her occasionally with a question as she told him the whole sorry story. Her marriage, Hank's affair, their divorce. How she'd used Hank's divorce settlement to set up her business. "After my parents and Hank, I needed to assert my independence. To have something that was mine. To prove I wasn't my mother or Hank's pathetic wife."

Ike held her close, stroking gently up and down her arm, encouraging her with his touch.

"Of course no one believed I'd survive even a full year. My father and Hank both said I wasn't capable of running a business, let alone one in such a competitive market. That's when I vowed that someday I'd be number one. Success would not only prove to him and everyone else that I could make it, but also prove to me I could be successful as a person."

After she'd finished, they sat quietly, each lost in their own thoughts. It was hard to tell what Ike was thinking about what he'd heard.

Finally, Tracy had to know. "I bet you're regretting you asked."

He shook his head. "Like I said before, everyone has a past. My childhood affected me and made me the way I am. I'm amazed you came through yours in such good shape."

She laughed. "Hardly."

"Most people would have folded after what you've

been through. Or repeated their mistake again and again. You broke the cycle and became your own person. What's more, you used your experiences to build an independent new life and a successful business. Sounds pretty good to me."

Stunned, she turned to look at him. It couldn't be that easy. Could it? "If I'd known you'd get it, I'd have shared all this before."

"I might not have understood back then." He gave a chagrined smile. "I've always been strong and self-reliant—I've had to be—and intolerant of those who weren't. This damn injury gave me a new perspective. Made me appreciate better what it's like to be vulnerable."

"But I could have tried."

"And I could have asked. What's done is done. I figure we've both learned enough from our mistakes not to repeat them."

"Or at least recognize when we're making them. Neither of us is perfect, after all."

"Speak for yourself. Kidding," he added quickly, when she reached for her wineglass.

She made a point of taking a long sip of wine before setting the glass down. "We also know to discuss issues when they arise, instead of hiding from them."

"Yeah. Great." He winced. "Hopefully we won't need to have any more deep discussions for a while. I think I've had my quota for the year."

Since she'd had enough angst herself, Tracy

moved out of his arms and shifted onto his lap, her knees on either side of his thighs. "Hmm. You must be quite worn out. That's a shame, because I've had this great idea." She leaned forward and whispered in his ear.

He laughed. "I may just have enough energy for that."

"Well, if you're sure." She slid down his body and proceeded to do exactly what she'd suggested.

IKE PULLED A sweater over his head, shook out his wet hair, then slipped his arms slowly into the sleeves. He'd been free of the splint for a couple of weeks, but was careful about how he used his still-healing arm. He had a decent amount of movement and flexibility now, and his arm was getting stronger all the time. He was also running and working out in his home gym daily. He was cautiously optimistic that this afternoon's appointment with Dr. Gibson would give him a date for when he'd be allowed to skate again.

The sooner, the better. Monty's run of strong play had continued and the Ice Cats were currently in a wild-card spot for the playoffs. Even the kid they'd brought up from the AHL was holding his own. All good news for the team, but it made Ike nervous.

Especially when there were rumblings that Hardshaw was after more scoring power and wanted to bring someone in before the trade deadline. With the Cats up against the salary cap, the only way the

GM could bring in a quality scorer would be a major trade or to shift salary. Sure, Ike's salary wasn't an issue right now, because he was officially on the long-term injured list. But who knew what might happen down the road when he was reactivated. If Hardshaw thought the current goaltending tandem was good enough, he might deal Ike.

Particularly if there was any doubt about Ike being as good as he used to be.

Which was why Ike was desperate to get back on the ice.

Marshaling his arguments for the surgeon, just in case, Ike headed downstairs to grab the lunch his housekeeper had left in the refrigerator. One good thing to come out of this whole mess was Marlene. Ike planned to keep her for as long as he could. Thankfully, she was happy to keep working for him. Tracy was working on a buyout of her contract with the employment agency so they could make the arrangement permanent.

Ike took out the soup, then grinned when he saw the lasagna and salad Marlene had made for dinner. Tracy was stopping by later. She had a long day of client meetings and he'd wanted to surprise her with a nice meal, so he'd asked his housekeeper to make something he could heat up easily.

Now that he understood what drove Tracy and why her business was so fundamentally important to who she was, he tried to do things like this to show his support. He still told her when he thought she wasn't getting the balance right, though he tried to do it in a more positive way.

The past couple of weeks had been unbelievable. Even better than when they'd been together before. After their intense conversation on the twenty-sixth, there had been a new closeness between them. They were adapting well to being together and they were compromising. They were also more relaxed with each other.

There was just one tiny fly in the ointment. Ike knew he shouldn't rush Tracy, but he was impatient to know where he stood. To have some reassurance that there would be a future for them. For him, the answer was obvious. He wasn't sure about Tracy. He understood why she was cautious and thought she was slowly coming around to the idea of commitment, but he had no idea what shape that commitment might take.

He'd thought about having one of those issue discussions she'd mentioned, but was wary of saying the wrong thing. Besides, with her so busy with work and him trying to regain his fitness, the timing never seemed right.

Perhaps that was a mistake. Perhaps he should tell her how he felt about her. What was the worst that could happen? She wasn't ready? She didn't feel the same? It had to be better to know for sure.

His front doorbell rang, interrupting his thoughts.

He was pleasantly surprised to find Tracy standing on the doorstep. "You're early. Did you miss me?"

She ignored his question. "Can I come in?" Despite her polite request, she looked ready to spit nails.

Curious and a little concerned, he stood back to let her in. "Sure."

In the front hall, Tracy turned to face him. Her anger erupted. "Do you know what your ass of a general manager just did?"

"Uh, no. I didn't even know you were seeing him today."

"I hadn't planned to, but he called asking for an urgent meeting, so I fit him in."

He opened his mouth to suggest they go through to the kitchen, but she cut him off.

"He gave me a whole song-and-dance routine about how he'd made a mistake taking my work in-house and giving so much responsibility to Lois." She paced the hallway. "Things have been getting steadily worse as I've handed things over to her. She hasn't been able to cope and the mistakes have been piling up. They'd become more than an inconvenience and were beginning to affect the efficient operation of the team. The final straw was when she tried to save money by changing the deal with the airline the Cats use for their charter flights. The airline retaliated by stripping out services. Apparently the trip back from Columbus last night was not good."

"So he wants to reinstate you?" he asked cautiously, not sure why she was so mad.

"Oh, yes." She stopped in front of him. "And he's sweetened the pot. A five-year deal with better financial terms and a longer notice period."

"That's good, isn't it?"

"No, it's not bloody good," she stormed. "He's set a non-negotiable condition."

"What kind of condition?" What the hell could Hardshaw have stipulated that would upset her so much?

"He's heard that you and I are seeing each other and doesn't approve. Nepotism or favoritism or conflict of interest or something. Anyway, the upshot is that I can have the contract or I can have you. Not both."

"Excuse me?" He couldn't have heard that right.

"If I want the Ice Cats contract, I'm not allowed to date anyone in the organization."

The logical side of his brain said it wasn't unreasonable. A lot of businesses frowned on in-office relationships. Unfortunately, logic wasn't ruling his emotions.

The uncertainty that had been nagging at him crystallized. He knew why he was afraid. Compromising on the smaller issues didn't mean a damn thing when it came to the security of their future.

His internal laugh was bitter and mocking. What future?

Why hadn't he brought up the dreaded *R* word? Man, was that ever coming back to bite him on the ass. Now it was too late.

Because one thing Ike knew for sure—when it came to choosing between her business and him, there would only be one winner. And it wouldn't be him.

CHAPTER SIXTEEN

"SO YOU TURNED him down." Ike tried to keep the sarcasm from his voice, but didn't quite manage it.

Tracy looked surprised and a touch offended by his tone. "Of course I did."

She'd chosen him over getting her Ice Cats contract back? No way. "You're kidding."

"I never kid about my business," she said crisply. "I won't let anyone dictate my personal life, least of all a client. Besides, I resented his implication that I can't be professional. Who I date would never affect how I do my job. So, yes, I told him his terms were unacceptable. He's stuck with Lois—he gets what he bloody deserves."

Tracy was serious. She'd said no. Ike had wanted proof that Tracy was ready for a commitment and holy cow—she'd just handed it to him, gift wrapped with a big bow. Happiness exploded in him.

"I'm… I don't know what to say." He'd been an idiot to doubt her. "How did Hardshaw take that?"

"He upped the ante, naturally." Her lip curled. "An introduction to the major sports teams in the area and his strong, personal endorsement for Making Your Move."

Ike's happiness dimmed. He should have expected that Hardshaw wouldn't let such an important contract go so easily. "That's some deal."

"It's amazing. Apparently it's one of those rare perfect storms—the Nets, the Mets and the Jets are all looking to outsource services and have been talking to the other teams in the area about who they would recommend."

Damn it. Ike had to hand it to his GM. That was a shrewd move. Hardshaw had given Tracy an offer she couldn't refuse.

Ike couldn't blame her. He understood that it wasn't just being number one, but what that success represented for Tracy that meant so much to her. Turning down Hardshaw's first offer had been an amazing gesture, but he couldn't expect her to reject a deal that would give her what she'd worked so hard for. Even if it meant ending their relationship.

"So you changed your mind," he said quietly, trying not to show his disappointment.

She frowned at him as if he were nuts. "No, I did not. I told him, politely, to stick his offer where the sun didn't shine."

Her retort should have pleased him, and it did in a small, selfish way. It also made him feel terrible—she was giving up so much for their relationship. For him. Too much. "If it worked out, you'd be the largest relocation services company in the area."

Tracy looked confused. "True, but at what cost? I told you—no one dictates how I run my life or my business."

"I appreciate that and I'm sure Hardshaw will think twice about trying anything like that again. But you can't turn down such an incredible offer."

"I can and I have." She softened her tone. "Our relationship is too important. I care too much about you to throw it away for a business deal. No matter how fantastic."

She was saying all the right words. Exactly what Ike had wanted to hear. Only instead of making him feel better, it made things worse. He cared too much to let her throw away such a huge opportunity. To pay such a high price.

He had to put this right. But what could he do? Callum Hardshaw had put them in an impossible situation.

Though it killed Ike to admit, there was only one solution. The problem was convincing Tracy to accept that. He had to take a leaf out of his GM's book—be ruthless and give her no choice. "I can't let you do this."

Tracy arched a haughty eyebrow. "Excuse me?"

"I can't let you make this mistake."

Anger flashed in her eyes. "You can't *let* me?"

"What I'm trying to say is it's unnecessary."

Her gaze narrowed. "And why is that?"

Crap, this was even harder than he'd thought it would be. When he said what he had to, there would be no going back. The line would have been crossed. For a moment, he was tempted to take the easy route. But only a moment. He had to be firm and do it right.

For Tracy's sake.

"I've been having second thoughts about us. I don't think it's working."

THIS COULDN'T BE HAPPENING.

"But...but that's not what you said this morning," Tracy stammered. "You were talking about celebrating two wonderful weeks together."

She'd actually thought he was on the verge of telling her he loved her. Oh, she'd told herself it was too soon for anything like that, but everything had pointed in that direction. Even the fact that he was making dinner for her. She'd even thought about admitting that she was falling in love with him, too.

What's more, she'd been planning to tell him that she finally felt ready to make a commitment to him. That she was no longer scared of taking their relationship to the next level. She'd imagined them talking about taking things steadily, but she'd been prepared to discuss a serious future together.

Ironically, the meeting with Callum Hardshaw had only strengthened her belief that she was about to do the right thing. Tracy had been furious that the GM had felt the need to lay down such a harsh condition. She'd never been anything but professional in her dealings with him, or any other client.

Once she'd put him in his place, she'd actually felt pretty good.

She'd come here expecting that Ike would be pleased with the decision she'd made. That he'd see how important he was to her. Instead… Well, she wasn't sure what this was.

She searched his face for a glimmer of hope, some sign that she'd misunderstood, but his expression was stony and cold.

"I'm sorry," Ike said. "I've had my doubts this past week, but I hoped I was wrong. I thought I could let things ride a little longer, just to be sure. That maybe with a bit more time and if I tried harder, it would make things right." He shook his head sadly. "Obviously, under the circumstances, that wouldn't be fair to you."

Tracy was stunned. "That's it? You're telling me we're over?"

"I think it's the best solution. The thing is, I really need to be focusing on my fitness. You know how important it is for me to get back on the ice. So I wouldn't have the time to work on a relationship, even if I wanted to."

The unspoken message being that he didn't.

It was truly over.

Tracy's temples started to throb. She felt sick. She reached blindly behind her to grab hold of the banister as she struggled to keep standing. What a naive fool she'd been, thinking that there might be a happy ending for her and Ike. That inner voice had been right all along.

Pride lit one final spark of rebellion within her. Pulling on every ounce of strength in her body, Tracy straightened. "You're right. This is the best way. Callum Hardshaw's deal is too good to turn down and I would have ended up regretting it. I'm sure he'll be thrilled to hear I've changed my mind. He was frantic at the thought of being stuck with poor Lois for the rest of the season."

She lifted her chin. "This was fun while it lasted. At least we know for sure we can't make this work and can move on with our lives."

For a moment, she thought Ike's emotionless facade would crack. There was a flicker of something in his eyes that she couldn't quite decipher.

But then it was gone.

She had to get out of there. Now.

She forced her legs to move. "Don't bother to see me out."

Even as she willed Ike not to follow her, she hoped desperately that he would. Hoped the sight of her leaving for good would change his mind.

Instead, he stood, solid and silent, as immovable and impenetrable as if he were in net.

As Tracy pulled the door closed behind her, the snick of the lock catching put a full stop on it all. White-hot pain seared through her body like a flash of forked lightning.

But in its wake came a numbness that dulled her

senses. As if those same nerve endings had been cauterized. Tracy didn't know how she made it to her car, or how she managed the drive home. She got out of the car, went into the house and upstairs to her bedroom on autopilot. Then she began to shiver, as though she'd caught a chill. Tracy toed off her shoes before slipping under the covers fully dressed.

Almost immediately, Moppet and Poppet leaped up onto the bed and snuggled in close to her. As she stroked their fur, the numbness vanished and she gave in to her misery.

SHELL-SHOCKED, IKE stood in the hall long after the door had shut behind Tracy.

It had all happened so quickly. Now it felt like that stunned moment in overtime, when the opposition scored. Motion slowed. Sound was muffled, as if it were traveling through water. And that terrible sinking feeling in the pit of his stomach that there were no more chances to put it right.

Just like that agonizingly miserable moment of defeat, his brain filled with if-onlys, even though he knew without doubt it had been the right thing to do.

That didn't make losing her hurt any less.

For a moment—one glorious moment—he'd known that he and Tracy could have a future. To have that snatched away was as hard to take as someone telling him he'd never play hockey again. It was a cruel irony that the team that was his career had shattered that hope.

Ike drew in a shuddering breath. Another mistake. Tracy's scent lingered, sending a spike of pain through him.

He had to get out of this damn hallway.

Slowly, he began to move. One foot in front of the other. Each step was labored, painful. He felt battered and bruised, inside and out. Yet he forced himself to keep going. He made it as far as the living room before his knees gave out and he crumpled to the floor.

Ike buried his head in his hands. A heaving sob escaped him. Then, as if a dam had cracked, tears burned their way down his cheeks. Instead of easing his pain, they amplified it. A dark cloud of misery descended.

He didn't know how long he stayed like that. He was barely aware of the lengthening shadows and graying light. Finally, a cramp in his leg forced Ike to move. He got to his feet slowly, his limbs aching.

Ike wandered through to the kitchen. He wasn't hungry, but he could use a beer or two. Or ten. He opened the refrigerator. The sight of the lasagna stopped him dead, reminding him of how he'd planned to spend the evening. He wanted to throw the damn dish across the kitchen. Instead, he emptied the salad into the trash, then grabbed the beer, wrenched off the top and tossed that at the wall. Not nearly as satisfying but better than nothing. And avoided having to explain the mess to Marlene in the morning.

He pulled out a chair and straddled it, taking a long drink of the beer. Unfortunately, his mind went stubbornly back to what he should have been doing with Tracy this evening. He'd sure as hell never expected it to end this way. Damn it—he'd never even gotten the chance to tell Tracy he loved her.

He drained his beer and got another one. Tracy didn't know—would never know—why he'd done what he had. That it was all because he loved her. He wished there had been another way, but no matter how many times he went back over it, he couldn't find one.

It was impossible. Ike or the contract, the endorsement and everything that went with it. What had possessed Hardshaw to make that condition? He had to have known that it might backfire. And if it hadn't, that he'd piss off his starting goaltender.

Had that been the point? He'd been worried about Hardshaw wanting to get rid of him. Had this been a way of getting him to waive his no-trade clause?

Ike laughed at the crazy thought. Paranoid, much? Knowing his GM, the bastard would just come out and ask. No need for dumb games.

He lifted his beer to his lips, then put the bottle down again as a thought occurred to him. Had he been looking at this all wrong? He'd been assuming that this had all been about Tracy and what she had to decide. But what if it wasn't? What if he turned the whole damn situation on its head? What if he took himself out of the equation?

What if he went to Callum Hardshaw and asked to leave the Ice Cats?

He drank his beer and went over his idea, looking at it from every angle.

The more he thought about it, the more Ike realized he had found the solution he was looking for—a way for Tracy to have what she needed and for him to have Tracy. He'd have to run it past his agent first. Andy might have an idea about the best approach to take.

Of course, it meant doing the one thing Ike had never thought he'd do. He'd hoped to retire as a Cat, but playing for another team wasn't the end of the world, as Tru had proved.

Maybe it wouldn't get that far. Ike couldn't help hoping that it wouldn't. That Hardshaw would change his mind and drop the condition.

But if he didn't, Ike was okay with that. As long as he had Tracy.

CHAPTER SEVENTEEN

"CARLA'S RIGHT—YOU look terrible."

As Maggie strode into the office, Tracy raised bleary eyes from the document she'd been staring at. The truth was she'd been shuffling papers all morning.

She'd hardly slept last night. Normally, insomnia would drive her downstairs into her office. There was always work to catch up on and even when there wasn't, it never hurt to be ahead of the game. But for the first time, she'd been unable to summon up the energy to get out of bed. The mere thought of her business had turned her stomach.

She'd never thought the day would come when she'd curse Making Your Move. The company that had been her salvation, the proof of how far she'd come and what she'd achieved, had become the instrument of her misery.

Once it was light, Tracy had forced herself to get up and get on with her day as if nothing had happened. If only she could keep her brain from reliving every moment of that awful scene in Ike's hallway.

"What's wrong?" Maggie dropped into the chair in front of Tracy's desk. "Are you ill?"

Tracy forced herself to straighten. "I'm fine. Got a lot on my mind." She tapped the file on her desk. "Business issues."

"Rubbish. Whatever's going on is more than just 'business issues.'" Her sister gave her a searching look. "Is there a problem with Ike?"

Trust Maggie to zero in on the problem.

"You could say that. We…uh… He…" Tracy cleared her throat to ease the tightness. "It's finished."

"What? Why? I thought it was going so well."

"You and me both." Tracy's eyes burned. "Apparently, we were mistaken, because Ike didn't think so."

Maggie swore, then jumped up and went around the desk to hug Tracy. "Okay, we're getting out of this office and going somewhere more comfortable so you can tell me all about it. And I can decide how painful I need to make Ike's demise."

Tracy gave a watery laugh, but allowed her sister to shepherd her down to the living room. She sank onto the sofa, thinking she might never move again, while Maggie made tea.

Her sister allowed her to drink most of the cup before asking, "What happened?"

"I don't know where to begin."

"You were fine yesterday morning," Maggie prompted.

It seemed so long ago that Tracy had been to see the Ice Cats, even though it had only been twenty-four hours. She hadn't even told Maggie about Hardshaw's call or their meeting. Since that had been the beginning of the end, it probably was the place to start.

"Callum Hardshaw rang me, asking if we could meet urgently. I'd heard things weren't going so well with Lois, so I went to see him."

"About time. Jake said the business was struggling to cope without us."

Tracy went on to explain the offer the GM had made and his conditions.

"What a jackass!" Maggie erupted. "I hope you told him what to do with his offer. As nice as it would be to have their business back, we're not playing by those ridiculous rules."

Tracy had known her sister would support her decision, but it made her feel better to hear it anyway. "I did. I also turned down his counteroffer."

Maggie's eyes widened when she heard what that had been. "Wow. He must be desperate. Serves him bloody right."

"It would have been a hell of a boost to our business."

"I know. And I know what that would have meant to you." Maggie's voice was full of understanding. "But I also know that giving into Hardshaw's conditions would have been a huge mistake. No success is worth that."

Tracy's laugh was bitter. "Turns out I should have accepted."

"Why?"

"Because the point about my having a relationship with Ike was moot." Tracy replayed the conversation with Ike for her sister. By the time she'd finished, the tears she'd tried so hard to hold back were falling.

"What nonsense. Ike's a bigger jackass than his GM."

Tracy swiped her damp cheeks with the back of her hand. "I don't follow."

"Anyone with eyes can see Ike's crazy about you and has been for years. I knew the first time I met him. He certainly hasn't gone off you since Christmas. In fact, I'd say the opposite. Since you've been together again, he's been the happiest and the most relaxed I've ever seen him."

Tracy wanted that to be true so badly, her heart ached. But it wasn't. "He clearly had us all fooled. Me especially."

Maggie waved her hand in the air as if brushing away that notion. "This is Ike we're talking about. He may like to think he's inscrutable, mysterious and impenetrable—which he is in his net—but off the ice, he's pretty easy to read. Smile for happy, scowl for unhappy. Believe me, he's been like a bloody Cheshire cat these past couple of weeks."

"Well, something changed his mind."

Her sister was quiet for several moments, thinking. "I wonder…" she mused. "Didn't you say Ike told you he wouldn't *let* you throw away Hardshaw's deal?"

Even through Tracy's misery, that single word still pissed her off. "Who does he think he is? I thought he'd changed, that he understood. We had a long talk and I told him everything about our parents and Hank. Where does Ike get off thinking he has the right to dictate what I do?"

Maggie smiled. "My point exactly."

"What point?" Tracy frowned, confused. Then it dawned on her. "You think Ike deliberately ended things? So I'd have a clear shot at Hardshaw's deal?"

Her sister nodded. "It's exactly the kind of idiot thing Jake would have done," she said fondly.

Tracy turned the idea over in her head. The more she went over it, the more she began to think Maggie had nailed it. That's the kind of man Ike was. He'd have felt responsible for her—especially because Hardshaw's impossible condition involved him—and taken it into his head that he had to do what was necessary. Making a noble sacrifice to ensure Tracy achieved her goal was Ike's way of looking after her.

Despite her irritation at his high-handedness, she felt hopeful. That had to mean he still cared for her. As much as she cared for him? As much as she loved him?

If that was true, things between her and Ike couldn't be over. She wouldn't let them be. The problem was how to convince Ike. She could see him stubbornly sticking to his guns, no matter what she said.

"The solution should be simple, but I can't see it," Tracy said. "I've already told Ike he's more important than the contract. Repeating it won't make any difference. I'd just be knocking my head against a brick wall."

"So don't tell him. Show him."

"I did that, too, when I turned down Hardshaw's bloody offer. Both times."

"What if you showed him you don't *need* the Ice Cats' contract?" Maggie suggested.

"I still haven't taken the deal. How else can I prove how serious I am?"

"By achieving your goal without it. Isn't that what you'd planned to do anyway?"

"Yes. I was certainly going to approach the New York teams. I don't need Hardhsaw's endorsement to do that. But that's a long game. It could take months even to get a foot in the door. That won't help me with Ike now."

"But I have an idea that might." Maggie smiled. "There are two other hockey teams in the area. We've always held back from going after their business because of concerns about conflict of interest."

"Without the Ice Cats' contract, there is no conflict of interest." Tracy could feel her excitement building. "Why stop with just those two? We could throw the net wider—Philly, Buffalo."

Maggie dusted her hands together. “My work here is done.”

Tracy bounced to her feet. “Thanks to you, dear sister, mine is just beginning.”

IKE’S FOOTSTEPS CRUNCHED in the newly fallen snow on Tracy’s path.

This was probably the moment in a movie when dramatic music would play to increase viewers’ tension. Ike didn’t need any help; his tension level was already sky-high. He was about to make the biggest play of his career. His life. It was bold and risky, but it was the right move. He had no doubts about that.

He just hoped it would be enough.

Ike had talked through his plan with Andy. His agent had gone over the ramifications with him and was on board. Ike had wanted to talk it over with Jake, too, but hadn’t wanted to put him in the tricky position of keeping it secret from Maggie.

At the foot of the front steps, Ike paused. Lights were on, so someone was up and about. He’d hoped to get here early enough that he’d catch Tracy before she headed out for any meetings. His breath misted in the frigid air.

Especially a meeting with Callum Hardshaw.

As far as Ike knew, Tracy hadn’t told the Ice Cats that she’d changed her mind about the contract and the endorsement, even though a couple of days had passed since he’d ended things with her. What Ike had to say wouldn’t affect that, but he wanted her to know where he stood before she went into such a meeting.

Which wouldn't happen unless he got his ass up those steps.

Time seemed to slow as he waited for someone to answer the door. Just like it did on the ice, as he waited for the ref to blow his whistle to start a shoot-out play. Unlike other players, who shuffled in place on their skates, Ike had learned to stand still. To appear confident, unmoved by the gravity of the situation. Right now, his feet wanted to shuffle. Which didn't work so well on a doormat.

When Tracy's intern opened the door, she stood for a moment studying him, her expression serious. "I hope you've come to do the right thing."

His tone matched hers. "I have."

"Good. About time." Carla stood back to let him in. "Tracy's in the kitchen."

Ike stomped the snow off his boots, then stepped into the warmth. As he walked down the hall, he wanted to blame the change in temperature for the trickle of sweat down his spine, but he knew that was crap. It was nerves, plain and simple.

Tracy did a double-take when she looked up from her seat at the kitchen table to see him. Luckily, the mug she'd been holding was almost empty, because it dropped from her fingers and landed on the rug. She ignored it and kept staring at him as though he were a ghost.

He stood staring at her, too, but for different reasons. It had only been a couple of days since he'd seen her, but it felt like longer. She looked good. No, she looked great. Ike searched for signs that she'd been through the same hell he had, but couldn't find any. Then again, she was made-up and dressed for action in her red power suit. Her stocking feet were bare, awaiting a pair of her favorite red-soled shoes, which lay by her chair. Only a hint of strain around her brown eyes suggested she wasn't as together as she seemed.

"I...uh...don't mean to interrupt." *Smooth start.* "Can we talk?"

She nodded once, sharply. "Help yourself to coffee."

"I'm good, thanks." Ike leaned his hip against the counter, trying to look at ease.

"What can I do for you, Ike?"

Her question made all his carefully rehearsed words fly out of his head. He had one chance to get this right. He couldn't blow it. The calm he relied on to get him through the toughest games had vanished. His mind was bombarded with snippets of all the things he needed to say, like pucks peppering his net. Where was his water bottle when he needed it? If ever he needed to buy time by squirting water over his face, it was now.

Focus, damn it!

He inhaled deeply and plunged straight in. "Hardshaw was wrong to put that condition on your contract with the Ice Cats and I'm not prepared to let him blackmail us. If we want a relationship, it's none of his damn business and we can't let him stop us."

"We no longer have a relationship," Tracy said. "You ended it."

He grimaced at her cool tone. "I lied. I know how much your business means to you and I understand why your success is so important. I'm proud of what you've achieved with Making Your Move. You deserve to be number one. I didn't want you to give that up for me."

"I see." Neither her tone nor her expression changed.

He plowed on. "I thought the only solution was to take myself out of the equation, but I also knew that unless I forced the issue, you'd never give in."

"You certainly did that very effectively. What changed your mind?"

"I couldn't stand losing you. So I found another solution."

"You did?" For the first time, her facade cracked and he could see the hope in her eyes.

It was surprisingly hard to get the final words out. Once he told Tracy, there would be no going back. No matter how much he believed in this plan, it was still the toughest thing he'd ever had to do. It would change his life and career forever.

But he loved Tracy so much, he thought he might burst. She was worth it. "I'm going to ask for a trade from the Ice Cats."

CHAPTER EIGHTEEN

TRACY DIDN'T KNOW whether to laugh or cry. To smother Ike with kisses or bash him over the head with a frying pan. The man always had turned her world upside-down. And he'd done it again.

What Ike was offering was huge. Amazing. Overwhelming. And absolutely crazy. To leave the team he'd been with since the day he was drafted, that he'd won the Cup with and whom he'd hoped to retire with, was more than a simple gesture of support. It was a serious declaration of his feelings. Despite the past, despite the bitter words, Tracy knew without a doubt that Ike loved her.

Of course, his offer was totally impractical. But it was the thought that counted.

Ike was watching her anxiously.

"I don't know what to say," she admitted. "I can't believe you're prepared to go to another team *for me*."

He shifted uncomfortably. "There will be stipulations. I won't go to just any team."

Tracy smiled. "Naturally. I didn't expect you'd want to cross the Hudson."

"The Rangers don't need me. I have the right to nix any team I don't want to play for, because of my 'no movement' clause."

"Still, it's a major career decision. And a major shift in your thinking."

"You were right when you said I had double standards for us." Color tinged Ike's cheeks. "If we were marr— together, I'd expect you to support me. Why shouldn't I support you, too?"

Her pulse tripped. She knew what he'd started to say. It was further confirmation of his feelings and reassurance that he saw a long-term future for them.

A future she wanted, too. Very much. This whole situation had made her realize that marriage itself wasn't the problem. Tracy and her mother had both allowed themselves be dictated to. Tracy knew now that no matter what the circumstances, she would never again let anyone else control her decisions, her life or her happiness.

Ike would always want to take care of her and there would be times when he'd frustrate her as he tried to do so. Tracy knew that she was strong enough to stand up to him and also to occasionally let him have his way. It was nice to have someone she could trust enough to lean on from time to time.

This wasn't one of those times. "I really appreciate the offer, but it wouldn't work."

"Why not?" Ike said, concern in his voice.

"It'll be a little hard to be together if you're not in New Jersey."

"I'd make sure I was at a team that was easily commutable back here. I'm sure we could manage that for a few years, right?"

Tracy nodded. "But you have more than a few years left to play."

"Who knows what'll happen with my next contract. If I even get another contract. I could get injured again or lose my starting position. I don't mind sharing the net, but I won't be a backup. I'd rather quit. We'll figure it out as we go. From now on, we tackle these problems together."

"I like the sound of that." If they were both committed, they'd make it work. "But asking for a trade really isn't necessary."

"Yes, it is." He walked over and crouched down in front of her chair. "That's how important you are to me."

His earnest words tugged at her chest. She laid her palm on his cheek and smiled gently. "You're important to me, too."

"I won't let you be bullied. Or let you give up an important contract for me. What's more, I won't let *myself* be bullied. The whole thing shows a major lack of respect for both of us."

"I know."

"Then we're good." It wasn't a question.

Tracy laughed. "If you'd let me speak, I could tell you that I haven't changed my mind about rejecting the Ice Cats' offer."

It was Ike's turn to be surprised. "What?"

"I won't be held to ransom over our relationship, either. I've done some research and made a few calls. It turns out I don't need Callum Hardshaw's endorsement, though obviously yours will still be useful. There's already quite a demand for my services, now that I don't have to worry about any conflict of interest with the Ice Cats."

His eyebrows shot up. "You spoke to the Rangers?"

She grinned. "The Islanders and Flyers, too. Funnily enough, they don't have a problem with me living with a player from another team."

"Yeah. So they're not idiots after all. They're..." He stopped and did a double take. "Wait. What did you say?"

"You heard me." Tracy tamped down her giddiness. There was a protocol to be followed, after all. "Although I could be jumping to the wrong conclusion here, as I don't recall being asked. In fact, I don't remember you saying three rather important words, either."

Ike's smile was slow and sexy. "You mean that I love you?"

Tracy had read about moments so special, so happy, they seemed to be sprinkled with fairy dust, but had never really believed in them. She'd certainly never experienced one. But the second Ike said those special words, her world lit up. The air sparkled and she swore she heard those fairies singing.

She stood, pulling him up with her. His arms wrapped tightly around her waist, as if he'd never let her go. Hers went around his neck, her hands cradling his head. They stood like that for several moments, staring deep into each other's eyes.

Then Ike lowered his head and touched his mouth to hers. A soft kiss, full of promise.

"Feel free to respond any time now." His voice was teasing, but uncertainty clouded his eyes. "Unless you don't… If it's too soon… You don't have… It's okay."

She stemmed the faltering flow of words with her finger across his lips. "It's not too soon. I was just savoring the moment."

"So you do…?" His lips brushed against her finger, sending tingles up her arm.

"I do." She smiled. "And to ensure there's no confusion—I love you."

"Thank God." He nipped her fingertip in punishment. "You had me worried."

"Turnabout is fair play."

"I guess. I'm still stunned by what you're giving up for me. What if your plans don't work out?"

"That would be okay. I don't need Making Your Move to define me any longer. I don't need to be number one to prove to anyone, least of all myself, who and what I am. Or what I can achieve. That's all in here." She patted her chest, above her heart. "I certainly don't need it to be happy and fulfilled."

"Kind of like I don't need you to marry me, now

or ever, to be happy and fulfilled. All I need is to know you love me."

"Which I do. Very much." Tracy laid her head against his chest.

Again, they stood silently. His heart pounded slow and steady beneath her ear.

Finally, he sighed. "I don't want to rush things, but I have to know—were you serious about us living together?"

She lifted her head and met his gaze. "Oh, yes. I'm ready to make that commitment."

"Hot damn!" He danced her round in a circle, making them both laugh.

A sharp cough interrupted them.

They stopped, breathless, and turned.

Carla stood in the doorway, smiling broadly. "If you don't need me, I have loads of errands to run, to the post office and the bank and so on. I'll probably be gone for the rest of the day."

Ike murmured his fervent approval beneath his breath.

Tracy swallowed a giggle. "I can manage without you."

"I thought you probably could." Carla's eyes twinkled.

As if by unspoken agreement, Ike and Tracy waited until they heard the front door close before moving. This time the kiss wasn't slow or gentle.

Ike broke away suddenly. "What time is your appointment?" he rasped.

"Not until two."

"Perfect." He grabbed her hand and pulled her with him. "We have some very important business to attend to before then."

"We'd better get onto that straight away. You know how I hate to let anything interrupt important business."

Laughing, they ran upstairs to Tracy's bedroom. As they tumbled onto the bed, she hesitated. "Are you sure this is what you want? That it'll be enough for you?"

Understanding filled his green eyes. "I meant what I said. Being with you is enough. I don't need a legal document to tell me what's in here." He mimicked her earlier action by patting her chest above her heart.

"I'm not saying never. Just—"

Ike pressed his mouth to hers, cutting her off. When he lifted his head, he said, "This is probably the last time I'll be able to do this, but I'm putting my foot down. We're not going to discuss that any further. Not until you tell me you're ready."

Tracy's heart, already filled to bursting with love, expanded just a little bit more. "This is probably the last time I'll let you dictate, but I'll do whatever you say."

"Whatever…?" Ike's grin was wicked, as he trailed a finger down her throat to the edge of the lacy camisole top beneath her red jacket.

She gasped as need shot through her. "Anything for…business."

"In that case, time to 'make my move.'" And then Ike proceeded to show her just how committed he was to the success of her business.

EPILOGUE

Two months later.

TRACY TWISTED HER fingers nervously and checked the dining room for about the thousandth time to make sure everything was just right. This was an important occasion and she didn't want anything to go wrong. There was a lasagna keeping warm in the oven. The table was set perfectly with candles, flowers and her best china. Champagne was chilling and a large, gift-wrapped box sat on Ike's place setting.

He was on his way back from the arena, where he'd been meeting with Coach Macarty and Callum Hardshaw. Dr. Gibson had called earlier to give her a heads-up that he'd cleared Ike for full contact practice and the team would activate Ike shortly from Injured Reserve, so he could prepare for the playoffs. The plan was for him to play some games with the Cats' AHL affiliate, before joining the team full-time.

Tonight's dinner was a celebration of the long road Ike had travelled and the fresh start he was making with the Ice Cats. Hence the new chest-and-arm protector and catching glove she'd bought for him, with a little help from the Cats' equipment manager.

It was a special celebration for Ike and Tracy, too. They'd been living together for one month. As nice as his town house was, they'd both preferred Tracy's Victorian.

Ike planned to sell his place at some point, but for the moment, he was renting it out to Kenny and JB Larocque. Tracy had also decided it was time her company had proper offices, separate from her home. She and Maggie had been checking out premises and hoped to sign the lease on a nearby building shortly. Which they would need as they were also in the process of hiring more staff. Carla was now a permanent employee, but as Making Your Move continued to grow they'd need more hands on deck.

As she walked back into the kitchen to check the lasagna, she saw an Ice Cats' file on the table and smiled. Callum Hardshaw had come back to her once more. This time, the deal had no mention of his stupid condition, so Tracy had accepted. It was nice to be back working with the Cats, but it was good to have the other hockey teams on board, too.

"Honey, I'm home."

Tracy's heart lifted, as it did every time she heard his teasing greeting. It was their private joke about Ike's previously old-fashioned views.

"Good day at the office, dear?" she called out with her usual response.

"Hell, yes. As of next week, I'll be back in net for the Cats."

She headed out into the hall, smiling. "Congratulations."

Ike grabbed her in his arms, kissed her and twirled her around. "Even that can't beat the sight of my beautiful woman greeting me in her apron." He lowered his voice to sexy growl. "Although, it would've been even better without that dress underneath."

Tracy batted her eyes at him with exaggerated seductiveness. "If you play your cards right, that can be arranged for dessert."

He turned to the hall table, picked up an enormous bouquet of brightly colored spring flowers and gave them to her. "Happy anniversary." He frowned. "Or should that be monthiversary?"

"Either is perfect." She smiled. "These look and smell gorgeous."

"Like you." He waggled his eyebrows suggestively. "How are those 'cards' looking?"

"Better and—" She broke off, when she saw a small business card tucked into the bouquet. "What's this?"

"The Sharks are in town and I know their coach from Juniors. He's from Jersey originally and wants to buy a summer place at the shore. I told him to give you a call and you'd sort it for him. Is that okay?"

"Of course it is." She reached over and pulled his

lips down to hers. “Thank you. I have something for you, too.” She beckoned him with a finger.

Ike rubbed his hands together with glee. “Awesome. I love presents.”

Nerves returning, Tracy bit her lip. “I hope you like this one.”

Ike draped his arm across her shoulder and they headed to the dining room together. “It’s from you. I’ll love it. Not quite as much as I love you, but close.”

Her cheeks flushed. “Always the charmer.”

As soon as he saw the box, his eyes lit up like a kid. “That’s a big present.”

“And they say size doesn’t count anymore.”

“Don’t kid yourself. Size always counts.” He dropped a kiss on her head, then rushed forward to open his gift.

Thankfully, he was happy. He was touched by the initial ‘T’ she’d stitched into the inside of his protector, so it would always rest above his heart. “New equipment’s a great idea.”

“I’m glad. I know how superstitious you net minders can be and was worried you’d insist on your old gear.”

Ike held up his now-healed arm. “Not when it means preventing this from happening again. Besides, I’ve still got my old leg pads.”

“For now.”

“What’s this?” Ike had picked up his new glove

and discovered the small box nestled in the mesh. "It'd better not be a cup—it's way too small."

Tracy shook her head, nerves tightening her throat.

Ike looked at her curiously, then undid the gift-wrap and opened the box. He stared at the contents, saying nothing for several moments.

Finally, he looked up, his expression carefully bland. "Are these what I think they are?"

She nodded, then cleared her throat. "Ike Jelinek, will you marry me?"

He caught the matching pair of gold rings on his forefinger and lifted them, so they glinted in the candlelight. "I'd ask if you're sure, but these prove the answer is yes."

She nodded again. "What's your answer going to be?"

His eyes blazed with the emerald fire she loved so much. "Yes."

"Are *you* sure?"

"Hell, yes."

Before she could respond, Ike swept her off her feet and into his arms.

"Put me down! You'll hurt yourself."

"Not a chance. I bench-press more than you every day."

"Don't blame me if you pull a muscle, net boy."

"Stopping a six-ounce hunk of rubber traveling at over ninety miles an hour is no walk in the park,"

Ike huffed. “So do we need to turn off dinner? I don’t want to be interrupted by the fire department.”

Tracy grinned. “We’d better make that stop first.”

He refused to set her down while she switched off the oven. He seemed unaffected by climbing the three flights of stairs to their room, though his breathing was a little ragged when he dropped her onto their bed.

“See, I told you I was heavier than a puck,” she teased.

“That may be, Tracy Hayden-soon-to-be-Jelinek. But now that I’ve caught you, I’m not letting you go.”

She wound her arms around his neck and pulled him down to her. “Me, neither.”

Just before Ike covered her mouth with his, he murmured, “Now, about that apron…”

* * * * *